ASH OF AGES

MEGAN O'RUSSELL

Ink Worlds Press

DEDICATION

For those who will change the world

ASH OF AGES

CHAPTER ONE

"I'm asking you to trust me, Lanni. Come with me. Please."

I studied Walsh in the dim light. The tree branches cast shadows across his face, but there was no laughter in his eyes, no teasing.

In that moment, the world seemed to disappear. There was no glass trapping us inside the Arc Domes. No Incorporation ready to destroy anyone who interfered with their perfect apocalypse.

It was just Walsh and me and a decision that would change everything.

He meant it. The werewolf I'd barely begun to trust wanted me to run away with him.

Not run away. Escape.

My heart froze as I took his hand.

A hint of a smile lifted the corners of Walsh's lips. "Thank you." He kissed the inside of my wrist. "I need you to get Mari ready. Don't try to bring anything with you. Just have her ready to run."

"Run where?" The trees started to sway around me. "Where are we going? Will Mari be safe? Will there be food?"

"Both of you will be safe. I'll protect you. And you're valuable. The pack will be happy to keep you fed and clothed."

"Why am I valuable?" I eased my hand out of his. Part of me wished he had held on, gripped so tight I couldn't have made the decision to pull away. "Because I'm a girl? I'm a good age for breeding?"

"No. The alpha would never allow anything like that." Walsh tipped his head to the side, listening for a moment, then stepped forward, leaning close to whisper in my ear. "You survived on the outside and managed to blend into the Arc Domes. You accomplished naturally what the pack trained me for three years to achieve. Mari's managed it, and she's just a kid. I need you to trust me, Lanni. Make sure Mari is prepared to leave. And be ready when I say it's time."

"That's all?" I grabbed Walsh's hands before he could back away. "Make sure Mari's boots are tied on tight?"

"I won't leave without you." He kissed my cheek. "Keep your head down."

Then he walked away, leaving me standing in the trees like everything was normal. Or as normal as things can be for someone pretending to be a kep right under the Incorporation's nose.

"This is a good thing." I closed my eyes, letting myself imagine what freedom might look like.

To not be trapped in the Arc Domes, pretending to be one of the monsters who had chosen to sacrifice the world for their own comfort. To not be in the city, waiting for the tainted air to destroy my lungs.

To live someplace where I didn't have to worry about where Mari's next meal would come from. And no one would ever try to take her away from me. And no one would lock me in a sterile room to breed. Or train me as a guard so they could use me to kill more innocent city scum.

Paradise. Jaime whispered the word in my mind.

"Walsh is a werewolf, not a god," I whispered back. "No matter what he promises, following him is a risk. There can't be a safe way to escape the domes."

You want to stay here? Jaime wrapped his arms around me, letting me rest my head on his shoulder.

"I want to get as far away from the Incorporation as I can. But what if I make the wrong decision and Mari gets hurt?"

It's a chance you have to take. You might never find another way out, and you know what will happen if you stay.

Images of a sterile white room with a white bed tore into my mind.

"Okay." I opened my eyes.

Jaime wasn't there waiting for me.

I studied the trees around me, trying to memorize the vibrant green of their perfect leaves just in case I never got to see a healthy forest again.

The war in my mind raged on as I weaved through the shadows back to the room Mari and I shared.

Our mother had sent us to the Arc Domes. This was where she'd wanted her children to be.

But I had to believe she hadn't known Project Progeny was even a possibility. If she'd sent us here knowing that I could be forced to breed with a stranger—

Pain sliced into my chest.

I couldn't be sure Mom hadn't known. I didn't know her well enough to be certain she hadn't understood what the Incorporation would demand of me and had just handed me to the kep anyway.

I pressed my palm to my heart, trying to make the pain stop. "Breathe, Lanni. You have to breathe."

In and out. In and out.

I made myself stay focused on breathing as I pulled my knife out of the purple flowers where I'd stashed it and opened the lock on our window.

Mari didn't stir as I climbed into our room.

I tucked the knife under my mattress before touching her shoulder.

"Wake up, Mar. I need you awake for just a minute."

Mari scrunched up her face as she rolled toward me. "What's wrong?"

I don't know what about my expression made her eyes widen.

"Nothing bad." I gave her the best smile I could manage. "I just need you to put your shoes on."

"Where are we going?" Mari clung to my hand.

"Trust me." I mouthed the words to her, too afraid of the Incorporation spying on us through the computer screen mounted in our wall to even risk whispering.

"They still haven't caught the one who killed the four Incorporation Guard," I said. "I just want to make sure we're ready in case they send us back to the bunker."

"Okay."

I leaned away from Mari, barely managing to keep my hand in hers as I grabbed her shoes from her side of the room.

"You know I'll always take care of you." I set her shoes beside her.

"Yeah." She kicked off the covers and put on her shoes, watching me like I was going to tell her to sprint for the door at any moment.

"I'm so proud of you, Mar." I glanced to the computer screen. "When we found out we were getting transferred here, you came without arguing, without asking any questions. That's how I know you can be brave enough to face whatever change is coming next."

"Just promise we'll stay together." Mari pulled me up to sit on the bed beside her.

"I promise." I kissed the top of her head.

"If there's time, we should both sleep."

I shook my head.

"Then just you sleep for a little while." Mari scooted over, giving me the center of the bed. "I got to sleep in the bunker last night while you were with the guards. We can't be ready for whatever comes next if you're too tired to move."

"I'm fine." Even looking at the pillow made me want to collapse.

"Sleep." Mari widened her eyes at me. "I'll wake you up if PAM has a message for you."

"Mar—"

"Sleep." She scrambled off the bed. "Now."

"Thanks, Mar." I checked that my bootlaces were still tied before lying down.

I was asleep before I could wonder if I should've made sure Mari knew there was a knife under the mattress.

CHAPTER TWO

"Lanni."

I jolted out of sleep, sitting up and opening my eyes as something thudded against the floor.

"Ow!"

I was on my feet before I even looked down to see where the *ow* had come from.

Mari lay between the bed and table, glaring up at me. "You didn't have to shove me off the bed."

"What's wrong?" I grabbed Mari under her arms, lifting her to her feet.

"Nothing was wrong until you knocked me down."

"Sorry, Mar. Are you hurt?"

"I just hit my butt." Mari pointed to the computer screen set into the wall. "PAM has a message for you, and I was too scared to open it, so I woke you up."

"Anything else happen while I was asleep?"

"You drooled. Then you twitched like you were having a bad dream."

Flashes of my nightmare burst through my mind.

A concrete box. Trapped in the box. The man, holding a knife, blocking my one chance for freedom.

We escaped once, Jaime whispered. *You can do it again.*

I gave Mari a quick hug, making sure she was actually real and with me before stepping over to the screen and tapping to open the message.

Schedule Adjustment for Lanni Roberts

Report to the Haven Dome at 5:00 p.m. for evening harvest session.

Report to the vehicle bay at 8:00 p.m. for guard training program.

"Why do you have to go to guard training at night?" Mari stepped in front of me to stare up at the screen. "You always go to training early in the morning."

"I don't know." I tried to sound calm for Mari's sake and for whatever Incorporation shit could be listening in on us. "Probably to make up for the training we missed this morning. That's probably why we're going to the Haven Dome to harvest, too. They don't want to get behind on food production."

"Can I..." Mari looked between me and the screen. "Can I go with you? I just got to come home again, and what if I go to Miranda's while you're busy and then the Domes Council says I can't live with you anymore? Won't it be better if I go with you?" She pointed down at the shoes I'd told her to wear.

"I don't know." I checked the time.

4:15 p.m.

I could go to Walsh, see if he needed me to keep Mari with me, and still make it to the Haven Dome by 5:00.

If Mari and I were even still going to be in the Arc Domes by 5:00. Walsh could come bursting in at any moment to tell us it was time to go. Then I'd just nab Mari and chase after a werewolf, hoping we ended up safe instead of dead.

"Lanni?" Mari tugged on my hand.

"Let's go see if Walsh got the same schedule changes as me." I pulled free from Mari's grip, pressing a finger to my lips as I went to the bathroom. "If he didn't, maybe he can take care of you. If he did, then we'll see if you can come with us to help with the harvest and watch training." I took a washcloth from the pile of clean towels.

"What if I can't come watch training?" Mari took her own washcloth from the pile.

I shook my head at her.

She scowled and shook her head back.

"Then we'll see if you can stay with Harper." I pulled my knife out from under my mattress, tucked the blade into the washcloth, and shoved the pathetic weapon into the ankle of my boot.

Mari opened the kitchen drawer and pulled out the smallest of our knives. The blade was only a couple of inches long, not meant for anything more than cutting fruit.

I gripped her wrist and shook my head again.

"I don't know if Harper's going to want me to stay with her. She has her appointment for Project Progeny tomorrow." Mari yanked her wrist away from me.

"Tomorrow?" The room swayed. I hadn't realized how quickly time had passed.

I'd promised Harper I would stop Project Progeny. That I wouldn't let them drag her into a sterile room. I was supposed to save her.

I'd failed.

I'd made it up into Incorporation Headquarters to plant the chip for Walsh, but I hadn't done anything to protect Harper.

And now I'm abandoning her.

"Harper's not going to be in a good mood today," Mari said. "I don't think even my cuteness could cheer her up."

"How do you know Harper's upset?"

"I know how to log into your messages." Mari shrugged.

"You read my messages?" I couldn't make myself move even as Mari wrapped her washcloth around the tiny blade and shoved it into her waistband, hiding the handle under her shirt like I'd done so many times.

"You didn't want to tell me what was going on, so I had to read your messages." Mari grabbed my hand, pulling me toward the door. "Don't worry, it's not like you sent love letters to anybody."

"We have to stop at Harper's room." I let Mari drag me into the hall. "We have to talk to her."

"I thought we were going to Walsh." Mari stopped.

I stared at Harper's door, but I didn't even raise my hand to knock. What could I say?

I'm sorry I betrayed you so I could run away? I'm sorry for abandoning the only friend inside the domes I've always been able to trust? I'm sorry for leaving you to be tormented by the Incorporation?

"Did you want to talk to Harper?" Mari jiggled my hand.

"No." It was my turn to drag Mari behind me. "There's nothing we can say that will help Harper."

As I led Mari down the tree-lined path, there was no hint that, only hours before, the kep had been scouring the Arc Domes, searching for the monster who'd managed to kill four Incorporation Guard without getting caught.

Everything in sight was beautiful and dome perfect. The scent of cherry blossoms filled the air, and the late afternoon sun gave the trees a beautiful glow.

But two Dome Guard were stationed at the stairs leading out of Bloom Dome. They watched Mari and me as we passed. It felt like they were glaring at me. I couldn't convince myself I was imagining it.

Sleepy kep hurried through the concrete corridors leading between the domes, like they were rushing to get to work after being mandated to make up for the hours lost hiding from the murderer the guards still hadn't found.

A pair of Outer Guard silently patrolled the hall, both wearing full riot gear as though they were ready to head into the city.

So they haven't given up on finding the killer.

I'd have to warn Walsh.

Another pair of Outer Guard came around the arc of the corridor.

"Excuse me." Mari dodged free from my grip to leap in front of them.

"Mar—"

"Is the scary murderer still hiding in the domes?" Mari wrinkled her forehead like she really was a kep kid and the killer was the scariest thing she'd ever faced.

And I'm trusting the killer with our lives.

I'm as much of a monster as Walsh. I'm the one who told him who to murder.

"Well?" Mari planted her hands on her hips. "Is the bad guy still hiding?"

Neither of the guards stepped around her. They didn't answer her either.

"Are you not answering me because the Incorporation is still listening to everything you say through your wrist bands?" She pointed to the black cuffs on the guards' right wrists.

"Come on, Mar." I took Mari's shoulders, pulling her away from the guards.

"Blink twice if you haven't found the killer," Mari shouted as I steered her down the hall.

"Don't harass the guards." I nodded at the next pair of guards we passed. This set was Dome Guard, but they were dressed like they were expecting some sort of battle.

Maybe the Incorporation finally figured out that desperate people might fight back.

"I was just asking the guards a question," Mari said. "If there *is* still a murderer on the loose, then I'm definitely staying with you. I don't care what anybody says."

"Everything is going to be fine." I stopped at the bottom of the stairs leading up into the Marsh Dome.

What if leaving Bloom Dome had been an awful idea? What if

Walsh was expecting us to be in our room and he came to get us so we could escape and we weren't there? What if he left without us?

The questions froze me in place.

"Lanni."

What if the kep had figured out Walsh was the one who'd killed the Incorporation Guard? If I took Mari to Walsh's room, would they realize I'd been in on it? Would they think Mari had something to do with it?

"Lanni."

Would the punishment for killing the guards be getting thrown out of the domes?

Should we tell them what we've done and offer to be exiled to the outside world?

"Lanni!" Mari smacked my arm. "Why did we stop?"

Because I'm not sure of anything anymore and I'm terrified of making things worse.

"I was just wondering if he'd be at home," I said.

"Well, let's go check." Mari ran up the stairs into the Marsh Dome, like she knew damn well chasing her was the only thing that could overpower my panic. "I don't know where he lives." Mari called from the top of the steps.

"Wait." I bolted up the stairs, making it all the way to the top before a ding sounded in the dome. "Mari, stop."

The swish of the tall grass rustling in the breeze created by the filtered air filled the second of silence.

"Outer Guard Trainees, report to the medical corridor." A female spoke through hidden speakers. "Outer Guard Trainees, report to the medical corridor immediately."

"Shit." I looked to the bridges that led to Walsh's room.

He was a member of the training program, too. He'd have to report to the medical corridor.

"Why do they want you to go to the medical corridor?" Mari went back to clinging to my hand.

"No idea." I counted to ten, watching the path to Walsh's room, waiting for him to come sprinting toward the stairs.

1, 2, 3—

He wouldn't leave without you. He's still in the domes.

—8, 9, 10.

"We'll find Walsh in the medical corridor." I headed back down the steps, keeping Mari right beside me.

"But what if they want you down there for Project Progeny?" Actual fear filled Mari's voice. "What if they're going to lock you up and make you get pregnant?"

"They won't." I dragged Mari to run faster. "You have to get a whole medical exam first. They do blood work and everything."

Blood work. That was how I'd convinced Walsh to help me. Not because he knew Project Progeny was evil, not even because we were friends.

Don't let doubt keep you trapped here, Jaime whispered.

By the time we reached the stairs leading down to the medical corridor, we'd joined the stream of trainees hurrying to obediently follow the Incorporation's orders.

None of them looked shocked that I was dragging my seven-year-old sister along with me. I didn't know if they were that intent on hating me or all so worried about what might be waiting for us in the medical corridor they didn't have the energy to care about Mari tagging along.

Four Dome Guard had been stationed at the bottom of the steps, and another pair flanked the door to Captain Tate's office.

"They're going to take me away," Mari whispered as she clung to my arm. "They're going to make me live with Miranda."

"No, they won't." I kept my pace steady, heading past the guards and toward the medical corridor. "Director Holbeck herself said you could stay with me."

"Lanni." Walsh stepped out of a storage room, like he'd been lurking, waiting for me.

Relief crashed into my chest. I raced toward him and hugged him with my free arm.

"We were going to go to your room to find you," Mari said.

"I didn't know what to do when they posted the schedule," I said. "I didn't want to leave Mari in our room."

"She shouldn't be left alone with a killer on the loose." Walsh nodded toward the guards lurking in the hall. "She should come to training with you. She'll be safer there than on her own."

"Good," Mari said. "I want to stay with Lanni."

"But..." I shut my eyes, trying to sort through all the doubts raging in my mind to find the path I'd regret the least. "But would it be better to have Harper come and wait with her while we're here in medical and then take her to watch our training in the vehicle bay?"

Two guards walked past. Both glared at us like they would have told us to get moving if they hadn't been forbidden to speak to Walsh and me since we were both in the guard training program.

"Harper wouldn't mind keeping Mari company while she watches us train. She could bring Mari to the Haven Dome, too, if we even make it up there for our harvesting time," I said. "And... and she needs an escape. She can't survive sitting in her room, worrying about Project Progeny."

He shut his eyes as his shoulders trembled. He flinched, like he could feel the echo of his alpha's orders stabbing through his mind.

"Please, Walsh," I whispered.

"Would she come without questioning why?" He kept his eyes closed.

"Absolutely." A little rush of relief swooped through the uncertainty crushing my lungs.

"Good," Walsh said. "Good. She's a driver. She can explain the trucks to Mari while we train."

"Yeah." Mari bounced on her toes like she was getting ready to bolt for the vehicle bay.

Walsh nodded before opening his eyes. "What about Alec? Would he come without asking why?"

The relief I'd felt vanished, replaced by a sharp pinch in my throat.

Alec had saved us from the city. Alec had protected Mari and me. He had cared for me. Had trusted me. Had wanted me.

"I think so," I said.

"You have to be completely certain." Walsh took my hand. "There cannot be any doubt. Even a hint of a question—"

"No." I blinked away the stinging in my eyes. "It's better not to bother Alec. I'm sure he's busy with the Outer Guard. Harper can sit with Mari in the bay."

"Okay." Walsh held my gaze for a moment before looking to Mari. "Can you run and get Harper on your own?"

"Yes," Mari said.

"She should stay with me."

"We have to get into medical before they start looking for us," Walsh said. "We don't have time to hunt for Harper."

"I'll see you in the bay." Mari tore her hand from mine and sprinted back toward the stairs.

"Mar—"

"Trust her." Walsh gripped my arm, keeping me tucked in the doorway beside him.

"She just ran off." I stared after her. "Four guards were killed yesterday and she bolted away from me."

"She's safe," Walsh whispered.

"But she doesn't know that. She's braver than I'll ever be."

CHAPTER THREE

"The unprecedented attacks on the Arcadia Domes have left Captain Pace with little choice." Guard Beck paced between the two lines of trainees. The soft thump of his boots against the floor sounded like a clock, ticking down to whatever doom they'd gathered us all into medical to face. "We have enemies lurking beyond the glass and a murderer threatening our lives within the sanctuary of our home."

"If we aren't safe inside the Arc Domes, why was everyone released from the bunkers?" One of the boys stepped forward, keeping his chin high as he met Beck's gaze.

Beck stopped and faced the boy. "The order came down from Incorporation Headquarters."

"So there isn't a killer in the Arc Domes?" the boy said.

"The Incorporation decided it was time for the Arcadia Domes' citizens to return to their homes," Beck said.

"While there's still a murderer lurking inside our domes?"

"The orders of—"

"The Incorporation is using Arc Domes citizens as bait for the monster who killed four Incorporation Guard." The boy spoke over Beck. "Captain Pace and Captain Tate couldn't figure out where the killer was hiding, so the Incorporation is lining us up to be the next victims. Maybe a higher body count will get the Incorporation the answers they want."

"You're out of line." Beck stepped toward the boy.

"However many deaths it takes to catch the son of a bitch, right?" The boy cut around Beck to face our group of trainees. "The Incorporation doesn't give a shit about us."

"Quiet. Now," Beck ordered.

"They're using us to breed, telling us the Arc Domes is in desperate need of new citizens, while putting our lives in danger," the boy said. "Tell me how that makes sense."

"Get him out of here." Beck looked to the two Outer Guard by the door.

"We are not disposable." The boy kept speaking as the guards grabbed his arms. "We're not animals to be bred and slaughtered."

I bit my lips together, fighting against all the things I wanted to shout as the guards dragged the boy from the room.

"The next person to speak will be joining him in the cells," Beck said. "Am I understood?"

None of the trainees responded.

Beck started pacing again like he hadn't been interrupted. "By order of Captain Pace, and under the guidance of the Incorporation, the decision has been made to temporarily assign all of you to Outer Guard duty."

Isn't that what happened when we patrolled last night? I pressed my palms to my legs, not letting myself speak. I couldn't afford to get locked up. I doubted even Walsh could break me out of the cells.

"Using the loudspeaker system to call you is ineffective," Beck said.

And tells the killer exactly where we're going to be.

I glanced to Walsh before I could help myself.

He stared at Beck with the stone face of a perfect kep minion.

Beck waved the doctor who'd been lurking in the corner

forward. "With your temporary assignment, you'll be receiving wrist bands for communication."

A tendril of fear wound around my lungs as my wrist began to tingle.

"With the chip band comes responsibility," Beck said.

The doctor pushed his cart to the first trainee in line. He pulled a black band from a tray, slipping it around the trainee's wrist and locking it in place like it wasn't anything more than tying a shoe.

The tingle in my wrist grew into a burning itch.

"You will be following the same edict from the Incorporation as the rest of the guards," Beck said. "There will be no communication with other guards, Dome or Outer, unless that communication is directly related to finding the one who killed the four Incorporation Guard."

One of the boys raised his hand. He'd already been trapped in his wrist cuff.

"Unless you know where the killer is lurking, do not speak," Beck said. "Yes, this order means you cannot ask a fellow guard how their mother is, what they thought about training, or any other blather. Your sole concern is finding the killer. Nothing else matters. Do you understand?"

The boy nodded and lowered his hand.

"Wrist, please." The doctor stopped in front of me.

I pressed my hands to my thighs even harder, fighting to keep myself from running or telling the doctor to go fuck himself.

"Wrist. Now." The doctor held a cuff out to me.

My hand shook as I raised my arm. I flinched as the doctor locked the band around my wrist.

The cuff was lighter than I'd thought it would be, much more comfortable than the metal chip band I'd been forced to wear back home in the city.

The simple black band was looser, too. It didn't chafe or pinch.

But I was still trapped. Stuck with a bit of kep tech locked around my wrist. With the little communication chip inside the band, I wouldn't be safe to talk anywhere. The Incorporation could listen to every word I said.

Only for a few hours. I'll be out of here soon enough. Just keep it together, Lanni.

The doctor reached Walsh.

Walsh held up his arm without argument, but I swear I heard a tiny growl as the doctor clicked the band closed.

"You will all be receiving your assignments through your wrist bands," Beck said. "If your assignment should require any equipment, report to weapons storage."

The doctor locked the last trainee's cuff in place.

"Am I clearly understood?" Beck stopped beside the door.

None of us spoke or even nodded.

I hoped the rest of the trainees felt the same level of rage I did toward Beck and all the shits who'd let this happen to us.

But I couldn't convince myself the kep had lost enough to truly understand what soul-boiling loathing felt like.

"All of you out," Beck said. "Keep to your currently assigned schedule until you receive new orders."

The lot of us began filing out of the room. I tried to hang back so I could position myself close to Walsh, but my wrist band beeped before I could join the flow of students.

"Lanni Roberts, report to the Root Dome." A little voice spoke from my cuff. "You have been assigned to guard the reconstruction crew."

A little beep came from another trainee's wrist band as I lifted my own to speak.

"Should I go to weapons storage first?" I glanced toward Beck to see if he would shout at me for daring to ask a question.

Beck just stood in the center of the room, glowering at us all.

The voice giving the other trainee his assignment was too faint for me to hear as I waited for a response.

"Yes. Yes, you have been assigned a weapon," the person speaking to me said, like they weren't really sure what I was supposed to do. But I guess the kep weren't used to getting more than twenty not-quite-guards to deal with all in one day. "Once you have your weapon, report immediately to the Root Dome."

I didn't bother thanking the voice.

Other trainees had stopped to listen to their instructions, creating a forest of frozen teens. I weaved between them, heading out into the corridor and turning toward the stairs.

Walsh had already disappeared.

I didn't know if that meant he'd been calm enough to walk while listening to his orders, or if he hadn't gotten any yet and had headed toward the Haven Dome for harvesting like PAM had assigned what seemed like hours ago.

A sudden fear squeezed my heart. I didn't know what time it was. Mari had run off to get Harper. She'd be waiting for me in the Haven Dome. But she'd go to the vehicle bay at eight.

If I was still stuck in the Root Dome...

"Fuck." The word slipped out. I hoped whoever was listening in on me had a fun time trying to interpret why I'd suddenly cursed.

Don't panic, Jaime whispered. *They want to hand you a weapon. Why not take it?*

I couldn't argue with his logic. My logic.

Even knowing Jaime was only a voice inside my head, hearing him speak was comforting. And I could worry about my slipping sanity once I'd gotten Mari away from the Incorporation.

I ran down the stairs, going past the guard barracks level and to the seed storage level where weapons storage and the entrance to one of the Arc Domes' two bunkers cut farther into the mountain.

I sprinted down the corridor, heading toward the entrance to the bunker.

Smack, smack, smack.

I turned at the sound coming from behind me. One of the other trainees slapped the wall again and pointed to an unmarked door before beckoning me toward them.

They opened the door and disappeared from view.

I ran back up the hall, stopping the door before it had closed behind them.

My breath caught in my throat just looking at the tiny space.

Bars boxed us in, keeping us from reaching the rest of the room.

Guns, rifles, clubs, helmets, vests—all the things you'd need to torment city scum—hung along the walls with bins of spares just waiting for the kep to stage a full-on assault on the outside world.

At the back of the room was another door. That one had a hand scanner to open the lock.

"Lanni Roberts?" A female guard stepped up to the bars. She glanced between her tablet and me, like she was matching my face to a picture on the screen.

I nodded for the woman but stayed planted in the doorway, unwilling to shut myself in the cage.

"You've been assigned a vest and a gun." The woman set the tablet down and pulled a weapon and vest from the wall.

The door shifted, moving away from my hand as the next trainee in line took their turn holding it open.

I stepped forward, taking my weapon and vest from the woman.

"These are now registered under your name," the woman said. "Bring them back when you've completed your assignment."

I peered through the bars, trying to catch a glimpse of the screen as the woman tapped on her tablet.

7:26. Thirty-four minutes until I had to meet Mari and Harper in the vehicle bay.

My weapon slipped in my hand as my palms began to sweat.

"Do you understand?" the woman said.

I opened my mouth to say *yes, ma'am* before biting my lips

together and nodding instead. I cut around the next kep in line and back out into the corridor. Even the concrete hall felt like a welcome relief after the cage in weapons storage.

What did the Incorporation think they were doing, banning us from saying anything as simple as *yes, ma'am*? But maybe I could've spoken, since the weapon I'd been issued was meant to protect me from the killer. If I was dumb enough to try and fight Walsh.

I pulled my vest on, feeling more strangled than protected by the thick material.

The trainee who'd been behind me in line sprinted past, charging toward their assignment, weapon in hand.

The Root Dome was above the vehicle bay. I'd have to pass where I wanted to be to reach my assignment.

Fuck. Fuckity fucks.

I ran up the steps.

Get to the Root Dome. That was step one. The faster I got there, the faster I could find an excuse to go down to the vehicle bay.

The still-healing injury in my calf ached as I took the stairs two at a time.

Don't panic. Just get to the Root Dome.

I sprinted down the corridor, bolting past Bloom Dome, not allowing myself to wonder if Mari and Harper were still in our building.

By the time the stairs leading up into the Root Dome came into view, the pain in my calf had sharpened enough to offer a stabbing distraction from my panic.

But the pain did more than draw my attention away from my racing heart. It was a visceral, undeniable reminder. I'd survived the bombing in the atrium. I'd survived living in the city back home. I'd survived the bombing at the depot, too.

Our fucking mess of a world hadn't managed to kill me yet. All

I had to do was survive for a little while longer and I could get Mari out of this kep-made, glass hell.

Voices carried from the right side of the Root Dome as I ran up the stairs.

"This isn't going to be finished in a day!" a man shouted.

"Our orders are—"

"We can't just slap some new glass in the gap and call it done." The man spoke over the woman.

I cut around the tiers of planting trays toward the voices.

A pack of twenty Outer Guard flanked a dozen maintenance workers who waited in front of the break in the glass, all looking somewhere between amused and annoyed as their supervisor stood opposite an Outer Guard, his hands on his hips as he shouted at her.

"I don't like there being a hole in our domes any more than you do," the man said. "But there's this little thing called *structural integrity*. The blast did more than shatter a few pieces of glass. It weakened the panes above the opening."

"Those panes can be fixed later." The guard stepped closer to the man. "Close the hole in the glass, now. Today. You can fix the rest of the structure once the domes are secure."

"That would be a waste of resources. We'd end up repeating the same work twice." The man pointed at the break in the dome.

All the shattered glass had been cleared away. They'd also taken down the blatantly cracked panes, leaving a gap twice the size of a kep truck between us and the outside world.

"A break in the glass is a breach in security," the guard said. "That gap is inviting trouble into our home."

And offering me a way out.

I stepped closer to the gap without even meaning to.

"You want me to do a shit job to make the guards happy?" the man said. "Have Captain Tate tell me herself. Until I hear the order directly from her, take a cue from the rest of the guards and shut the hell up."

The guard stayed frozen for a moment before lifting her wrist to her mouth. "Get me Captain Tate. Now."

She glanced at me as she stalked past, snapping her fingers and pointing for me to join the other guards near the gap. She didn't bother watching to see if I did as she'd instructed.

She could have spoken the order. Blocking the gap keeps the killer from escaping.

Maybe she's just as scared of stepping out of line as the trainees are.

The tiny flicker of sympathy nudging at my chest vanished as I took my place alongside the guards at the gap.

The Incorporation had made the whole world their enemy, and the kep profited from the Incorporation's massacres.

The kep deserved fear and confusion. It was only a tiny taste of what Mari had suffered growing up in the city.

Most of the guards were positioned facing in toward the center of the Root Dome, ready to stop anyone from trying to escape. The few facing the outside carried rifles, like they were waiting for a horde of enemies to charge up the mountain's slope to attack.

I faced toward the center of the dome, trying to look like I was afraid of the killer coming to slaughter us all even though I knew damn well that since Walsh hadn't already arrived in the Root Dome he hadn't been assigned to guard the gap, so we wouldn't be seeing the murderer.

I started counting in my head, trying to keep track of how much time had passed. I needed to get down to the vehicle bay without anyone wondering where I'd disappeared to.

The easiest thing would be to get myself sent to medical. It was on the same level as the bay, and I could just head the wrong direction at the bottom of the stairs.

I could trip. Or puke. If I pretended to faint, they might try to have someone carry me, and I couldn't afford to waste time convincing anyone I could walk on my own.

Be more inventive, Lanni.

Pretend to find a shard of glass. Slice my hand on the knife hidden in my boot. Get sent down to the medical corridor to have the wound healed.

I picked a spot on the ground ten feet outside the pack of guards, far enough away I'd be able to cut my hand without the kep catching a glimpse of my knife. I took a step toward the spot, tipping my head like I was trying to figure out if I was actually seeing something.

Shed a little of my blood and I could get down to Mari.

Easy. Quick.

I took another step.

Something warm spattered the side of my face. I reached up to wipe my cheek as the kep in front of me toppled to the ground, a knife sticking out of his throat.

CHAPTER FOUR

Someone behind me screamed.

I stepped toward the downed guard, staring at the knife in his throat even as I raised my gun.

It didn't make sense. Walsh needed to be in the vehicle bay. He couldn't be in the Root Dome killing people.

Another knife whipped through the air. Someone else screamed.

The pop of kep guns filled the dome as the guards fired on our attacker.

"Guards down. Medical, we have guards down! Back line, stay on the gap," a guard shouted over the chorus of pops. "Morris, Hunter, block the stairs. Everyone else, fan out. Let's find this fucker."

The shooting stopped as the front line of guards stepped slowly forward.

I knelt beside the first guard who'd been hit. He was already dead. I pulled the knife from his throat. It had started out as a kitchen knife, but someone had sharpened the blade on both sides, fashioning a far better weapon.

"What the hell are you doing?" The guard who'd been giving

orders grabbed my arm, yanking me to my feet. "Never remove an object from a wound."

"He's already dead." I held the knife out to the guard. "And the handle looked familiar."

"We already knew what the murdering bastard was using." The guard grabbed the knife from me and shoved me forward. "Now start searching."

It only took me five quick steps to join the rest of the guards who stalked steadily forward. They spread out in an even pattern as we reached the planting trays, like fanning out to search was something they'd practiced.

Would have been nice if they'd included that in training.

I veered left of the path that should have been mine, cutting closer to the stairs.

"Guard down!" The shout came from deeper within the dome. "Medical, we have another guard down in the Root Dome."

I kept moving toward the stairs, searching the shadows for any hint of a killer. If someone had decided to use Walsh killing the Incorporation Guard as inspiration for retaliation against the Incorporation, I didn't want to become their victim. But I was the spokesgirl for Project Progeny. The most hated girl in the Arc Domes.

A flash of movement caught my eye. A body rolled from the tallest tier of the planting trays.

I raised my cuff to call for medical before realizing the corpse had landed on its feet.

Walsh straightened up, grinning before stabbing himself in his already bloody stomach.

"No!" I leapt toward him as he gasped and tore the blade back out.

"Help!" His hand shook as he tucked his knife into his waistband. "I need help." He reached for me.

"I've got you!" I ran forward, grabbing his arm as he tipped toward me.

"We have another wounded." A guard spoke into her wrist band as she sprinted toward us.

"I saw the killer." Walsh choked, spitting blood out onto the clean kep ground. "He went toward the back of the dome."

"The killer is heading east in the Root Dome," she shouted into her wrist band.

Walsh sagged toward the ground.

The guard lunged forward to catch him.

"Go." Walsh spat out more blood. "Lanni's got me. Go get this fucker."

The guard nodded and headed toward the back of the dome.

"Help me get to the stairs," Walsh said.

"Are you sure you don't need to rest?" I looped my arm under Walsh's, fighting against his weight as I dragged him to his feet.

"There's a killer on the loose in the Root Dome." Walsh winked at me. "Let's wait for medical at the bottom of the stairs."

You're a fucking idiot.

I gripped Walsh tighter, holding him upright as he stumbled toward the steps.

The guards at the stairs gaped at Walsh, guns raised and mouths open, like they couldn't understand how Walsh was still on his feet.

"We need more medical to the Root Dome. Now!" one of the guards shouted into his cuff.

"I'll get you down the stairs." I focused my gaze on the steps, willing the guards not to stop us. "We'll get some pressure on the wound and wait for medical. You're going to be okay."

"I know you won't abandon me, Lanni." Walsh coughed, but blood didn't spatter from his mouth. "I would never abandon you."

He squeezed my shoulder, easing his weight off me as we took the stairs one at a time.

As soon as we got to the bottom of the steps, he pulled me out of view of the guards in the Root Dome. He let go of me, glancing up and down the hall before peeling off his bloody shirt. He had a red shirt on underneath, folded up to his chest where the blood hadn't reached.

He wiped his hands and stomach off on his bloody shirt and tossed it to the ground before pulling down his relatively clean red shirt to hide the still-healing wound on his stomach. He gave me a wink, took my hand, and dragged me down the hall.

You stupid fucking werewolf. You stabbed yourself in the gut!

He let go of my hand as two doctors came charging down the corridor.

You just stabbed yourself to get me out. Thank you, you stupid fuck.

As we reached the stairs, a pack of Outer Guard ran up the steps, blocking our path. They were all armed, ready to find the monster hiding in the Root Dome.

A head of bright blond hair appeared near the back of the horde. My heart pummeled up into my throat as Alec reached the top of the steps.

He met my gaze before looking down to where Walsh had reached across me, protecting me from the stream of kep. There was no mistaking the hurt in Alec's eyes.

I hadn't even noticed my shoulder pressing against Walsh's, like the two of us were a unit. I'd gotten too used to being near him.

I watched Alec disappear with the rest of the Outer Guard, knowing that abandoning him to the Incorporation would cause a much deeper hurt than my being near Walsh but unwilling to risk speaking to say I was sorry for all the damage I'd done.

He asked to be moved to group one in Project Progeny.

I tried to comfort myself with the thought as I followed Walsh down the steps.

He only did it because he was mad at you.

It didn't matter. I couldn't be sure Alec would want to leave the Arc Domes. I couldn't even be sure he wouldn't turn us in for trying to escape if I offered him a chance at freedom.

As we reached the medical corridor and vehicle bay level, two more doctors ran toward us, heading for the stairs.

The second doctor stopped, almost tripping over herself as she grabbed my arm. "You're bleeding. Where are you hurt?"

"I'm fine." I tried to pull away from the doctor, but she switched her grip to my shoulders.

"Were you in the Root Dome?" the doctor asked.

"I was in the Root Dome, but I wasn't injured." I shook free from the doctor's grasp. "The blood isn't mine. It's bad up there. There are at least three down."

"Shit." The doctor bolted up the steps.

I looked at my hands and my shirt, but I couldn't find any blood.

"It's on your cheek." Walsh grabbed my arm.

I didn't fight him as he dragged me toward the vehicle bay.

Six Outer Guard blocked the thick metal doors.

Walsh let go of my arm and pushed on my stomach, shoving me a step behind him. But he didn't slow as he neared the guards. He charged forward like he was just going to plow right through the center two.

The Outer Guard all raised their guns, pointing them at Walsh. One of the guards raised his free hand, too, gesturing for Walsh to stop.

Walsh shook his head and picked up speed, barreling toward the guards. He reached for his waistband.

I only saw a flash of bloodstained metal before Walsh sank his blade into the side of a guard's neck. He shot another guard with a silver dart before he'd even pulled his knife out of his first victim.

"Backup. We need backup by the bay!" the third guard shouted into his wrist band. He leveled his gun at Walsh.

I shot that guard in the neck as Walsh kicked the weapon out of the fourth guard's hand while shooting the fifth in the arm.

The fourth stumbled.

I shot him in the chest. The dart didn't penetrate his vest.

He lunged toward me, knocking my gun from my hand.

My vision blurred as he punched me in the jaw.

He wrapped his hands around my neck as he slammed me against the wall.

My lungs seized before I'd even begun to run out of air.

I pulled my knee up.

The guard shifted to the side, like he thought I was going to knee him in the crotch.

I yanked my shitty knife from my boot and stabbed up into the guard's armpit.

He shouted as he let go of me.

I kept ahold of my knife, yanking the blade from his flesh as he stumbled. I dragged in a deep breath, preparing for the next attack.

The guard jerked sideways, shock filling his eyes as hands grabbed his head, twisting sideways. He crumpled to the ground.

Walsh stood behind him, not even out of breath, surrounded by the six downed guards.

He grabbed two guns from the floor and waved for me to follow him into the bay.

I grabbed my own gun, snatched the weapon from the fucker who'd tried to choke me, and followed Walsh.

He stopped just inside the first bay door. As soon as I was through, he shoved the thick metal door closed.

I'd never seen the door closed before. Not in all my times coming into the bay for guard training.

A shout came from inside the vehicle bay.

Walsh snapped his fingers, pointing me toward the inner door that led into the massive bay. He cracked his weapon against the computer set into the wall, striking twice before managing to shatter the screen. He grabbed the wheel set into the door, spinning the lock closed by hand.

The siren blared to life all around us.

Walsh glanced over his shoulder, his eyes widening as he looked where he'd pointed before.

I spun around, raising the weapon in my right hand.

Two Outer Guard sprinted toward us.

"Open that door!" one of them shouted. "We have guards in distress in the corridor."

I shot that guard, my dart barely sinking into the side of his neck.

"Freeze!" The other guard raised his weapon, aiming for me.

A dart flew over my shoulder, hitting the guard in the eye.

Walsh shoved me forward.

I leapt over the downed guards and into the vehicle bay.

Walsh tossed the guard blocking the inner door aside before slamming it closed. He shattered the screen beside that door then cranked the lock by hand, just like he'd done with the first.

I hadn't even known the doors could close that way. I'd never bothered to look.

You haven't been planning your escape, either.

The sound of running came toward us from beyond the line of trucks, barely carrying over the blare of the siren.

Mari!

I wanted to call for her. To make sure she'd made it safely into the bay.

A woman wearing a maintenance uniform sprinted around the corner, like she was evacuating to the bunker.

Walsh shot her in the chest.

A man in a maintenance uniform skidded to a stop beside her. He managed to scream before Walsh shot him, too.

I held my breath, waiting for Mari to appear. To come running toward me, ready to jump into my arms.

I searched the shadows. No Mari. No Harper.

I ran down the line of trucks.

Walsh dashed in front of me, blocking my path.

Heat burned in my eyes as panic crushed my throat even worse than when the guard had choked me.

If Mari hadn't made it into the bay, if we'd left her outside the door...how could I get to her? There would be too many guards.

I shouldn't have let Walsh close the doors. I'd abandoned my sister.

Walsh shut his eyes and took a deep breath.

I opened my mouth, wanting to scream but too afraid of letting the Incorporation shits hear me.

He tucked one of his guns into the back of his pants and grabbed my arm, dragging me toward the front of the line of trucks.

I tried to pull away, but he tightened his grip, squeezing my arm hard enough to hurt.

He didn't stop until we reached the third truck from the front of the long row.

He wrenched open the passenger's side door.

Harper sat hunched on the floor, shielding Mari with her own body.

A sob hitched in my throat.

"Lanni!" Mari wriggled out of Harper's grip.

Walsh knocked on the door and pressed a finger to his lips, shushing Mari.

"But—"

Walsh held up his wrist, showing Harper and Mari his black cuff.

Mari's eyes widened in horror.

Walsh pushed me toward the truck, like he wanted me to climb in.

Harper slid up and over, taking the driver's seat. I had one foot in the truck before the siren stopped.

For one terrifying moment, silence rang in my ears.

"There is no way out." Director Holbeck's voice filled the bay. "Congratulations. You're trapped, Connor Walsh."

CHAPTER FIVE

I froze. My body, my brain, my entire being. Like I had dived beyond panic to a place where thought had become impossible.

"In just a few moments, the Arc Domes' guards will swarm the vehicle bay." Director Holbeck sounded calm, cheerful even. "They will kill you, Connor Walsh."

Walsh shoved me into the truck and slammed the door behind me.

"Let them fucking try." Walsh didn't bother speaking into his wrist. He said it like Holbeck was standing behind him, a weapon aimed at his heart.

"The only chance you have of surviving the next five minutes is to let the girls go," Holbeck said. "Return the hostages in good faith, and I will order the guards to spare your life."

Walsh met my gaze through the open window.

I opened my mouth to speak.

He gave the tiniest shake of his head before pounding on the side of the truck. "Drive to the outer door. Now." He grabbed the roof of the truck, hoisted himself up to perch in my window, and aimed his gun at my head.

"Lanni, what—" Harper said.

"Do what he says," I cut across her. "Just go to the door."

Harper's hands shook as she started the truck.

"Move it," Walsh said.

Harper tightened her jaw and drove toward the door.

"What exactly is your plan, Connor Walsh?" Director Holbeck said.

A low bang came from the doors leading into the corridor.

I twisted to see past Walsh as Mari scrambled into my lap. The inner door still looked solid.

"You want to kidnap three girls and drag them out of the domes?" Holbeck said. "Will you murder them on the outside?"

Mari whimpered.

I kissed the top of her head, daring to whisper, "Just like before, Mar. Breathe."

Mari relaxed in my arms.

"There is no version of reality where the Incorporation will allow you to hurt these girls and survive," Holbeck said. "I would have thought someone clever enough to get away with murder would understand that."

Harper stopped the truck just inside the bay door.

Walsh jumped down from the window, reaching the computer screen beside the door in two long strides.

"You can't open that door, Connor Walsh." Laughter filled Holbeck's voice. "I've already told you, there's no way out."

Walsh started tapping on the screen. A low beep came from the door, but it didn't open.

"They locked it." I shifted Mari out of my lap and dove for the window. "I heard Holbeck say it when I was in her office. The Incorporation locked the outer bay door themselves. It sounded like some kind of master lock Holbeck controls."

"Shit." Walsh glanced back at me, a hint of doubt on his face for the first time. "Shit."

I opened the door and jumped out of the truck. "There's got to be a way."

"This door doesn't have a manual lock to override the computer," Walsh said.

"Lanni Roberts," Holbeck said, "have you been helping this murderer?"

"Only because I threatened her," Walsh shouted to the ceiling. "I lured Mari here. I wanted Lanni to build a life with me on the outside."

"Walsh." I took a step toward him.

He pointed his gun at me. "But we don't have to die together. I care too much about you to let the guards kill you. Get back in the truck. Stay there until it's over."

Another, louder boom came from the doors leading into the domes.

"No." I mouthed the word.

Walsh shuddered. The muscles in his neck tensed like it was taking every ounce of strength he had to fight whatever orders were screaming in his head.

"Go back to Mari." Walsh spoke through gritted teeth.

We were trapped. Locked in a concrete box with no way out.

"I'm sorry," Walsh said.

"Move." Harper shoved her door open and cut in front of the truck, running toward me.

He aimed his gun at her.

"They aren't dragging me back in there. If you want to get through this door, get out of my fucking way." Harper grabbed the weapon from my hand. But she didn't aim it at Walsh. She darted behind him and smashed the butt of the gun against the computer screen. It didn't even crack. "Shit." She hit the screen again. "Fucker."

Another boom came from the door to the domes.

"Let me." Walsh punched the computer, smashing through the screen.

"Nice." Harper shoved him aside and reached into the wiring behind the shattered screen. "Everybody who wants to leave, get in the truck."

"Harper, how—"

Walsh grabbed me around the waist, tossed me into the truck, and slammed the door behind me, still acting like I was his prisoner.

Just in case it's the only way he can protect me.

I can't let them kill you. I don't want to lose you.

"Walsh, get ready to drive," Harper shouted.

Walsh vaulted over the hood of the truck and leapt into the driver's seat.

"Don't you dare leave without me." Harper twisted over her shoulder, looking back at Walsh, wires from inside the wall clutched in her hands.

"Wouldn't think of it." Walsh eased the truck forward, angling us so Harper was within arm's reach of my open window.

"Get on the floor, Mari." I shifted as close to Walsh as I could.

Another bang came from the dome door. The clack of concrete hitting the floor shot bile into my throat.

"Do it," Walsh shouted.

With a crack of sparks from the wires, the outer bay door began grinding slowly open.

"Come on!" I reached for Harper.

"Patience." Harper kept holding the wires together, her gaze fixed on the door. "Keep moving, you fucker."

The door opened wide enough for the truck to pass through.

"Harper!"

"Wait for it." Harper edged toward the truck. "Now!"

The instant the bay door had fully opened, Harper dropped the wires. She launched herself toward my window as Walsh stomped on the gas. Her fingers grazed the seat, but she slipped back, falling away from me.

"Harper!" I grabbed her wrists, keeping her moving with us. "I've got you!"

Her weight jerked me toward the window as the bay door shot toward us, trying to slam shut.

"Shit!" I yanked on Harper, terrified the bay door would smash her against the truck.

But Walsh hadn't slowed for me to help Harper.

The bay door crashed into our back bumper.

Harper screamed as the truck swerved.

"Hold on!" I planted my feet against the truck door, trying to pull her up.

"I got it." Mari grabbed the back of Harper's coat, using every bit of strength she had to help me drag Harper through the window.

Harper laughed as she landed on top of me.

"That was stupid," Walsh said.

"But it worked." Harper squished the air out of my lungs as she crawled over me to sit beside Walsh.

"You can't tell me that wasn't brilliant," Harper said.

"It was great," Walsh said. "Now crawl over my lap and take the wheel."

"Gladly."

I sat up, shifting as close to the door as I could while they switched places.

We were in a tunnel carved through the heart of the mountain whose eastern slope was the base of the Arcadia Domes and Incorporation Headquarters.

Lights glowed from the ceiling, but there were patches of darkness in between, letting the shadows swallow us every other heartbeat.

"How far—" I began.

"Not yet." Walsh slid into the seat beside me. "Sorry if this hurts." He took my wrist, digging his fingers in on either side of my black guard cuff. His knuckles bruised my skin as he pulled, cracking through the band.

I bit my lips together and shook out my hand. Even though the cuff hadn't weighed much, my wrist felt so much lighter.

He tossed the broken cuff past me and out the window. "Mari, get on Lanni's lap."

Mari climbed up, wrapping her arms around my neck. The poor kid was shaking.

I held her tight.

Walsh bent over, pressing his palm to the floor of the truck. Without even taking a breath to prepare, he stomped on his own hand, breaking his thumb joint.

Mari whimpered.

"Shit." Harper glanced down at him.

Walsh slid the cuff over his broken hand and held it close to his mouth. "Director Holbeck, consider this my resignation from the guard training program and Project Progeny." He tossed his cuff out the window.

Harper whooped with joy.

"Don't celebrate just yet," Walsh said.

"Any moment of freedom from that hell is worth a fucking celebration." A smile lit Harper's face as she raced through the tunnel. We hadn't even made it to the open air and she was already beaming.

"Just don't slow down." Walsh kneaded his broken thumb like he was coaxing the bones back into place.

"I can wrap your hand to keep the bones set." Mari didn't loosen her hold on me. "I know how to do that."

"I'll be fine." Walsh winced as he opened and closed his hand a few times. "I'm a fast healer."

A crackle came from the dash of the truck as the radio lit up. "Harper Kemp, return your vehicle to the bay."

"Shut up." Harper turned the radio off.

"Slow down when we get near the end of the tunnel," Walsh said. "Lanni, I need to get to the window."

I lowered Mari to the floor and squished in to kneel beside her.

Walsh crouched on my seat, leaning out the window, aiming his gun at something.

I twisted, trying to peek over the truck's dash. I couldn't see anything but the lights set into the stone of the ceiling.

Harper slowed as the darkness in front of the truck deepened.

"A bit slower," Walsh shouted. "Keep us steady."

My heart raced as the truck slowed. We needed to go faster. We needed to run and keep running.

I heard Walsh exhale just before he started shooting.

Pop, pop, pop.

Clink.

A spark flashed on the ceiling of the tunnel.

"Go!"

Crack!

The sound almost swallowed Walsh's shout.

Harper stomped on the gas as Walsh slid back in through the window.

Crack!

The tunnel trembled around us.

"Lanni." Mari buried her face in my shoulder.

Boom!

Bright light flared behind us as the tunnel shook.

"Shit!" Harper shouted.

The truck rocked as the ground beneath us shifted.

"Shit!"

The crash of falling rocks chased us out into the open.

The sky spread out in front of us as we raced into the night.

"Yes!" Walsh pounded on the side of the truck.

There were no lights lining the winding road, but a glow filled the basin at the bottom of the slope.

"Shit." Harper shook her head as she steered us around the curves, going so fast it didn't seem like the truck should have been able to stay on the road. "Shit."

"Get us into the city," Walsh said. "We'll ditch the truck there."

"What in the shitting fuckery was that?" Harper said. "Did you just blow up the tunnel?"

"Yes," Walsh said.

"How in the ever-loving fuck did you do that?" Harper said.

"Short story?" Walsh said. "My pack planted my exit plan."

"Pack?" Harper said. "What the—"

"That part's a long story." I twisted, sliding up onto the seat beside her, while still letting Mari cling to me. "All you need to know right now is that Walsh could have escaped without us and he didn't."

"How does a kid from the Ice Domes have friends with explosives?" Harper asked.

"Harper—"

"No." Harper stomped on the brake. "I'm all about getting out of the domes, but I'm not going to run from one hell straight into another."

"You need to keep driving," Walsh said.

"You need to start talking," Harper said.

Walsh looked down at his hands. I couldn't tell if he was looking at the kep weapon he was holding or the bones he'd just stomped. "You drive, I'll talk."

"Deal." Harper pressed on the gas.

"I'm a member of the Alliance, a group that's been working against the Incorporation for years," Walsh said as Harper tore down the road. "Until this point, everything the Alliance has done has been small. Little steps to try and protect the people on the outside from the atrocities of the Incorporation. But tonight changes everything. I was sent into the Arcadia Domes with a very important mission."

"What mission?" Mari peeked up at Walsh.

"I can't tell you that," Walsh said. "But I can promise that what I did is going to help a lot of people on the outside."

"We're just supposed to believe that?" Harper said.

"Yes," I said. "We have to."

"I completed my mission," Walsh said. "The explosives in the tunnel were a part of the exit plan provided by my commander."

"Blow up a tunnel to give you more time to escape?" Harper pushed the truck faster as the road straightened out at the bottom of the slope.

"Give me time to escape and cut off the Arc Domes' access to the city," Walsh said. "When we get to the city, we're going to get rid of the truck and continue to the rendezvous point on foot. Lanni and Mari are coming with me. We're going to my pack's base camp.

"You can come with us and trust the place I'm taking you will be a hell of a lot better than staying in the Incorporation's grasp and letting them torture you in the worst possible ways. Or, you can wait in the city and see how long it takes the Outer Guard to find you. Either way, I'm grateful for your help. We would have stayed stuck in the vehicle bay if you hadn't managed to open that door."

"Okay." Harper nodded. "Okay, so I follow you to the Alliance and then what?"

"You join the fight," Walsh said. "You get to help us stop the Incorporation for good."

"Fuck yeah." Harper grinned. "I'm in."

CHAPTER SIX

There are things I know I'll never forget. The way you wrinkled your nose when you were trying not to laugh. The rhythm you'd drum with your fingers when you were nervous. The perfect way you fit into my arms, as though we were born two pieces of one beautiful whole.

The details of you, I will never forget. But there is beauty in this world I wasn't wise enough to make myself remember.

The inconsistency of the wind. How quickly it gusts and settles. The vastness of the night sky when the Incorporation's glass isn't blocking your view. The power of knowing you can chase the horizon.

Our world is a dark and bloody place filled with so much pain and want, I'd forgotten to appreciate the glory of the things humanity hasn't managed to destroy.

I will never be foolish enough to forget those wonders again.

I am free of the Incorporation's grasp. I have completed the mission I spent so long training for.

What comes next?

I don't know what's happened in the Alliance while I was trapped inside the glass. How many of my brothers have fallen while I slept in comfort? Who in my pack is still alive?

What will this life demand of me next?

I clung to my mission for so long, success and freedom have left me fumbling in the dark.

I will report back to the Alliance. I will rejoin my pack. I will allow them to choose my next purpose.

They will give me a path to follow and save me from drowning.

I promise I will cling to enough of myself to remember the scent of your hair and the feel of the wind.

See you in the embers,

~C

The road cutting through the center of the city didn't have a piece of trash to mar its Incorporation-planned, pristine beauty. Trees grew between the streetlights, planted in straight rows like the kep wanted to inspire the people of their servant city to stay perfectly in line.

The roofs of the concrete buildings all angled south, letting their shiny black solar panels catch the most sun during the day. Even though it was nighttime, the lights in the building labeled *Manufacturing 1-B* were still on, like the night shift was hard at work making things for their kep masters lurking on the eastern slope of the mountain that towered above them.

All the buildings we passed were labeled. The kep had even used the same font that gave directions in the corridors of the Arc Domes to mark which of the city's buildings was for what.

"Where do you want me to go?" Harper asked.

"We should ditch the truck near the southern edge of the factories," Walsh said.

"Got it." Harper turned left at a building marked *Agriculture 1-D*. The next street was just as perfectly kept as the first.

"They trim the trees." Mari pointed out the window, her eyes wide with something between fear and excitement. "I didn't know people outside the glass did that."

"The Incorporation built this city to support the Arc Domes and Incorporation Headquarters," Walsh said. "They designed everything to be efficient, self-sufficient, and capable of surviving. Of course the glass butchers demand the trees be kept trimmed. How else could they take pride in the outsiders they force to work for them?"

"Then why didn't we get a pretty city back home?" Mari bit her lips together like she wished she could swallow her words.

"It's okay, Mar," I said. "Walsh knows."

"The city you're from, by the Plains Domes, wasn't meant to survive forever," Walsh said. "The Plains Domes were built near an existing city. The Incorporation packed workers in to build the domes and help the Incorporation stockpile goods. Once the butchers got the work they needed from the population, they always planned to let the city fall. Either by letting desperation tear it apart—"

"Or by murdering people." Mari sat up straighter on my lap. "I hate the kep. They killed my mom and they killed Jaime. They're evil, and I hate them."

"I'm sorry." Harper turned down a narrower side street. There were no trees on that road, only patches of vegetables grown right up against the buildings. "I'm sorry the domes are filled with awful people."

"Not completely filled," I said. "You managed to be a decent human."

"I had a solid barrier of booze to protect me." Harper stopped the truck next to the loading bay of *Storage 12-D*.

The building was huge, as large as the Root Dome at least, but there weren't any lights on.

"We should move fast." Harper opened her door, hopping out

before reaching in for Mari. "They don't load the trucks at night, but there's still security."

I passed Mari to Harper and climbed out after her as Walsh jumped out his own door.

"What will security do when they find the truck?" Mari asked.

"Call the Incorporation," Harper said. "But better to leave the truck here than on the curb."

"This way." Walsh waved us toward the street.

I pulled my weapon back out of my waistband. "Harper." I passed her the gun I'd stolen from the guard who'd tried to choke me.

"Thanks." Harper checked the clip.

"Keep the guns out of sight." Walsh stopped at the corner, looking both ways before heading north. "If anyone sees us, we don't want them to be suspicious."

"Who would see us?" I tucked my weapon away. "We haven't passed a single person."

"Why not?" Mari gripped my hand. "Are the people in this city not allowed to go outside at night?"

I waited for Harper or Walsh to explain.

"Let's just get where we're going," Walsh said.

As soon as we reached the next cross street, Walsh headed east, back toward the mountain.

"You do have a plan for where we're going," Harper said. "Right?"

"We have to get to the rendezvous point." He paused beside a building labeled *Processing 11-C*. "From there, we'll be taken to base camp."

"Fancy," Harper said.

The faint sound of voices came from behind us as we headed farther east. Not shouted orders or screams of fear, more like the angsty conversation of people who didn't want to be where they were.

Walsh tipped his head as he walked.

I held my breath, trying to catch whatever his altered ears were hearing.

"We need to move faster." Walsh picked up his pace.

Keeping up took an easy jog for me, but for Mari it was a full-out run.

She furrowed her brow, her gaze locked on Walsh's back as he led us into the slim shadows beside the buildings.

We headed south at the next intersection.

"I thought we needed to go north," Harper panted.

"Too many people to the north." Walsh spoke easily. "They sound like they're close to the rendezvous point."

"Was the rendezvous point near where the street got blown up a while back?" Harper asked.

"No idea." Walsh led us east on the next street. "I've been locked in the Arc Domes. The last time I heard from my pack was before the depot attack."

My breath caught in my throat as I waited for Harper to ask if Walsh's pack had been the ones to attack the depot. I'd barely forgiven him for his part in the bombing that could have killed Mari. I didn't know if Harper was desperate enough to follow someone who had come close to murdering her.

"If we're skipping the rendezvous, what's your plan?" Harper asked.

I took a deep breath, trying to calm my aching lungs.

"We go with plan b," Walsh said.

"Which is?" Harper asked.

Mari's pace changed. She gripped a stitch in her side.

"I've got you, Mar." I bent low, ignoring the throbbing in my calf as I slung Mari up onto my back.

"I can do it. I'm good at running," Mari said, even as she wrapped her legs around my waist.

"I know you're a good runner, Mar. You just need a little break." I fought to keep my voice steady as I ran, ignoring my body shouting that it didn't want to carry the extra weight.

Walsh glanced back at me, like he knew damn well carrying Mari was more than my calf wanted to do. But he didn't offer to take her.

We cut south again, onto a street lined with thinner, taller concrete structures. Something about them made me sure they were apartment buildings, like well-groomed, kep-designed versions of the place I'd grown up in back home.

The buildings had plenty of windows, but all of them were closed tight against the cool evening air, and only a few of the lights were on.

"Keep going south." Walsh pulled out his weapon, darting around us to head north before I even heard the woman behind us shout.

"I found them! I claim the bounty!"

"Fuck." I pulled my gun from my waistband, running as fast as I could with Mari clinging to me.

Pop. Pop. Pop. Pop.

The shouting was replaced by a terrified scream.

I hoped Walsh had been the one doing the shooting, but I couldn't look back.

"They're here!" The shout came from a man that time.

A door opened in front of us. A girl barely younger than me stepped outside, holding a board like a weapon.

I slowed just long enough to shoot a dart into her neck.

Pop. Pop.

The gunfire came from behind us.

I sprinted after Harper.

"I can run." Mari started to slide off me.

"No, Mar." I clung to her feet with my gun-free hand. "Stay where you are."

Bang.

The sound chased us up the street.

Bang. Bang.

Bark flew off the tree in front of me as a bullet struck its trunk.

Pop. Pop. Pop.

Bang.

"Go east," I shouted to Harper, not caring that people could hear me, just desperate to get away from whoever was shooting at us with an actual, old-fashioned gun.

Bang.

Pop. Pop. Pop.

Bang.

Mari tensed, tightening her legs around my waist. She coughed.

Her grip around my neck went slack. She toppled backward, falling away from me.

"Mari!" I twisted, trying to catch her.

She slipped out of my grip, landing face first on the ground.

Blood spread from a bullet wound in her back, swallowing the pink of her shirt as she coughed and went still.

CHAPTER EIGHT

"Mari."

Bang.

"Mari!" Her name tore from my throat.

"Mari!" The world tipped. I fell to my knees. "No, no. Mar, you have to wake up."

Pop. Pop, pop, pop.

I pressed on the wound on her back. She was so tiny. Fragile.

"We have to go." Someone grabbed my arm, trying to drag me away from Mari.

"I can't leave her." I yanked my arm free. "I have to pro—" A sob swallowed my words.

Bang.

Pop. Pop.

A scream echoed down the street. I wasn't sure if it was mine or someone else's.

"We need cover." Someone pulled Mari away from me.

"No!" I dove toward Mari.

Arms wrapped around my chest, hauling me to my feet.

Walsh had Mari in his arms. He sprinted down the street, moving faster than any normal human could.

I plunged my elbow back, breaking free from the one who held me, chasing after Walsh.

He disappeared around the corner.

Mari.

I'm so sorry, Mari.

My breath came in shuddering gasps as I ran.

There was screaming behind me. Sounds of fear and pain.

I wanted to burn them all. I wanted to cut their throats.

I could drown in their blood. Then maybe the pain in my chest would ease.

I tore around the corner.

I couldn't see Mari or Walsh.

"Mari!"

"Over here," Walsh called.

I followed the trail of my little sister's blood.

He'd stopped, hiding behind a staircase. He'd laid Mari face-down on the ground.

"Watch the street." Walsh tore the leather tongue off his boot and the sleeve off his shirt. "Lanni, watch the street."

"I've got it." Harper crouched beside the steps, aiming her weapon in the direction of the people who'd shot Mari.

Walsh pressed the leather to the place where the bullet had torn into my sister.

"Mar." My legs gave out. I crumpled beside her.

Harper fired her gun.

Walsh ripped away the bottom of his shirt. "Either watch the street or put pressure on the wound. You don't get to fall apart, Lanni. Not when Mari needs you."

I didn't know I still had a weapon in my hand until I dropped it. I pressed on Mari's back.

Her chest shifted just a little. A hint of a breath.

Pop. Pop.

"We need to go," Harper said.

Pop.

"They're getting ballsy again." She pulled the trigger, but nothing happened. "Shit."

I kicked my gun to her.

Walsh moved my hand, pressing the bundle of his torn sleeve on top of the leather. "You need to lift her, so I can wrap this around."

My hands shook as I propped Mari up.

"As soon as we get this tied, we're running like hell." Walsh wrapped his shredded shirt around Mari's chest. "I'll carry Mari. You two keep up."

I wanted to scream that I had to carry Mari. She was my responsibility. But I'd already failed her.

Walsh tied off the bandage. He lifted Mari, cradling her in his arms like she was nothing more than a baby. "Lanni, grab the empty gun."

"But—"

"We don't waste weapons where we're going." Walsh peeked out onto the street.

I grabbed the gun, gripping it like I might be able to make it useful through sheer force of will.

Pop. Pop.

"Now would be a good time to run." Harper stood.

Walsh bolted down the street.

I followed him.

I could barely see Mari—just a bit of her hair shimmering in the streetlight.

Black hair. Like mine and Mom's.

I don't know which direction we ran or how far or what buildings we passed. I couldn't even feel my feet hitting the pavement. The only thing in the world that mattered was following Mari.

I didn't know Walsh had slowed down until I managed to reach out and touch Mari's hair. The light had gotten too faint for me to properly see her. We'd left the city's streetlights behind and entered a concrete corridor like the ones I'd been walking for months in the Arc Domes.

"Keep moving." Walsh led us into a room whose only light came from a window high up in the wall. As he turned to close the door, I caught a glimpse of Mari's face. She was so pale.

I wanted to touch her cheek, but Walsh turned again.

He started pressing on one of the walls in the tiny room, using his knuckles like he didn't want to taint the space with the blood that stained his hands.

There were pruning shears in the room, and rakes and brooms.

Click.

Part of the wall shifted, forming a doorway I wasn't sure Walsh would be able to fit through.

"Careful on the stairs." He crouched to ease himself through the gap. "Harper, make sure the door is shut tight behind you. I'd rather not lose this path if we can keep them from finding it."

He disappeared into the darkness.

I ducked through after him, not caring where the door led. I needed to be near Mari.

Dim bulbs had been pushed into the dirt walls, barely lighting the roughly made wooden steps. The tunnel was tall enough for me to stand in, but Walsh had to hunch over Mari to keep from hitting his head.

"This might as well be here," Harper murmured.

As soon as she'd shut the door behind us, Walsh ran down the stairs, moving faster than I could manage without tripping on the uneven steps.

"This tunnel will lead you out into the open," he said. "I will be there waiting for you. I promise I won't leave you behind, but I need to help Mari."

"Go!" I shouted.

At the bottom of the steps, Walsh took off, bolting down the twisting tunnel, carrying Mari out of sight.

A sob drove all the air from my lungs.

"Keep your shit together," Harper said. "Run now. Cry later."

Another sob shook my chest.

"Crying doesn't help Mari." Harper shoved me in the back, pushing me to run faster.

I swallowed my tears and followed Walsh as fast as I could.

Even with all the running I'd done in guard training, the end of the tunnel was still nowhere in sight when my body screamed for me to stop.

It had to have been two miles, maybe more, and we were still in the same tunnel, with packed-dirt walls and wooden beams keeping the whole place from collapsing on our heads.

If they can dig a tunnel like this, they can help a little girl.

My calf had given out and I'd started limping before I finally heard Walsh's voice from up ahead.

"Just keep her alive until we get back to base camp," Walsh said.

"That's a hell of a lot easier said than done," a woman answered. "Demetrius didn't send me to help the strays you brought with you. This isn't part of my mission."

A different sort of light shone on the staircase up ahead.

"Please, Bell. She's just a kid," Walsh said. "Trust me. Demetrius will thank you for helping her."

"It's a good thing you're cute," Bell said.

"Mari." I took the steps two at a time. A trapdoor led up to the open air. "Mari."

Mari lay next to a tree, facedown on the ground. A woman shoved a needle into Mari's arm.

"No!"

Walsh caught me around the stomach as I dove toward Mari.

"She needs fluids," Walsh said. "Bell is helping her."

"Which really isn't my job." Bell attached a tube and a bag to the needle. "Who wants to hold the bag while I steer?"

"Harper can do it." Walsh scooped me into his arms. I hadn't even realized he'd been holding me up.

"Great," Bell said. "Harper, shut the door behind you. Then you carry the bag and I'll carry the kid."

"I can do it." I shoved against Walsh's chest. He didn't seem to notice. "I'll carry Mari."

Harper shut the trapdoor. It had roots and moss attached to the top, like someone had built it to blend into the forest floor. She ran to Mari and took her IV bag, holding it over her head while Bell carried Mari through the trees.

"Put me down." I spoke through gritted teeth. "I need to carry Mari. I need to be with her."

"You can be with her while we travel," Walsh said.

"Just let—"

"You're shaking, Lanni." Walsh carried me through the trees. "You look like you could pass out any second. We need a steadier set of hands holding the bag and Mari."

I looked down at my hands. They were shaking and covered in blood. Mari's blood.

How could such a little person bleed so much?

The forest opened up onto the bank of a river. A black boat waited in the water.

I forced myself to take a slow breath. "I'm fine. I need to be with her."

"You can sit with her," Bell said. "But the other one holds the bag."

The boat had been parked beside a line of boulders that cut out into the water. Bell carried Mari over the rocks and into the boat, waiting for Harper to get in before setting Mari down.

Walsh kept me in his arms as he jumped on board. The engine of the boat roared to life as I scrambled out of his arms.

The world rocked as we sped into the darkness.

"I didn't even know there was a river here." Harper knelt

beside Mari, holding the IV bag up with one hand and gripping the side of the boat to stay steady with the other.

I crawled toward Mari. I wanted to hold her, but I knew she couldn't be moved.

"The Incorporation doesn't use any of the few boats they have on this river," Bell said. "At least, not that we've ever seen."

I lay down beside Mari, touching her hand. "Just keep breathing, Mar. I can't lose you."

"We have a doctor at base camp." Walsh dug into the crate at the back of the boat, pulling out a rifle. "She'll be willing to help her."

"Of course," Bell said. "She's got nothing better to do than care for stray kids."

"She isn't a stray. She's my sister!" I shouted.

"You're both strays," Bell said. "The Alliance doesn't have unlimited resources. They can't go around treating runaway Incorporation brats."

"They aren't Incorporation." Walsh stood on the back of the boat, searching the night for anyone who'd managed to find our path. "Lanni and Mari snuck into the Arcadia Domes. They're outsiders."

Bell gave a low whistle.

"Trust me. Demetrius will want to meet them," Walsh said.

I brushed Mari's hair away from her cheek. There was no blood staining her face. She looked like she could be sleeping.

"I love you, Mar," I whispered under the rumble of the boat's engine. "You are the strongest, bravest person I know. You've just got to keep fighting."

"We're almost there," Walsh said.

"Can you warn your people that we need a doctor?" Harper asked.

"We can't use radios this close to the domes," Bell said. "Too easy for the Incorporation to track."

The engine started to slow.

"Do you even remember where the infirmary is?" Bell asked.

"I'll get her in. Harper, watch the banks." Walsh took the bag from her and passed her the rifle.

My arms shook as I pushed myself up to my knees.

"I'm going ahead. I'll get Mari to the doctor. Bell will help you find me." Walsh bit the top of the IV bag, holding it in his teeth as he lifted Mari. He jumped, landing on the bank five feet away before Bell had even stopped the boat.

"Mari." I lunged toward the water.

"Don't even think about it." Bell eased the boat up next to the bank. "You jump wrong and end up in the water, the propeller could slash you to pieces."

Walsh disappeared into the darkness.

"How far away is the doctor?" I kept staring at the trees, searching for any hint of salvation.

"Close." Bell turned off the engine then froze for a split second, like she was listening for something, before grabbing a rope and jumping to the bank. "Leave the rifle behind." She tied the rope to a tree.

I stepped up onto the side of the boat and jumped for the bank. My legs gave out, and I landed on my hands and knees.

Harper landed on her feet beside me.

"Put all your weapons on the ground," Bell said.

I scrambled to my feet.

"I'd rather keep mine," Harper said.

"I can't take you to the girl until you drop all your weapons." Bell had a gun in her hand. I wasn't sure where it had come from.

I tossed the gun from my waistband onto the ground and pulled the shitty knife from my boot.

"You, too." Bell aimed her weapon at Harper.

"How do I know you're not going to shoot me the second I'm unarmed?" Harper sidestepped to stand in front of me. "We don't know who you are or where the fuck we are. We need to talk to someone who's in charge and make a deal for our safety before—"

"Please, Harper." I gripped her shoulder. "I have to get to Mari."

"Fuck." Harper tossed two guns onto the ground.

"Anything else?" Bell said.

"No. Now just take us to Mari," Harper said.

Bell whistled. The trees rustled as five people dropped from the branches.

All of them held some kind of weapon. Guns, knives, even a sword. All of them wore black. All of them looked like they'd have loved nothing more than to kill us.

"Take the redhead to Demetrius's tent for questioning. Take the other one to the infirmary," Bell said. "Her sister should be in surgery by now."

"But Harper—" I began.

"Go." Harper shoved me toward where Walsh had disappeared. "I'd love to get some answers. I'll find you."

"Thank you." I squeezed Harper's hand and ran into the trees.

———

CHAPTER NINE

———

Tree branches tore at my hair and scratched my arms as I ran through the darkness. The forest was thick and healthy, like the one I'd been able to see through the glass of the Arc Domes. I hated the trees for blocking my path to Mari.

"Since you don't know where you're going, maybe I should lead?" A man sprinted in front of me, moving too fast to be plain human.

"I'm sorry." I panted out the words. Pain pulsed in my chest as I fought for each inhale, but it didn't seem possible for me to be breathing. Not when someone could be slicing Mari open.

I stopped to vomit beside a tree. I wiped my mouth as I chased after the man.

"Lovely." He slowed to match my pace as he veered to the left. The space between the branches widened, like he'd led me onto a narrow path even though I couldn't see any hint of a trail on the ground.

"Can your doctor help my sister?" I asked.

"How old is she?"

"She's only seven." The words broke in my throat. "She's just a kid."

"Then Vamp and Lycan aren't an option," the man said. "You can't survive being changed into a blood sucker or a wolf before puberty."

"Walsh said you had a doctor."

"We do." The man veered farther left. "And our doctor is good. But we don't have all the resources the Incorporation's hoarded."

"She has to be okay." Soul-crushing pain pressed on the front of my throat.

I can't lose her.

I couldn't push the words out.

A dim slit of light appeared right in front of us.

"I've got a girl to bring to medical," the man called.

The light widened as something like a curtain was pulled aside.

The silhouettes of four people waited beyond.

"She one of the rats Walsh led home?" one of the silhouettes asked once we'd gone past the curtain.

"Yep." The man stopped.

We were inside some sort of tent. The back wall was made of raw stone with an oddly shaped door blocking our path.

"Walsh's always had a soft spot for damsels," the silhouette said.

"Clear for light." A voice spoke from behind us.

The door in the rock wall opened, spilling light into the tent.

I stayed right on the man's heels as he stepped into the tunnel beyond.

"We've got one more straggler," the man said. "She's to go straight to Demetrius."

One of the people in the tent gave a low whistle.

The man shook his head, like the whistler was funny.

I wanted to scream at the man to stop shaking his head and run, but I couldn't make any sound. And, even if I'd known how to get to Mari, I couldn't have cut around him in the narrow passage.

The tunnel was short. I could hear voices coming from up ahead, but none of them sounded like the urgent orders of someone trying to save Mari's life.

The ground sloped down as the tunnel ended. The man kept walking, but I froze, like my brain couldn't process the scene in front of me and keep my body moving at the same time.

The tunnel had let us out into a massive cavern. Tents lined the sides of the space. Some were small, barely big enough for a person to crawl into. Most looked large enough for two or three people to comfortably share. A few were the size of our room in Bloom Dome. On the left side of the cavern, one huge canvas tent was surrounded by guards.

The guards all had old-fashioned guns, like the one that had shot Mari.

My body remembered how to move.

I followed the man through the center of the cavern. Everyone stopped what they were doing to stare at me. Still holding the weapons they'd been training with, or the laundry they'd been carrying, or the cup in their hand—all the little things that made it seem like I was intruding on their lives.

But there was something about their faces. Something wrong.

A woman carrying a wooden crate met my gaze as she stepped out of my path.

Her eyes were a violent, bloody red.

So were the man's who leaned against his staff as he waited for me to get out of his way so he could fight a knife-wielding woman.

She had red eyes, too. Like a demon, or a nightmare...or a werewolf.

I fixed my gaze on the back of my guide's head. It didn't matter if the wolves wanted to tear me apart.

I deserved every bit of pain they could offer.

Just get to Mari.

The floor of the cave sloped farther down as we walked beyond the tents to an area where niches cut into the walls. Supplies had been stacked in most of the nooks, but one had a desk and chair, like someone was using it as an office. Another had sleeping bags laid out, like it had been claimed as a home by people who didn't have tents.

But none of the nooks had a surgeon or any hint of a medical team.

The man glanced behind, checking to make sure I was still with him before heading into a tunnel at the very back of the cavern.

I didn't know if he thought I might've wandered away to explore the underground lair or if he thought someone might've ripped my throat out before I managed to cut all the way through the camp.

The new tunnel was wider than the first and had a steeper slope as it wound deeper underground. The walls were rough, the stone left as nature had formed it.

This is where they're going to try and save Mari.

She should be in the medical corridor, being taken care of by the best doctors the Incorporation has to offer.

The pain in my chest sliced all the way to my spine, stealing the air from my lungs.

I'd made the choice to drag her away from the Arc Domes. I'd been stupid enough to think I could keep her safe.

I choked on a sob. The sound of it bounced down the tunnel.

"We're almost there." The man said it in a kind way. He didn't know it was my fault a seven-year-old had been shot.

The tunnel led us into another cavern almost as large as the first. Wooden structures had been built in the space. Five of them. Each had two people guarding its door and wires running down from the ceiling to give whatever was inside the shacks more electricity than just the sparse lights hanging from the ceiling.

"This is it." The man stopped in front of the largest of the shacks with the most cables running power to it.

I reached for the doorknob.

"Step back." One of the guards planted herself between me and the door, pulling a knife from the sheath on her belt.

"I—" I coughed on my tears. "My sister is in there. Mari's so little and—"

"Are you a doctor?" the guard asked.

"No, but—"

"Then you're not going through this door," the guard said.

"But my sister needs me."

"She really doesn't." The guard raised her knife, aiming for my throat.

I looked behind me, ready to ask the man to help me get past the guard, but he'd already walked away.

"You're useless to that bleeding child." The guard pointed to the side of the building. "Find a corner to curl up in and stay out of the doctor's way."

My legs started to shake.

"Don't make things worse for that kid," the guard said. "Go."

I stumbled around the side of the shack, fighting to keep my legs beneath me.

I had made everything worse.

I reached the stone wall at the back of the building. There wasn't even a crack in the shack I could peek through.

She's better off without me. All I've done is hurt her.

I slid down the jagged wall, pulling my knees to my chest. I wedged myself in the corner like I could somehow keep my soul from shattering at the pain of knowing I'd failed my sister.

"I'm sorry." Tears blurred my vision. "I'm so sorry."

I'd failed them all. Mom. Jaime. Mari.

"I'm sorry." The words strangled me.

"Lanni."

Sobs tore at my chest.

"Lanni." Someone touched my cheek. He brushed away my tears.

I blinked, clearing my vision enough to see his face.

"You're safe." Jaime gripped my hand.

"I'm sorry." I leaned forward, collapsing into Jaime's arms. "I thought I was protecting her. I wanted to get her away from the Incorporation."

"I knew you'd find a way out." He held me tight, keeping me from slipping away from the world.

"She was riding on my back. They were shooting at me. That bullet was meant for me." I clung to him as sobs swallowed my words. "I'm so sorry."

"You're okay." Jaime started to shake with tears of his own.

"I can't lose her. I can't lose Mari."

"I've been trying to get to you. I swear I have." I could feel his skin against mine as he took my face in his hands. "I spent every day—"

"No." I tore myself away from him, shaking my head, trying to slam my mind back into reality. "No, no, no. Get your shit together, Lanni. Mari needs you."

"Is Mari in with the doctor?" Jaime looked at the shack. "They said someone in your group was hurt."

"She lost so much blood." A fresh round of sobs shook my chest.

He took my hand. "Mar is strong. If any kid can make it, she can. They have a doctor here, Lanni. A real doctor, not just some back-alley butcher with a stolen med kit."

"Stop!" I yanked my hand from his. "Please stop. I wish you were here right now. I need you here with me. But I can't afford to fall apart, and imagining you're here won't make Mari better." I closed my eyes, letting my tears spill down my cheeks.

"I *am* here, Lanni." His fingers were cold against my skin as he brushed my tears away. "I'm right here. And I'm not going to lose you or Mari ever again."

I opened my eyes.

He gave me a crooked smile. "I've missed you, Lanni."

"Jaime." I laid my hand against his chest. His heart beat against my palm. His shirt was soft from wear. His hair was longer than it should have been. He leaned into my touch as I traced the new scar on his cheek. "Jaime?"

"We found each other." He touched my lips and tucked my hair behind my ear. "I knew we would."

I threw myself into Jaime's arms, sobbing as I held him close enough the universe should have known we were one person who had finally put themselves back together again.

CHAPTER TEN

I don't know how long I clung to Jaime. Even when I'd run out of tears, I stayed in his arms, too afraid that if he let go, he'd disappear.

We waited, wound together in the shadows beside the shack that hid my sister. He sat with his back to the corner, and I leaned against him, my head on his shoulder, his arms locked around me like he was just as terrified that I'd slip away.

Neither of us spoke. There was so much to say, but none of it was as important as Mari.

I stared at our hands, at the way our fingers twined together without even meaning to.

He had a new burn scar on the back of his hand. I hadn't been there to wrap his wound.

I burrowed deeper into his arms.

Jaime straightened up before I heard the door to the shack open. He lifted me to my feet but kept an arm around me as the doctor stepped into view.

The doctor was old with white hair to match her white coat. Fresh blood stained her sleeves.

Jaime tightened his hold on me as I swayed.

"Should you leave?" The doctor narrowed her red eyes at Jaime.

"Your patient is family," Jaime said. "I'm not going anywhere."

The doctor pursed her wrinkled lips.

"Mari." I made myself speak. "My sister, is she okay?"

"Your sister is very lucky to have had Walsh protecting her." The doctor finally looked at me. "If she'd lost much more blood, there wouldn't have been anything I could do to help her. As it is, she'll be under my care for quite some time. But barring any infection, I see no reason the child shouldn't recover."

My knees buckled.

Jaime caught me before I hit the ground.

"Can I see her?" I asked.

The doctor stepped close to me, staring into my eyes like she was studying me. "You can go in for a few minutes. My infirmary is for patients, not visitors."

"Thank you." I forced my legs to stay strong as I took a step toward the door, still clinging to Jaime's hand.

"He stays out here." The doctor pointed to Jaime.

"Mari would want to see him," I said.

"No," the doctor said. "It's bad enough he's in the lower cavern at all."

"I would never hurt Mari or Lanni," Jaime whispered. "They are everything in this world to me."

"Hunger overwhelms reason," the doctor said.

"I fed before I came down here," Jaime said. "I would never put them in danger."

"Clearly, you don't understand the words I'm saying," the doctor said. "Under no circumstances will you be entering my infirmary. There are some risks only fools take."

"Jaime, what's she talking about?" I looked up at him, right into his black eyes.

Their deep brown that I had always known had been swallowed by darkness.

His fingers trailed across my palm as I eased my hand free from his grip. The cold of his touch throttled pain into my chest.

"Jaime." Whispering his name broke my heart.

"Let me explain." He reached for my hands. Mari's blood still stuck to my skin.

"I have to see Mari."

"I'll come with you." Jaime's voice shook, like his heart was breaking, too.

"Vampires are not allowed in my infirmary," the doctor said.

Jaime flinched at the word *vampire*, at being called the thing he'd become. "I would never, ever hurt Mari."

"If you don't like my rules, take it up with Demetrius." She strode back to the infirmary door.

I took two steps to follow her before turning back to Jaime. "Promise me you'll still be here when I come back out."

"If you want me to be." He held my gaze. I could see the test in his eyes as he waited for me to flinch.

"Good." I hurried after the doctor, too afraid of failing Jaime's test to risk staying with him a moment longer.

An awful feeling of relief tainted with guilt pressed on my lungs when I closed the door behind me. Then I looked around the infirmary, and all I could feel was helpless fear.

Mari lay on a table surrounded by bloody scraps. There was a tube down her throat hooking her up to a machine that forced air into her body. They'd tucked her in with a blanket like she was sleeping, but in the bright light of the bulbs hanging from the shack's ceiling, she looked too pale to be alive.

A man set a bowl beside Mari. He dipped a cloth into the water, wringing it out before wiping away the blood and filth that stained Mari's arm.

She looked like a doll made of spun sugar, too delicate to survive being touched.

"I should do that." I made myself step closer to her.

"No." The man didn't look at me.

"She's my sister. It's my job to—"

"You're not touching her." The doctor pulled off her blood-stained coat.

"Of course I am." I walked right over to the side of the bed.

Mari was so tiny, like a toddler. An innocent little child who I'd failed.

"You're covered in filth." The doctor scrubbed her hands in the makeshift sink in the corner. "It's hard enough to maintain a clean room to operate in. You are not lingering in my infirmary, and you are most definitely not touching my patient."

I looked down at my hands. They were covered in dirt and blood.

Mari's blood.

"I'll wash my hands," I said. "Let me clean up, and I'll take over."

"You have filth on your clothes, in your hair, and for all I know, you could be ill and contagious," the doctor said. "*Clean* is more than not having blood under your fingernails."

The man wiped the dirt from Mari's palm.

A hateful part of me was grateful I wasn't allowed to wash her. I was too terrified of her skin feeling unnaturally cold to truly want to do the job myself.

You're a fucking coward, Lanni Sampson.

I swiped the tears from my cheeks.

"I have to stay with her," I said. "It's my fault she got hurt. I have to make sure she's okay."

"Didn't know Walsh had dragged a new doctor back to base camp," the man said.

"I'm not a doctor," I said.

"Then you're not going to be much help in keeping your sister alive." The man took his bowl and cloth to the sink.

"Mari's just a kid," I said. "She can't be in here alone. She needs to know I'm here."

"She's incapable of *knowing* anything right now." The doctor finally stopped washing her hands. "And you should be grateful for it. If I didn't have the drugs to properly knock her out, your sister wouldn't have made it through surgery."

"But I need to know she's okay," I said.

"Because your feelings are more important than your sister's health?" The doctor dried her hands. "Go find somewhere else to feel guilty. If anything changes, I'll find you. If you haven't heard from me in twelve hours, you can come back and check in."

"But—"

"You're trying my patience. Just get the fuck out," the doctor said.

"I'm so sorry, Mar," I whispered.

"Out. Now." The doctor snapped her fingers and pointed toward the door.

There was something in the motion that made me want to tear off the doctor's hand and shove it down her throat.

"Take care of her." I let out a shuddering breath. "I love you, Mar. I'll be back soon."

I stepped out of the infirmary and closed the door, leaving my little sister behind.

I blinked in the dim light of the cavern, trying to force my eyes to adjust after the glaring lights of the infirmary.

The air smelled different outside the shack, fewer chemicals to mask the scent of silty moisture.

I tried to focus on the scent as I made myself breathe, needing something tangible to cling to as I fought the spiraling panic that wanted to drown me.

"She made it through surgery," I whispered. "She escaped the Incorporation. She's strong enough to heal."

The two guards at the corners of the shack stepped closer to the door, both of them eyeing me as they gripped their weapons.

I swiped more tears from my cheeks. "Thank you for protecting my sister."

A fist squeezed my heart as I stepped around the corner of

the infirmary. I didn't know if I was more afraid that vampire Jaime would be there waiting for me, or that I'd imagined him and he'd only been a ghost my mind had conjured to comfort me.

The fist squeezed even tighter as I saw Jaime standing in the shadows at the back of the shack, like he was hiding from the light.

"I..." I tucked my hands into my pockets, hiding Mari's dried blood. "She's alive. They won't let me stay with her."

"She made it through surgery. That's the important thing." Jaime stayed in the shadows.

"They said they'd find me if there were any changes, but I'm not allowed to check on her again for twelve hours." My voice shook.

He rocked forward on his toes, like he was fighting the instinct to come closer to me. "I can send you somewhere to get washed up and get some sleep."

"How am I supposed to sleep when she's in the infirmary without me?"

"You're right. I'm sorry."

"Don't be. You're not the reason she's hurt."

"I would never hurt Mari." Jaime sank farther into the shadows. "I would never, ever hurt you. Please believe that."

"You're a vampire." I stepped toward him.

"That doesn't make me a monster."

"But it makes my sister a potential meal."

He winced like I'd hit him.

"Mari's blood is all over the infirmary." I pointed at the shack I'd been banished from. "She has an open wound, Jaime."

"I know that."

"You're a new vampire. Can you honestly tell me you wouldn't have the instinct to feed?" The words burned in my throat.

"I would never hurt you or Mari." Jaime shifted closer to me. Pain filled his eyes as I backed away. "Even at my worst, I'd have enough control to not feed on the two people in this world who actually matter to me."

"I can't trust that."

"Neither can I. Which is why I fed before I came down here to see you. I'm not an idiot, Lanni. I know what I can handle. And I will take every precaution in the world to keep Mari safe. Vamp changed a lot, but there are some parts of me no drug could ever steal."

"I want that to be true, Jaime. You have no idea how much I've missed you."

"I'm right here, Lanni." He held out his hand. "A little stronger, a little colder. But I'm right here."

I reached out, trailing my fingers across his cold palm. "How could you do this to yourself?"

"Injecting Vamp into your heart isn't easy, but I managed it." He gave a tiny smile as he said it, like he thought I could believe it was a joke.

"But why?"

"It was the only hope I had of finding you."

CHAPTER ELEVEN

*I*ce *burned through my veins when the Lycan changed my body.*

Now I feel nothing but fire. Embers of rage glowing just beneath the surface, tempting me to attack with every breath. The urge to fight and kill calls to me. And resisting the blissful relief of bloodshed takes more strength than I can spare.

The pack is my salvation.

The orders of the alpha pound through my mind. His voice tells me not to attack. His words are more powerful than the instincts Lycan has given me.

The word of the alpha rules our pack of blood-hungry brothers. We are bound by the nature of what we are. The pack calls to us. I can feel the pack pulling on my soul just as I can hear the alpha shouting in my mind.

I am a wolf. The longer I spend with my pack, the stronger my bond to them will grow, the less I'll recognize the person you knew.

Even as I think of you, I crave violence. I want to rip the monsters of the Incorporation open and see how long they scream. I find joy in antici-pating the warmth of their blood on my hands.

But this is not the time to fight. This is the time to plan, to build. That is what my alpha commands. My dreams of Incorporation blood must wait.

We will attack. I will slaughter the monsters who made this world the hell that tried to break me. Slicking the ground with their blood will be all the more satisfying for having had the patience to wait.

See you in the embers,

~C

CHAPTER TWELVE

Jaime's tent wouldn't have been able to stand up to any kind of rain. Scraps of old cloth had been sewn on to cover the holes in the faded orange fabric. The sounds of people training and talking invaded our tiny haven, but I still glanced at Jaime every few seconds just to make sure I really wasn't dreaming.

"I can try and find you something better to wear while your clothes dry." Jaime dunked the shirt I'd worn to escape the domes back into the bucket of water he'd managed to find somewhere. He'd found a bowl of warmish water for me to wash up with and a sliver of soap, too.

"Want your clothes back already?" I stopped washing my hands as he looked at me, his gaze shifting from the t-shirt to the pants he'd lent me. The shirt was soft and held Jaime's familiar scent. The pants, we'd had to tie with a rope at the waist to keep from falling off.

"You can keep them as long as you want," Jaime said. "But I should have something cleaner for you. Or at least pants that fit."

"I don't give a shit about clothes, Jaime."

"I'll find something. I'll go see what I can trade—"

"Don't." I dried my hands on my borrowed pants. "You're not leaving me to go on a clothes hunt."

"You deserve—"

"You're alive." I lifted Jaime's hands away from the bucket. "You found your way to the Arc Domes. Do you know how much of a fucking miracle that is?"

"None of it was a miracle." Jaime kept his gaze fixed on our hands.

"Can you tell me what happened?"

"I took the Vamp so I could come find you." He tried to slip his hands away from mine, but I held on tighter.

"That doesn't explain how you found out where I was or how you got here."

"I'm a vampire now, Lanni. None of the rest of it matters."

"Yes, it does." I tipped his chin up, making him look at me. "I'm sorry I can't let you near Mari while she's hurt. I know how much you care about her."

"Mari is family."

"You're right, you are our family. And you're here. And you're breathing. And if the only way you could stay alive was to take Vamp, then I'm glad you did it."

"I'm not sure you mean it." A horrible sadness filled Jaime's black eyes. It would have been easier if he'd raged at me.

"Of course I mean it." I knelt in front of him, taking his face in my hands. "I thought you were dead, and I missed you so much I started having full on conversations with an imaginary version of you. I was terrified and alone, and talking to the you in my head was the only thing that kept me together."

"You're really not kidding." A hint of the hurt faded from his eyes.

"I wish I was." I wrapped my arms around his neck, daring him not to hold me. "You kept me alive. And vampire Jaime is much better than imaginary Jaime."

He pulled me into a hug. I rested my head on his shoulder, and he sighed, like he'd finally found relief from some terrible pain.

"The night the kep stole you, I heard you scream my name as they dragged you into that van." He pressed his cheek against the top of my head. "I swear that sound ripped my soul out."

"I'm so sorry."

"I chased the van for as long as I could. But I wasn't fast enough. When I lost the van, I went to your apartment."

"Did you see my mom?" I looked up at Jaime. There were tears in his eyes. I hadn't known vampires could cry.

"She said I had to leave it alone. I couldn't ask her any questions. She tried to throw me out, but I wouldn't go. Finally, she told me she'd sent you away. You were going to become a kep and live where you and Mari could be safe."

A wave of nauseous loathing rolled through my gut.

"She said if I cared for you, I should never talk about you again. You were better off, and I had to forget you'd ever existed." Jaime laid his hand on the side of my neck, trailing his thumb across my cheek like he had to be sure he wasn't imagining me. "But I couldn't believe you'd want to be with the kep. I'd heard you screaming for me when they took you away."

"I didn't want to go with Al—with the kep." I sat up straight, needing to look Jaime in the eye. "I wanted to come back to the city. But they promised they'd keep Mari safe and healthy, and I couldn't send her away on her own. I begged them to let you come with us. I swear I did. I never wanted to abandon you, but I had to protect Mari. I thought going with them was her best chance."

"It probably was. Things in the city got worse after the kep bastards burned the trade hall and the Misery Drain. The guards started raiding factories and homes, not telling anyone what they wanted, just causing chaos. People started fighting back. It only took a week for things to get bloody. That's how I managed to get here. I fought with the resistance."

"Jaime." I pressed my hand to his chest, needing to feel his heart beating, even if it was in an unnaturally slow rhythm.

"The kep guards were all over the city. I wanted to capture one so I could question them to find out where the caravan you'd been put on had gone. I managed to corner one, get his gun away from him, but he fought back so hard, he ended up dead before I could capture him."

"Jaime."

He pressed my hand to his chest, keeping me from pulling away.

"I grabbed the guard's gear, but there was something wrong with his earpiece, and he didn't have a tablet. I decided to see if I could take what I'd gotten from the dead kep to make a trade. I needed a better weapon. The guard's gun was useless, he'd barely had any darts, so I at least needed ammo. I went into the worst places the underground had left. Almost everywhere had been raided, but I found some people who still had real guns. They wouldn't trade me for the kep gear, but they said they knew where the caravan had gone. They'd tell me if I fought with them.

"They were going to try and take the water tanks back. The kep had cut us off. They were letting people die of dehydration to prove there was nothing city scum could do to fight back." Jaime's voice got low, like he'd somehow aged a lifetime right before my eyes. "We were winning the fight. We drove the kep away from the tanks. But they'd planted bombs under them. They blew up the tanks. I don't even know how many people died in the blast.

"I took shrapnel in my leg. I should have bled out, but one of the resistance fighters grabbed me and hauled me back to the underground with the other survivors. They patched me up and thanked me for trying to help them. Then they told me you'd been sent to the Arcadia Domes, so far away I didn't have a chance in hell of reaching you.

"It felt like I was watching you get dragged into that van all over again." He started to shake. His heartbeat sped to a near-human rhythm. "I begged the resistance leader for help. Said I'd do anything to get to you. He handed me two doses of Vamp and told me if I survived the change, he'd send me to people who could help me reach the Arc Domes."

"And he kept his word." I touched Jaime's cheek. "You're here. We're together."

"I should have gotten to you sooner. I tried, Lanni. I swear I did. I came here on foot and tried every day to convince Demetrius we had to get you out. When I found out about Project Progeny and what the kep were going to do to you—"

"How do you know about that?" I shied away from him without even meaning to.

"Information sent digitally between domes locations isn't as secure as they think." Jaime sat back on his heels, leaving a gap between us like my fear took up actual physical space. "I wanted to storm the glass to protect you."

"I don't know if I deserve your protection." I stared at my hand still pressed to his chest. "You shouldn't have taken Vamp just to come find me. I'm not worth that, Jaime."

"You're worth everything." He tipped my chin up and looked into my eyes. "I'd have swum to the other side of the world to find you, Lanni. And I don't even know how to swim."

A tiny laugh eased the pain in my lungs. I leaned into him, burying the things I wasn't brave enough to say under the comfort of feeling his arms around me.

"We're going to be okay." He kissed the top of my head. "Mari will heal. And we'll find a place where we can be safe. We'll take care of her together. Just like I promised we would."

I sat up just enough to be able to study his face.

Black eyes. Cold skin. None of it mattered.

He was Jaime. My Jaime. The person who had managed to make living in the hell of the city feel like something more than a hopeless battle.

My heart stopped as I dared to brush my lips against his.

The whole world froze as I waited for him to shove me away and say I was only a friend, a sister in his found family, and he could never see me as anything more.

A tiny bit of my heart broke as I pulled away from Jaime.

He just stared at me.

My mind raced as I tried to find the words to apologize.

He touched my cheek, tracing the line of my jaw. He trailed his fingers down the side of my neck.

"Lanni." He whispered my name like it was something bigger than just a word.

And then he kissed me. Gently, like he wanted to make sure I was more than a fragile dream that could be shattered by a careless touch.

He met my gaze. Pure joy lit his face.

I wanted to memorize the beauty of his bliss, but I needed to kiss him.

I leaned closer to him, pressing my chest against his.

He lifted me, shifting my hips so there was no space between us.

I laced my fingers through his hair, wanting to wrap myself so tightly in Jaime no nightmare could ever rip him away from me again. I teased his lips, daring to deepen our kiss, shivering as his hands drifted under the back of my borrowed shirt.

There was strength in his hands I didn't recognize and a need in me I hadn't understood when we'd lived in the city.

He kissed the side of my neck, tracing his nose across the skin I knew damn well smelled like a meal to him. He tightened his hold on me.

I closed my eyes, trying to block out any reality where he could want my blood more than he wanted me.

But he didn't linger near my veins. He tipped me back, laying me on the ground.

I claimed his lips again, my moment of doubt slipping away

more quickly than it had come. I pulled up the back of his shirt, wanting to explore the strength the fabric hid.

A happy rumble purred in his throat as he arched into my touch.

"Lanni." His lips brushed against mine as he whispered my name with such longing a part of my soul I didn't know existed caught fire.

I twisted, rolling to sit on top of him.

Jaime lifted the bottom of my shirt, easing the fabric up.

"Lanni," Walsh called from just outside the tent.

CHAPTER THIRTEEN

"Walsh." I scrambled off of Jaime. My knee dug into his stomach as I lunged toward the tent flap. "Is Mari okay?"

The zipper on the flap fought to stay closed, catching on the rusty metal.

"Let me." Jaime lifted me away from the zipper. "You have to do it slowly."

"Walsh, is Mari okay?" I shouted.

He didn't answer.

Jaime slid the zipper high enough for me to crawl out.

Walsh stood right beside the tent, his hands tucked behind his back like he was trying to impress Guard Beck.

"Have you heard anything about Mari?" I lurched to my feet, tripping on the cuffs of my borrowed pants.

"The last report from the doctor said she was still sedated and resting well. I've been sent—" He paused as Jaime climbed out of the tent. "I've been sent to bring you to Demetrius. He'd like to meet the girl who helped my mission to succeed."

"Will the doctor still be able to find me if anything changes with Mari?" I asked.

"I'm sure everyone will know you've been taken to see Demetrius." Walsh's lips curved into a tiny smile. "There's no such thing as privacy in base camp."

"Then let's go," I said.

"I'm coming with her." Jaime put his hand on my shoulder.

"Demetrius told me there was a vampire who'd been looking for Lanni." Walsh's smile broadened, making him look more like an animal baring its teeth than a human feeling joy.

"This is Jaime." I nudged him closer to Walsh. "He's my friend from back home. Walsh is the one who got Mari and me out of the Arc Domes."

"Then I owe you my gratitude." Jaime nodded to Walsh.

"Your gratitude belongs to the pack. And Demetrius didn't invite you to the meeting with Lanni. She'll have to find you later." Walsh stepped aside, bowing me toward the path that cut down the line of tents.

"I'll wait for her outside Demetrius's tent," Jaime said.

"There's no point," Walsh said. "Lanni will be safe with me. She doesn't need a baby bat to protect her."

"Walsh." I shot him a glare as Jaime made a noise like a growl.

"Don't worry, Lanni." Walsh looped my hand through his elbow. "Werewolves and vampires work together in the Alliance. We all have a role to fill in the camp. I'm sure Jaime understands his position. Don't you, Jaime?"

"Of course." Jaime's fingers grazed the back of my free hand. "I'll find you later, Lanni."

"This way." Walsh led me down the path.

I waited until we'd crossed through the center of the cavern where people were training with weapons and fists before daring to whisper, "What the hell was that?"

"I have no idea what you're talking about."

"I tell you that my best friend, who I thought was dead, is here and alive, and you're a shit to him?" I pulled my hand away from Walsh.

"Demetrius doesn't take well to people invading his tent." Walsh cut between two taller tents then stopped and turned to me. "Your friend wasn't invited."

"You could have been nice about it." I swatted his arm. "I just got Jaime back, and separating from him—"

"Must be difficult. I can tell how much he means to you. His scent is all over you."

"What?"

"Nothing." Walsh scrubbed his hands over his face. "This isn't the Arc Domes. Things are different now. I get it."

"Get what?" I took his hands, guiding them away from his face. "Walsh?"

"I got too used to pretending." He kissed my cheek and whispered in my ear, "Be careful trusting your life to the vampire. We may all fight for the Alliance together, but not all altered humans are forged the same. We're living in pack territory now."

"What does that mean?"

"That I'll miss pretending." He took my arm, gripping it more like I was a prisoner than a friend as he led me toward the largest tent in the cavern.

The guards holding old-fashioned guns still stood at the front corners of the tent. They bowed to Walsh as he neared them.

"I guess they're happy you're back," I whispered.

"They respect me," Walsh said in a normal tone. "They'll respect you, too, once Demetrius tells them what you did for us."

The guards shifted their gaze to me.

I hated feeling their eyes boring into the back of my neck as Walsh pushed the canvas flap aside and led me into Demetrius's tent.

Lights with mismatched bulbs hung from the ceiling, casting an uneven glow over the space. Along one side, three computer monitors all showed images of the Arc Domes and surrounding area. An empty cot and desk took up the other side of the tent.

In the center of the space, four strangers sat at a round table that could have held twice as many. Harper sat with them, studying the papers in front of her.

"I've brought Lanni," Walsh said.

All the people at the table looked up.

Harper stood and ran around the table to pull me into a one-armed hug. "Is Mari still out?"

"She is," Walsh said.

"She's going to be okay." Harper squeezed me one more time before letting go.

She'd been put in a borrowed shirt, too, and she had a bandage on her right arm.

"What happened?" I tried to remember Harper having been hurt. My brain got stuck on Mari.

Mari shot. Mari bleeding.

"A bullet nicked me while we were running for our lives." Harper shrugged and winced.

"I didn't even notice. I'm so sorry."

"You had more important things to worry about," Harper said.

"And we still do." A man with curly brown hair stood from his seat at the table.

"Sorry." Harper cut back around to her chair.

"Demetrius"—Walsh bowed—"this is the one who planted the chip that allowed us to break into the Incorporation's computers."

"Lanni." Demetrius studied me from my kep-issued boots to my unbrushed hair.

I studied him right back.

He didn't have any scars I could see to make him look like a battle-hardened warrior. He was younger than I'd pictured, too—he didn't look like he could be more than twenty-three. But if Lycan slowed a werewolf's aging the way Vamp did to vampires, he could have been fifty and I wouldn't have known.

Demetrius smiled once he'd finished examining me, displaying all his perfect white teeth. There was an oddly inviting charm in the expression that made me feel like I'd won something by gaining even a shred of his approval.

"You're not what I pictured from Walsh's account of your work on our behalf," Demetrius said.

"What did you picture?" I stepped closer to the table, like that could somehow prove my bravery.

"A child filled with rage and bloodlust," Demetrius said.

I tucked my hands into my pockets, digging my nails into my thighs rather than give in to the temptation to glare at Walsh. "I'm not a child. But the rage part is dead on. I've seen kep hurt enough people to know better than to mourn Incorporation dead."

Harper pulled the papers she was working on closer to herself.

"If it hadn't been for Harper," I said, "my sister and I would have been killed by the Plains Domes kep. She's saved my outsider ass more than once."

"So I've heard." Demetrius didn't look at Harper.

"Well, thank you for taking Harper, Mari, and me in." I swallowed the stone that rose in my throat just from saying Mari's name.

Walsh shifted beside me. I barely caught the movement out of the corner of my eye.

"We can begin by pretending things are that simple if you like. Sit." Demetrius pointed to the chair opposite his.

Suddenly, it felt like I was back in the Arc Domes' Council chamber, waiting for them to hand down some new edict proving they had total control of my life.

"The chip I planted"—I slowly sat—"did it work?"

"It worked quite well." Demetrius took his own seat. "Our people were able to dive deeper into the secrets of the Incorporation than even we knew the vile pit of their evil ran."

"Those files are going to help us save a lot of lives." Walsh stood beside me, lurking over my shoulder. "You made a real difference, Lanni."

"Good." I pressed my palms to the scratched-up tabletop. "I'm glad I could help."

"I'm sure there are many more ways you can be useful." Demetrius gave me another smile.

I glanced up at Walsh without meaning to.

He laid his hand on my shoulder, steadying me.

"The path the Incorporation has handed us is not a peaceful one," Demetrius said. "If the world were a different place, now that we have the information we need, we could slip away without the Incorporation ever knowing we were here. But our mission is to defend the world from the butchers that have slaughtered hundreds of thousands of innocent people so they could build glass palaces where they can comfortably watch while the rest of us suffer and die."

Harper shuddered.

"If we leave the Incorporation's power and assets intact, they will continue to abuse and murder outsiders until there are none of us left," Demetrius said. "They've given us no choice. We have to ensure the Arcadia Domes and Incorporation Headquarters are no longer a threat before we can leave this base."

"I don't know how much I can help with that," I said. "I had a little guard training, but I'm just plain human."

"You're a plain human who lived inside the Arcadia Domes and managed to get up into Incorporation Headquarters," Walsh said. "We need to go through every detail you remember—every person you met, every place you went inside the domes, every abandoned corner you found to hide in at night."

"Isn't all that in the Incorporation files you stole?" I asked.

"There's a difference between what a computer has been told and what a person remembers." Demetrius pushed a stack of blank papers and a pencil toward me. "Start with when you went up into Incorporation Headquarters. How many guards did you see?"

"I'm not sure." I looked down at the paper. "There were some at the elevator and some at the door."

"How many?" Demetrius said.

"I don't—"

"Try zoning out." Harper didn't look up from her papers. "Don't think too hard. You'll remember better."

I stared down at the blank paper.

The Incorporation Guard had come to get me in the atrium. They'd taken me to the elevator that carried us all the way up to Headquarters.

"I started with six guards." *Six in atrium,* I wrote on the paper. "There were more when I got into Holbeck's office."

"You were in Director Holbeck's office?" Demetrius said.

"That's where I planted the chip." I looked up at him.

"How many doors were there?" He leaned across the table toward me.

"One, I think," I said.

Walsh tightened his grip on my shoulder.

"Don't think, just zone." Harper set her paper aside and started on a new sheet.

I shut my eyes, remembering standing in front of Holbeck's door to record a video.

One door, I wrote on the paper. *On the walls, art and screens monitoring all the domes. Computers that come out of the top of the desk. Fancy soft carpet on the floor.*

CHAPTER FOURTEEN

What furniture did Captain Pace have in his office? How many people did I see when I roamed the domes at night, trying not to wake Mari up when I couldn't sleep? How many rooms had been converted into sterile breeding cages for Project Progeny?

Every time I finished writing out an answer, Demetrius would ask another question.

Walsh stayed beside me, never sitting, just standing like a guard as he prompted more questions. I couldn't tell if he was protecting me or making sure I didn't run.

They brought me food—grilled meat and some kind of boiled root. I tried not to wonder where the meat had come from. I'd have to get used to not having perfect food delivered to my door every day.

You gave that up. Tossed away a life of decent food and medical care and got Mari shot.

Demetrius finally agreed to let me have a break when my hand started shaking too badly for me to write.

When Walsh escorted me out of the tent, Harper was still working on her growing stack of papers.

He led me toward the center of the cavern, past the new pack of people who'd taken over the training area.

"Do they ever stop?" I asked.

"Not really." Walsh touched my back, guiding me around the far side of a pair who seemed determined to shred each other with knives. "Too many wolves and vampires packed into a tight space. Training helps keep actual fights from breaking out. We all heal quickly, so as long as we don't ruin the weapons, there's no harm in it."

One of the pair leapt forward, sinking his knife into his opponent's gut. Blood leaked out around the blade.

The rock beneath my feet seemed to lurch. "Can I see Mari yet? I don't know what time it is."

"We'll make it time." He wrapped his arm around my waist, keeping me close to his side, like he knew I was about to tip over. "I'll find some bedding for you and a place where you can sleep in the lower cavern."

"I should get Jaime. He'll want to know how Mari is."

"He won't be allowed to go with you."

A curl of self-loathing broke through my fatigue. I still didn't want Jaime near Mari. Even if he was my Jaime, he was also a vampire.

"He can wait outside the infirmary." I tried to stand up straighter and not lean on Walsh, but the cavern had started to sway.

"Vampires aren't permitted in the lower cavern." Walsh slowed our steps as we reached the guards at the opening of the tunnel. "Jaime shouldn't have been allowed down there in the first place, and the guards have been reminded of the protocol."

"Yes, Walsh," both guards said.

"Good." He gave them each a nod.

"Why not?" I whispered once we'd entered the tunnel.

"Why not what?"

"You know damn well what." I stopped, pulling away from Walsh, bracing myself against the wall to stay upright. "Why can't Jaime come down to wait outside the infirmary?"

"Rules of base camp." Walsh leaned against the wall opposite me. "The lower cavern is off-limits to vampires."

"But isn't Jaime a part of this camp?"

"Sure." Walsh shrugged. "We've got about a dozen vampires who've joined with Demetrius's pack to form this cell of the Alliance. Other cells are all or mostly vampire. Your friend is a valuable member of this camp."

"But?"

"But he's still not a member of the pack." Walsh reached out, brushing his fingers across my wrist before letting his hand fall to his side. "The pack follows Demetrius's orders, completely and without hesitation. We are one unit of brothers. The vampires are under Demetrius's command, but it's not the same. They can be unpredictable. They don't follow the same rules as the pack. They can't be allowed free access to our weapons, supplies, or our new human population. It keeps us all safer."

I looked back up the tunnel. "Can someone tell Jaime where I am?"

"Sure." Walsh reached for me. "I'll take you to him after you've gotten some sleep."

"I don't need sleep," I said even as I leaned against him so I could keep moving.

"You're an unchanged human who hasn't slept in well over a day. Yes, you do." The laughter I'd expected didn't rumble in his chest. "I need you to stay down here until I come back to get you."

"But Jaime—"

"Can wait. I promised I would keep you and Mari safe, and I will. But you need to acknowledge that you are humans living in a cave of vampires and wolves. I can only protect you if you let me.

I need you to trust me, Lanni. You don't understand how things work here."

"I do trust you. And you're right, I've never been in an Alliance camp before and you're the first werewolf I ever met and the only one I really know." I reached across Walsh, taking his hand. "But I've known Jaime since—"

"Who you want to screw around with is your own business."

I stumbled as Walsh let go of my waist.

"But now isn't the time." Walsh walked faster as we headed into the cavern.

"You're right." My legs ached as I jogged to keep up with him. "Now is the time to make sure Mari is safe."

"Well, you forgot that in his tent didn't you?" Walsh stopped twenty feet in front of the infirmary. "I'll find some clean clothes for you, too."

"What happens between Jaime and me is none of your business."

Anger flared in Walsh's eyes.

"Why do you even care? You don't have to lie and pretend we're a couple. We're not posing for the Incorporation's cameras anymore. There's no one here to order you to kiss me." I held his gaze, refusing to flinch. "And thank you for the offer, but these clothes are just fine."

"No, they're not. You reek of vampire."

One of the guards outside the infirmary chuckled just loud enough for me to hear.

Walsh silenced him with a glare then strode to the infirmary door and knocked.

I lifted the front of my shirt, sniffing the fabric.

"You wouldn't be able to smell it," the chuckling guard said, "but you stink of week-old blood."

Bile rose in my throat as the doctor opened the infirmary door.

She looked from Walsh to me and back again before speaking. "It hasn't been twelve hours yet."

"Lanni has been meeting with Demetrius," Walsh said. "She needs to sleep so she can get back to her work for the Alliance, and I know she won't sleep until she's gotten to see her sister."

The doctor held Walsh's gaze for a moment before stepping aside. "Three minutes, then I want her out of here."

"Thank you." I cut around Walsh and into the infirmary.

"I'll go find you some bedding," he said.

I reached back, grabbing his hand without thinking. "You're not coming in to see her? She'd want you to."

I don't want to be alone in here.

Something in Walsh's face shifted, like maybe he understood my fear of breaking at the sight of Mari lying in the infirmary bed.

"Sure." Walsh looked to one of the guards. "Kinley, find some bedding and a tent for Lanni. Tell Val I sent you. Tell her to take from my pile."

Kinley bowed and ran to follow Walsh's orders.

"Why did he do what you asked?" I said once Walsh had closed the infirmary door.

"I outrank him," Walsh said.

"I thought you were here to see your sister," the doctor said.

"I am." I stepped farther into the infirmary, trying to convince myself to look at Mari's bed. Panic shook my hands.

If she'd gotten worse, if she'd withered into some horrible, decaying doll, it would be my fault.

"Her color's better," Walsh said. "And it's good to see she's breathing on her own."

I finally looked at Mari.

She was so tiny in that big bed, but the tube wasn't in her mouth anymore. And the deathly pale tinge of her skin had lost some of its horror.

"She's on antibiotics and something to keep her asleep," the doctor said. "She's so young, she needs to stay sedated for a while longer. If she wakes up in pain, she could easily get upset enough to fling herself around and undo my work."

"But she's going to wake up." I stepped toward Mari.

"I told you before," the doctor said, "barring infection, she should make a full recovery. *Full recovery* generally entails regaining consciousness."

"Thank you, Doctor," Walsh said.

Tears burned in my eyes. I reached for Mari.

"Still no touching," the doctor said. "Your comfort is not worth the risk to my patient."

I stepped away, bumping into Walsh. He touched my hips to steady me and I leaned against him, instinctively seeking comfort in his strength.

"She's going to be okay, Lanni," Walsh said. "Mari will recover, and you'll both be safe here. She'll even have a scar to show off when she tells the story of the time she escaped the Incorporation."

"Thank you." I wrapped my arms around Walsh's neck, pulling him into a tight hug. "Thank you for saving us from that hell. I'm sorry I didn't say it before. I should've—"

"You were worried about Mari." He held me close. "And besides, I didn't save you. You saved yourselves. I just offered you a ride."

I tucked my head onto his shoulder. Tears slipped down my cheeks as I laughed. "Don't pretend I don't owe you."

"Your three minutes are up." The doctor opened the door. "You can come back in *twelve hours*."

I let go of Walsh and faced the doctor. "Thank you for saving my sister."

"Yes," the doctor said. "I'm very talented. Now get out."

I kept laughing through my tears as Walsh led me outside.

"Think you'll be able to sleep now?" He looped my arm through his.

"Definitely."

"Good." He led me toward the other side of the cavern.

The guard, Kinley, knelt beside a tent he'd just begun setting up.

"You didn't have to get me a tent," I said.

"It'll be better this way. Camp gets crowded when you don't have a private corner. Trust me. And once Mari is out of the infirmary, you'll be able to share."

"I keep having more to thank you for." I slid my arm away from Walsh as we reached my new fabric home.

"I don't think you understand how much good you did for the Alliance." Walsh pulled a red sleeping bag out of the pile Kinley had brought.

Kinley gave a low laugh.

"What?" I asked.

"Nothing," Walsh said. "Kinley has nothing to add."

"Yes, Walsh." Kinley popped the last tent pole into place and stood. "Anything else I can do for you?"

"Guard the infirmary," Walsh said.

Kinley bowed and ran back to the infirmary.

"He's an ass, but he'll keep Mari safe," Walsh said. "Her protection was ordered by Demetrius."

"I'll have to thank him, too."

"Sleep." Walsh handed me the sleeping bag. "Getting some rest so you can go back to answering questions—that's the best thanks any of us could ask for."

Holding the sleeping bag made my fatigue seem heavier, like concrete had taken the place of my limbs. "You'll tell Jaime that Mari's doing better?"

Walsh's jaw tensed. "I'll"—his shoulders went rigid—"He'll be informed."

"Thanks." I held his gaze for a moment, wanting to say something, but my brain was too tired to figure out what it should be. "Wake me up when Demetrius needs me."

I went into the tent and zipped the flap closed behind me. It wasn't until I'd crawled into my sleeping bag that I realized I'd seen something strange in Walsh's eyes.

I fell asleep before I could sort through if the look had been anger or fear.

CHAPTER FIFTEEN

"It's not enough." Demetrius planted his palms on the table, staring down at the stack of notes Harper and I had created over the two days we'd spent in his tent answering every question he threw our way. "There are still too many things we don't know."

"I don't know what else you want to hear." I dragged my fingers through my gritty hair. "I didn't know I was supposed to be looking for things to tell you. I was just trying to blend in as a kep."

"And you learned what you needed to know to pass as an Incorporation citizen from a tablet?" Bell leaned across the table, glaring at me.

"She's already told you that." Harper sat back in her chair, her eyes closed like she might fall asleep at any moment.

They'd been harder on her than they had on me. I'd been allowed two breaks to check on Mari and get a few hours' sleep. Harper had only been allowed to sleep once. If they weren't careful, she'd end up in the infirmary.

"All of your lessons were on a tablet?" Bell said. "Did you have access to any books?"

"Not really." I dug my fingers through my hair again, like that could somehow get rid of the grit from escaping the domes. "Jaime would get books through his trading stall every once in a while. If I had time, he'd let me read them before he traded them again. But between working in the factory, doing my lessons on the tablet, and taking care of Mari, I didn't exactly have a ton of time to worry about extra reading."

"While you were in the Arc Domes, did you ever encounter a mobile power supply?" Demetrius asked.

"I've already told you, as far as I ever saw, in my entire life trapped inside glass, the only mobile power supplies are on the trucks," Harper said. "Everything else is built into the domes' systems. Everything charges off the power supply there."

"I didn't ask you," Demetrius said. "I asked Lanni."

"Right." Harper laid her head down on the table. "Wake me up when you need me to answer more questions. The tent is spinning. If it doesn't stop, I might puke."

"I never saw a mobile power source," I said, cutting off Demetrius before he could respond to Harper. "Maybe there are some in the warehouses below the Arc Domes, but I never went down there."

Bell and Demetrius looked at each other.

"We need to make up a map." Walsh stepped out of the shadows in the corner of the tent. "Figure out what we know and where the holes are. Give the three of us time to work. We can figure this out, Demetrius."

"Can I please sleep for, like, an hour first?" Harper said. "Or ten minutes while you lay out paper?"

"What do you need a map for?" I asked.

"Currently, that isn't your concern," Demetrius said.

"But if I knew what you were trying to do, I might be able to help you more," I said. "I managed to weasel my way into Incorporation Headquarters. I can be useful if you let me."

"If I may, Demetrius?" Walsh waited for Demetrius to nod

before taking the seat beside me. "There are too many pieces you'd have to be able to put together before you could understand our end goal."

"I'm listening." I leaned back in my seat.

"It's not time," Walsh said. "Not yet."

"'Cause that's not cagey as fuck," Harper murmured.

"It's not. I promise. I just need you to trust me." Walsh laid his hand on my shoulder, giving it an almost imperceptible squeeze. "You trusted me when you planted the chip. You trusted me when I asked you to come here. We just need a little more time to sort through the information we gained from the Incorporation's computers—"

"Enough." Demetrius didn't shout, but somehow it felt like he had.

"Fine." I looked straight at Walsh, trying to pretend everyone else in the tent had disappeared. "I trust you. I'll help you with the map and whatever else you need."

"After sleep, right?" Harper said. "Because I'm either going to vomit or pass out if you don't let me sleep."

"Bell, take Harper to the lower cavern to sleep," Demetrius said. "I want her back here in four hours."

"Sounds great," Harper groaned as she got to her feet.

"Walsh, take Lanni and see what good she is with our weapons." Demetrius began sorting through the stacks of papers where Harper and I had written out every detail we could remember.

"You're going to let me touch your weapons?" A bit of the fear that had been scratching at the edges of my stomach disappeared.

"Of course." Demetrius gave me one of his perfect, inviting smiles. "Everyone in my camp earns their keep. I can't afford to feed people who don't contribute. And, should the time come, everyone will be expected to fight."

A shiver ran down my spine. "But not Mari, right? She's just a kid."

"We're not monsters," Bell said. "There are other ways your kid sister can be of use."

"We'll have her cooking and darning socks in no time," Demetrius said.

"You're in luck with Mari." Walsh stood. "She's already a great cook."

"Yeah, she is." I pushed myself to my feet and followed Walsh out of the tent. I waited until Harper and Bell passed us to speak. "They really aren't going to make Mari fight, right?"

"No. She's way too young." He shifted to walk closer to me as we passed a group of people sitting around some sort of dice game. "Everyone in the Alliance is required to learn a secondary skill besides fighting. Mari will work on that until she's old enough to train with weapons."

"What's your secondary skill?" I asked.

"Learning everything I needed to pass as a student in the domes was my secondary skill." Walsh took my arm, leading me through the sparring pairs. "It'll be my job to pass on as much of that knowledge as I can."

"You trained to be a teacher?"

"I trained to teach and lead. All that time we spent learning about planting and animal husbandry is going to come in handy, too."

I laughed. The sensation felt strangely wonderful.

"Is farming funny?" Walsh furrowed his brow.

"Picturing werewolves farming is funny."

"We're not vampires." Walsh stopped in front of the woman who was doling out weapons. "We eat actual food."

"Blood is food."

I turned at the sound of Jaime's voice.

"Only for bloodsuckers," the weapons woman said. "Wolves don't stoop that low."

"At least my mind is my own," Jaime said. "I'd rather drink blood than let an alpha control me."

The woman growled.

"Is your mind really your own?" Walsh stepped closer to Jaime. "You can't be trusted in the lower cavern. The temptation to feed burns through your veins."

"Walsh, don't," I said.

"I would never hurt Mari." There was no pain in Jaime's voice, only sharp anger.

"Jaime, I know you care about Mar." I cut around to stand in front of Walsh. "And once she's healed—"

"He still won't be allowed in the lower cavern," Walsh said.

"You'd tear Mar's throat out if your alpha commanded it." Jaime stepped closer to me, pinning me between himself and Walsh like he'd forgotten I was there.

"What the hell is wrong with you two?" I tried to elbow my way free.

"My alpha would never hurt a child," Walsh said. "You'd drain Lanni for a snack."

"I'm in love with her, you sick fuck!"

"Jaime—"

I don't know which of them pushed me, but I flew sideways. Pain pounded through my shoulder as I slammed against the hard, stone ground.

"Shit." I rolled to my hands and knees, trying to make sense of the chaos in front of me.

Jaime dove at Walsh, hitting him in the face and landing another punch in his stomach.

Walsh stumbled back but blocked Jaime's next attack. He grabbed Jaime's arm, flinging him up and over his head then smashing him against the ground.

"Jaime!"

Neither of them noticed I'd screamed as Jaime leapt back to his feet. He kicked low, aiming for Walsh's knee, but Walsh jumped out of the way, bringing his fist around to hit Jaime in the kidney.

Jaime growled like some sort of feral beast as Walsh locked his arm around Jaime's neck.

"Don't leave your scent on something you can't defend," Walsh spat.

"Stop it!" I got to my feet, ready to try and break them apart.

The weapons woman caught me by the arm. "Best to not."

Jaime shot his elbow back into Walsh's stomach as he twisted, tossing Walsh aside.

Walsh let go of Jaime, falling to the ground and rolling back up to his feet in the same smooth movement.

"I can defend her." Jaime charged forward.

Walsh dodged and caught Jaime behind the legs, sending him crashing to the ground. He leapt on top of Jaime, plunging his knee into Jaime's gut and punching him in the face.

"Stop!" I fought against the woman's grip.

"If you really believe that, you're a fucking idiot." Walsh punched him in the face again.

"Walsh, please!"

He looked up at me, blinking, his hand pulled back to hit Jaime again.

"Walsh," I whispered. "Don't."

He leapt to his feet and backed away from Jaime. "If you can't beat one werewolf, then you better get your shit together. You're too weak to survive."

He shoved his way through the crowd I hadn't noticed forming around us and stormed into the tunnel that led to the open air.

I couldn't convince myself to speak until he'd disappeared. "Jaime, are you okay?"

The woman kept her grip on my arm as she slid in front of me, standing between me and Jaime.

"I'm fine." Jaime got to his feet and wiped the blood off his lip. The wound beneath had already begun to heal. He rolled his shoulder like he was checking for damage.

"What you are is lucky," the woman said. "Don't pick fights with wolves. You're lucky Walsh didn't whale you into the ground. It's not in a werewolf's nature to back away from a fight."

"I'm not the one who started it," Jaime said.

"Yeah, you are." The woman finally let go of my arm. "And if you think any of us are dumb enough to not see what's going on, you really don't have a chance of surviving. Now get the fuck away from my weapons, both of you."

"No problem." I grabbed Jaime's arm, dragging him through the dwindling crowd and toward his tent. I hadn't been back there since I'd kissed him. Hadn't gotten to do more than wave to him as Walsh ferried me from the lower cavern to Demetrius's tent and back again. I searched the sea of tents for the orange of Jaime's fabric home.

"He's wrong, you know." Jaime took over leading, weaving a path through the lines of tents. "I can survive here. I've spent my whole life surviving."

"I know you have. Hell, you've saved my ass more than once."

"I can protect you." Jaime stopped beside his tent. He laid his hand on my shoulder.

I winced at his touch.

"What's wrong?" He backed away from me.

"I'm fine." I carefully poked the sore spot on my arm. "When I got knocked over so you and Walsh could brawl in peace, I landed on my shoulder."

"Did I—" Jaime dragged his hands down his face. "Was it me?"

"I don't know." I fought the instinct to shake out my shoulders and pretend I was fine.

"You should go down to the infirmary."

"It's a bruise." I circled my arm. "It'll heal on its own. I'm an unchanged human, not porcelain."

"That doesn't keep me from worrying about you." He offered me his hand. "I'm so sorry I got into a fight anywhere near you. I should know better. I'll do better. They're just...he's keeping you away from me. I finally get you back and I barely get to see you."

"I've been in Demetrius's tent getting questioned. He's the one who sent me to use the weapons. I was over there to train. We're going to end up in the same fight eventually." I twined my fingers through his. "Just try not to get into another brawl with Walsh. He's done a lot for Mari and me."

"More than we've managed together?" Wrinkles pinched between his eyebrows.

"It's not a competition." I touched his cheek, not letting myself pull away from the cold of his skin. "We have plenty of enemies without you and Walsh trying to tear each other apart for no fucking reason. Who eats food and who drinks blood shouldn't matter. We're hiding in a cave filled with people who want to fight the Incorporation. Let's just focus on that and getting Mari healthy."

"And when we get out of the cave?" Jaime pressed my hand to his cheek.

"I have no idea what happens next."

"We should stay together." Hurt flashed in Jaime's black eyes.

"That's the easy part. I'm supposed to have a secondary skill besides fighting." I curled myself into Jaime's arms. "The only thing I'm good at is stealing, which doesn't seem helpful."

"The Alliance will find a way for you to contribute. I hunt to feed the wolves."

"But you don't eat meat." I tipped my chin to look up at him.

"I drain the animals to feed me and hand the meat over to feed the pack."

I wrinkled my nose, trying not to picture Jaime drinking the blood out of a still-fluffy rabbit. "I guess that's a good way to save resources."

"It's not as glamorous as having a booth in the trade hall, but I can skin and butcher animals now. I've even started to learn about tanning leather."

"What the hell am I supposed to do? Be a farmer? A cook?" A tingle of panic crept through my limbs. "I don't have any usable skills. I—"

"You could make a decent weaver. And I don't think there could ever be too many farmers." Jaime gave me a crooked smile. "Don't worry. They'll find a skill for you to learn. You're smart. You're capable. Everything will be fine."

"Promise?" The childish question wobbled in my throat.

He brushed his lips against mine. "We're together. We can figure everything else out."

I kissed him, my body melting against his as I let his strength keep me from dissolving into a puddle of useless fear.

He sighed, like me clinging to him offered him just as much relief as it did me.

"Lanni!"

I flinched as someone shouted my name.

"Lanni." Bell stalked toward us. "Demetrius ordered you to train."

"Yeah well, shit happens." I let go of Jaime and turned to face her.

She glared at me.

"Walsh left," I said.

"Then congratulations." Bell grinned. "I'm your new trainer."

CHAPTER SIXTEEN

We'd laid out rows of paper in Walsh's tent, one for each level of the Arc Domes, with only two pieces left above the rest for the little information I could provide about Incorporation Headquarters.

I sat on the ground beside the row of housing domes, staring at the sketch of Bloom Dome. It was the right size and in the right place, Demetrius had been able to get that information when they'd hacked into the Incorporation's computers, but something about the picture made it seem like a place I'd never been.

"You okay?" Harper knelt beside the row that held the vehicle bay, working on a rough sketch of where everything was stored in the room for vehicle maintenance.

"Yeah." I drew in the fountain at the center of Bloom Dome. "Just weird to see it all laid out like this."

"The more we know, the better off we'll be." Walsh leaned over the four pages that made up the atrium.

"Better off we'll be for what?" Harper asked, not even looking up from her work, like she already knew what Walsh's answer would be.

"For whatever becomes necessary," Walsh said.

"Great." Harper scooted closer to her drawing. "Just as long as we're clear."

I gave up on Bloom Dome and moved on to the Salt Dome. The walkway over the tanks had already been drawn in.

"The Incorporation knows that four people who lived in the Arc Domes escaped," Walsh said. "They know two of us were training with the guards. Every bit of security in that place will have been tightened."

"Then, random idea here, let's run far away from the Incorporation and never look back," Harper said.

"That's not the mission the Alliance has given us." Walsh marked the spot in the atrium where we'd met more than once—out of view of the path, where the noise of the stream kept us from being overheard.

I fixed my gaze back on the picture of the Salt Dome, drawing in the shadowy corner of the beach where I used to meet Alec. I hated the strange sadness that rolled through my chest. Alec wouldn't have wanted to be in Walsh's tent plotting against the Incorporation, even if I could have found a chance to ask him to come with us.

I shaded in the place where the pumps for the tanks hugged the glass of the Salt Dome.

"What's that?" Walsh asked.

I tensed as he shifted to kneel beside me.

He watched me for a moment, like he was waiting for me to tell him to back away. But as much as I knew that being afraid of a brawling werewolf was smart, I couldn't bring myself to feel unsafe beside him.

"It's the gap between the pumps for the tanks and the glass of the dome." I drew a hard line on the beach side of my shading where steel beams blocked the path. "It's a tight space, but I managed to squeeze into it when we were searching the domes for the one who'd killed the Incorporation Guard."

"Good." Walsh nodded. "That's good."

"So little hiding spots are helpful?" I looked up at him. A bit of blood stained his collar even though all his wounds from his fight with Jaime had vanished.

"Very." Walsh reached across me to draw in the willow tree in Bloom Dome.

The place where he'd kissed me and made me forget there were Incorporation cameras snapping pictures of him touching my breasts.

My breath caught in my chest as he leaned even closer to draw the stand of twisted trees where we'd hidden together and it'd felt like maybe we could hide forever.

"There are a few unused classrooms." I scooted away from Walsh. "But I can't honestly remember which ones they are."

"It's just too secure." Harper set her pencil down. "You can keep not telling me what you're planning, but I can promise you it won't work. There are chokepoints on the stairs leading between levels. So, trying to get into the warehouse below the domes is a suicide mission at best.

"Even if we could cut off someone's hand and use it to get up into Incorporation Headquarters, Lanni says there's a hall right off the elevator leading to the Incorporation's atrium. We'd be taken down before we even made it out into the open."

"You're talking as though the pack fights like plain humans," Walsh said.

"So you are planning a fight." I took Walsh's hand without meaning to. "I get that the Incorporation is fucking evil and sitting on a hoard of supplies, but you can't—"

"I can and will do whatever my alpha orders." Walsh tightened his hold on my hand.

"We barely escaped. You can't go back in," I said.

"Demetrius will be given all the information we have, then he will decide how the pack and everyone else in this camp will proceed," Walsh said.

"Fighting the kep inside the Arc Domes would be suicide." I pulled my hand from his. "We need to slip in, get what Demetrius wants, and get the hell out. Tell me that's what we're making this map for."

"Demetrius's plans aren't for me to share." He looked down at the map. "The Alliance is counting on us. Our mission is about more than just the people in this camp."

"You can't bring Mari and me here and then jump straight into planning to let the Incorporation murder you." I took Walsh's face in my hands and leaned sideways, blocking his view of the map.

"I thought you wanted your vampire to protect you." Walsh lifted my hands away from his cheeks.

A tiny pain shocked through me.

"What the hell is wrong with you?" I tried to keep the pain out of my voice.

"Don't." Walsh dropped my hands and stood, backing away from me.

"And I suddenly have the urgent need to pee. Good luck, kids." Harper bolted out of the tent.

"Wanting you to stay alive isn't about my protection," I said. "You're my friend. Mari cares about you."

"When she wakes up, she'll be so ecstatic the vampire is here, she'll forget I even exist." Walsh backed farther away from me.

"That's not true, and you know it. Jaime being here doesn't change anything."

"Are you genuinely naïve enough to believe that?" Walsh flexed his hands and started pacing.

"It's not naïve to want to keep your friends alive." I looked away from him and down at the drawing. My gaze landed on our hiding spot. "We are friends, aren't we?"

"You don't understand." Walsh dug his knuckles into his temples. "Do you have any idea how hard it is for me to be in this tent right now?"

"Why would that be hard?" I stood.

"The vampire left his scent all over you." He kept pacing. "That blood sucker is looking for a fight. He gave you his clothes. He kissed you. The entire pack knows."

"Why would the pack care who I kiss?" Heat rushed to my cheeks. "It's not like you and I were ever a real couple. You only ever kissed me when you had to."

"It left my scent on you. It's still there, lingering under the vampire's stench."

I sniffed my hair. The only thing I could smell was stone.

"The wolf inside my head wants to rip out the vampire's heart and claim you as mine."

"I'm sorry, what?" I let go of my hair. "I'm not a meal to be claimed."

"You would be safer with me." Walsh kept talking like he hadn't heard me. "The pack would protect you if you were my mate. The vampires won't take care of you. All the bloodsuckers do is hunt for their next meal. You'd be better off with me."

"Let me get this straight." I dug my nails into my palms. "I should be your *mate* and stay away from Jaime so your scent can mark me like a cat pissing on its territory?"

"Lanni—"

"Because if you *claim* me, I'll have a pack of wolves protecting me like I'm your favorite chew toy?"

"You don't—"

"I don't what? I don't understand why you'd even suggest that I should fuck you to keep your pack happy? I ran from the Arc Domes so they couldn't tell me who to spread my legs for! Or maybe you think I really don't give a shit who I fuck. I'm just a whore's daughter, so selling sex for comfort should come naturally to me."

"The last thing I want is for you to have to use sex to stay safe."

"Then what do you want, Walsh?"

"You. I want you. You safe. You alive and happy." He gripped the top of his head. "And the wolf in my mind keeps screaming that I should tear apart everyone who might take you away from me. I'm stronger than that vampire, I'm the better protector, the better mate. I can't make the wolf stop."

"Walsh—"

He backed away from me before I even knew I'd stepped closer to him.

"You don't want me. Not really." I reached for him, wanting to soothe him like I would Mari when she'd had a bad dream. "We're friends. We trust each other. But you're not in love with me."

"How do you know?" He didn't fight when I lifted his hands away from his head.

"Because you would have told me." I let go of his hands and took his shoulders. "Just take a breath, Walsh. I can't imagine how hard it is for you to be back with your pack—to be back with Demetrius—but you're still you. Don't let the wolf in your head tell you what you want."

"I want you."

He was kissing me before I could breathe. The warmth of his hands burned through my borrowed shirt, lighting a fire in my chest I wasn't smart enough to fear. He pulled me close to him, letting me feel every ridge of his body so there was no way I could question how desperately he wanted me.

The world tumbled away as I kissed him. Nothing existed but him and me.

He kissed the side of my neck as his hands slid down to my hips.

A sigh escaped me as I threaded my fingers through his hair.

He froze for a heartbeat, going still as death, then backed just far enough away that our bodies weren't touching.

"It's not just the wolf that wants you, Lanni." He looked into my eyes, holding my gaze. "I'm in love with you. It started the first time we snuck into the trees in the atrium."

"No. No, you're just confused." Cold dripped into the fire in my chest. "We trust each other. We're friends. You wouldn't keep a secret like that. If you were in love with me, you would have told me."

"When? While you were with Alec? When I thought I was leaving you behind?"

"When you asked me to escape with you would've been a good time."

"That's when I knew for sure I could never have you. The wolf in my head is only going to get stronger the longer I'm with the pack. The wolf wants to claim you. The human I have left loves you too much to want you to be with a werewolf." He brushed his lips against my cheek. "I'm glad you're here, Lanni. I'll do what I can to keep you and Mari safe. But you should stay away from Jaime and me. He'll put you and Mari in more danger. And I'm..." His shoulders sagged as he backed farther away from me. "The Walsh you knew is fading, but that'll only make the wolf want you more."

He turned to look down at the rows of papers on the ground.

"We need to keep compiling more information. The sooner we can finish the Alliance's work, the better off you'll be."

"I'll—" I let out a shaky breath and swallowed the knot in my throat. "When Mari wakes up, she'll have more to add. Her class went different places than ours, and the kid's got a great memory."

"Good." He stepped toward the tent flap. "It's light out right now. The river water is safe enough to bathe in. You should go scrub down. Get rid of as much of my scent as you can."

"Walsh—"

"Be careful with the vampire. You're better off without either of us."

He slipped out of the tent, leaving me with a scattered map of the home we'd fled and his taste on my lips.

CHAPTER SEVENTEEN

The woods around the cavern looked different in the daytime. Less like a terrifying maze and more like a place the kep would approve of.

Demetrius himself had to give permission for Harper and me to be let out of the tent that surrounded the entrance to the cavern, and Harper had to beg Bell for a bit of soap to bathe with.

I held the clothes I'd worn when we escaped the domes in front of me as Harper and I made our way to the river, trying not to get anyone's scent on the fabric. My gaze kept flicking down to the faded red stains every few steps.

How much blood had Mari lost?

The idea of wearing clothes still marked with her blood made my stomach roll.

It's the scent that matters, not the stains.

"Can I sound like a complete asshole for a second?" Harper said.

"Always," I said.

"I never really thought about not being able to shower." Harper stopped and looked up into the leaves of the trees and the open sky above. "In all the times I wanted to run away from the domes, I always assumed I'd be dead before I had to worry about something like bathing, so I never really considered how people on the outside got clean."

"A lot of times, you don't." I stepped around Harper and toward the sound of the river rushing just out of sight. "You wash the stinky bits if you have spare water and if you don't, well everyone around you probably smells just as bad."

"This is going to be a steep fucking learning curve."

"Wishing you hadn't come with us?"

"Never."

I winced as Harper knocked her shoulder into mine.

"You could eviscerate me right here and I'd still be grateful for having gotten out of that hell."

"Good." I gave Harper the best smile I could.

"Mari is going to be fine, you know. Being patient is rough, but Mari will wake up. The doctor said so, and I trust the scary lady."

"I do, too." I stopped at the edge of the trees, scanning the riverbanks for armed kep before daring to step out into the open.

"Then why do you look halfway to a panic attack?" Harper set her spare clothes down and sat beside the water.

"Nothing life or death." I dropped my bloodstained clothes and kicked off my boots.

"Not everything has to be about survival to matter." Harper poked the water and gasped. "Shit that's cold."

"I kissed Walsh." I pulled off Jaime's shirt and tossed it on the ground, away from my other clothes. "Well, I guess *he* kissed *me*, but I enjoyed it."

"That doesn't sound like a problem."

I looked around one more time before taking off my pants. The feel of the sun against my naked body seemed more threatening than walking through an alley of vampires.

I slogged out into the shallows of the river. The cold of the water bit my skin, tensing my muscles and setting my teeth to chattering. I let out an involuntary squeak when the water got up to my breasts.

"Throw me the soap." I held my shaking hands out to Harper.

"Tell me why enjoying kissing Walsh is a problem." She tossed the soap from hand to hand.

"Harper, just give me the soap."

"You wouldn't let me drink myself to death, I'm not going to let you brood. That's how friendship works."

"Jaime is alive." I spoke through chattering teeth. "He's my best friend, and he's alive."

"Which is another good thing."

"I kissed him." I sank into the water up to my shoulders like the cold might act as some kind of penance. "I kissed Jaime, and he's my best friend, and it was great. Then Walsh kissed me. He's a warrior who's saved my life, and I trust him, and that was also great."

"Was this before or after they tried to kill each other?"

"Jaime was before, Walsh was after, and now I have to wash their fucking scent off me before they get into another fight because apparently that's something changed humans do."

"Well, shit." Harper threw me the soap. "Scrub away."

"Thanks." I lathered my arms.

"Happy to help keep the peace."

"I'm not sure that's going to be possible." I scrubbed the nasty-tasting soap on my lips. "I ruin everything."

"I wouldn't say that." Harper cringed as she dipped her feet into the river. "Mari's a pretty great kid, and you've had a lot to do with that. You fucked things up for the Incorporation, which is a major win in my book."

"Thanks." I dunked my head beneath the water, scrubbing my fingers through my hair, trying not to miss the kep soap.

The cold of the river clenched around my chest in an oddly comforting way. I came back up to the surface and dragged in a breath before starting to shiver in earnest.

"Can I say something?" Harper pulled off her shirt. "Like, really say something you're not going to like?"

"I guess." I scrubbed my legs. I couldn't tell the difference between my goosebumps and the dirt stuck to my skin.

"Has it occurred to you that maybe, somewhere in that clever ass brain of yours, you have some fucked up ideas when it comes to sex?"

"I'm pretty sure I know exactly how sex works." I dunked under the water again, giving my hair a second scrub.

"Sure, but hear me out." Harper stepped into the water. "Fuck, this shit is cold. Okay, so Alec helps get you and Mari out of the city. He's nice to you in the domes. You try and get in his pants."

"It wasn't just about sex with Alec." I ducked beneath the surface one last time and slogged back toward the bank.

"You need information from Gideon, you throw yourself at him so he wants to get in your pants. You and Walsh need an excuse to be close so you can work together, you basically tear off each other's pants."

"That was for a photo shoot." I stepped up onto the bank to wring out my hair.

"You find your long-lost bestie and, once again, pants are in danger of being ripped off. There's a very clear pattern here, Lanni. Guy enters life, finds a place for sexual tension in the relationship"—Harper splashed water on her arms—"you jump straight to sexy time if you want someone's help or just want to keep them around."

"That's not—"

"I'm not done. I don't want to imply that I know more about your childhood trauma than you do, but has it occurred to you that your daddy drama and *my mommy is a sneaky sex worker...no wait maybe she lied to me my whole life* trauma, might have really fucked over the way you connect with men?" Harper dunked her head under the water. "Fucking, shitting hell this water is cold."

"You're wrong, Harper." I yanked on my pants.

"About which part?" She scrubbed her arms.

"Things with Gideon and Walsh were complicated, but I cared about Alec." I made myself ignore the bloodstains as I pulled on my shirt. "And Jaime is my best friend."

"Are you in love with Jaime?" Harper splashed back to the bank.

"Of course I love him." I grabbed my boots and sat on the ground.

"Not what I asked." Harper shivered as she pulled on her shirt. "Are you *in love* with him?"

I froze with my boot halfway on my foot. "I don't know...he's Jaime. He's my Jaime."

"Are you in love with Walsh?" Harper pulled up her pants.

A pang of sadness cut through my gut. "Walsh isn't even Walsh anymore."

"Did you love Arc Domes Walsh?"

"Why does it even matter?" I tied my boots.

"Because maybe before you worry about whose tent you want to crawl into for lots of sex, you should worry about who you're in love with." Harper sat beside me. "And not because they're helping you or protecting Mari or anything else. You don't have to buy protection or friendship with your body. You can think about who you actually want to be with."

"How am I supposed to know who I'm in love with?"

"Fucked if I know." She yanked on her boots. "Who do you want to spend time with even if no one's trying to kill you or Mari? Who makes you laugh? Who would you pick if the world wasn't a shit place?"

I stared at the river, trying to picture a world where survival didn't have to be my first consideration.

I couldn't manage it.

"What if I'm not built for falling in love?" I leaned my head on Harper's shoulder.

"Then pick which one you think would be better at rolling

around in a tent and go with that." Harper leaned her head on top of mine. "Or ask if you can just alternate between their tents."

"That would never work."

"Ask if the three of you could all pile into a tent together."

"Harper!" I laughed.

Harper took my hand. "We managed to escape Project Progeny. You have a chance to make choices and build a life you actually want. If you want to build that life with Walsh or Jaime, don't mess up your chance with them by racing into naked time with whichever one seems like the better alpha male. Which has a very different meaning when you're living with a pack of werewolves, but you get what I'm saying."

"Yeah, I do." I twisted to give Harper a damp hug. "I'm really glad you left the Arc Domes with us."

"Thanks for inviting me to the grand escape."

"Promise you'll come with Mar and me when it's time for the camp to leave?"

"Sure." Harper stood. "I have to travel with someone who appreciates my home brewing."

CHAPTER EIGHTEEN

I try not to think about the man in the box. Sometimes I can go weeks without remembering the stench that clung to the concrete walls. But he's always buried deep inside my mind, waiting to terrorize my nightmares.

It started with shoes. Simple as that. Mari had outgrown her shoes.

I had to take her with me to the school at the factory every day. Try and keep her busy while I worked during lessons. I could carry her to the factory, but I had to put her down once we got inside, and there were always bits of metal on the floor.

I'd asked Mom to find her new shoes, and she'd promised she would, but things like that were hard to come by in the city. Mom had said to be patient, she'd bring shoes home. In the meantime, she'd cut up one of her shirts and stitched together slippers for Mari to wear.

The fabric wrapped around my baby sister's feet had eased my worry. I let myself get distracted in class, and Mari got away from me.

There was just this scream from over by the wall. My heart

shot into my throat, and it was like I'd never be able to breathe again. I knew it was her before I even turned to look.

I knocked over the tray of bolts I'd been sorting as I ran to her. There was blood on the floor, and her face was screwed up in pain, and she just kept screaming. I could barely get her into my arms to see where she'd been hurt.

She'd stepped on a hunk of sharp metal anyone but a toddler would have known to avoid. It had sliced straight through her slipper and into her foot.

I asked the foreman for a bandage. He said Mari wasn't a student. The kep only allowed bandages for students working on the floor.

I sat in the corner, holding Mari in my lap, trying not to cry as hard as she was.

Then Jaime came. The minders told him to go back to his place and keep working, but he didn't listen. He pulled Mari's ruined slipper apart and helped me wrap it into a bandage for her foot. When he was done, she wriggled out of my arms and clung to Jaime, holding onto her hero.

But slippers and bandages aren't shoes.

Jaime started searching for a pair that would fit Mari. I still don't know who he talked to to find the woman with the shoes.

I snuck out to meet Jaime, bringing everything from water to a fancy glass bottle of scented oil my mother had gotten from one of her *friends*.

We met the woman in an alley. She had the shoes with her, and we made the trade. She accepted water and a tomato plant. I didn't even have to offer her my mother's scented oil.

I remember thinking how nice the woman was. I was almost giddy that Jaime and I had succeeded. Maybe that joy was why I didn't see the man at the end of the alley until he grabbed me and threw me down into that concrete cell.

Pain crashed through my entire body when I hit the ground.

By the time I could think to look around, Jaime had been thrown down the hole, too.

The man closed the trapdoor above us, locking us in the darkness.

We clung to each other, Jaime and I, twined together in the concrete box. It didn't matter how many times I told him I was sorry I'd gotten him locked in that awful tomb, he said his place was with me. He and I were supposed to face every danger together. We'd fight our way out.

The man brought a knife with him when he finally climbed down the ladder into the concrete tomb. The dim light filtering in from the street above glinted off the blade. He told us not to scream, or he'd cut out our tongues. Said to take off my clothes or he'd kill Jaime.

I set the shoes we'd gotten for Mari on the ground and stood, hating losing the comfort of Jaime as he backed away from me. I held the man's gaze as I pulled off my shirt. He smiled as I reached down to unbutton my pants.

The man was so determined to see me naked he didn't notice Jaime sneaking closer to him until Jaime'd sunk the jagged neck of the shattered oil bottle into the man's throat.

In my mind, time slows down as the man drops his knife and grabs at his neck while Jaime stabs again and again. The light trickling in through the trapdoor glistens off the blood leaking from the man's wounds.

He coughs, and blood spatters the ground.

"Lanni!"

I hear Jaime shout my name as the man chooses to use his last bit of strength to fight back. He lets go of his own wounds to wrap his bloody hands around my friend's neck.

The man's dropped knife lies on the ground, a discarded bit of sacred magic made for stealing life.

I grab the knife and slash at the man's arm, like I can sever it from his body.

The man stumbles as he looks at me. The hatred in his eyes makes me feel stronger.

I ram the blade into the side of his stomach.

He finally lets go of Jaime as he sags to the ground.

"We have to go." Jaime stumbles to my shirt and tosses it to me. He tucks the shoes we'd nearly died for into his pocket. "Lanni, you have to climb."

I tuck the knife into my waistband and pull my shirt back on.

Jaime makes me climb up the ladder first. We ignore the blood tainting our skin and hold hands as we sprint back to my home.

Mari's already asleep. Mom's furious we stayed out after dark. She yells the whole time she washes the blood off our hands. She doesn't stop yelling until we show her the shoes we'd gotten for Mari. Then Mom starts to cry.

Neither of us tells Mom about the concrete room. We don't talk about it with each other, either.

But something between us changed in that horrible place.

There are limits friendship isn't meant to survive. I thought we'd left those barriers behind when we climbed back out of the darkness.

CHAPTER NINETEEN

The lights on the ceiling blurred above me as I flew backward and hit the ground. I rolled sideways, forcing my lungs to drag in air as I got to my feet.

I tightened my grip on my knife, waiting for Bell to charge me again.

"You okay?" Jaime asked from ten feet behind me.

"She's fine." Bell paced in front of me. "She just needs to learn to duck faster."

"Easy for you to say." I twisted my spine, testing my ribs for damage. "I'm just a plain old human."

Bell spun toward me, kicking me behind the knees and slicing her wooden practice knife across my arm.

I drove my knife back as I fell, hitting her in the hip. "Lucky for me, the kep are unchanged humans, too."

Bell took my arm and hoisted me back to my feet. She leaned close to whisper, "If you think you'll never have to fight anyone but the Incorporation's demons, you're not half as smart as Walsh made you out to be. You're a lost little girl in a world of blood-thirsty monsters. If you want to survive, you're going to need to be able to defend yourself from every kind of evil the world has to offer."

"Then I guess I should be grateful for your taking the time to beat me up." I stepped just far enough away from Bell to be able to leverage her weight before reaching out to shake her hand. I grabbed her forearm instead, ramming my shoulder into her stomach and flipping her up and over my back.

Bell was on her feet again before I could turn to face her.

She kicked me in the stomach, knocking me ass-first to the ground.

"At least you're a decent shot." Bell glared down at me like I was the epitome of disappointing.

"As long as you don't shatter all my bones, I'll get better at hand-to-hand, too." I pushed myself back up to my feet, trying not to wince at the pain that shot from my ass to my skull.

"You'd better. Everyone in the Alliance pulls their weight," Bell said.

"Lanni has been—"

I held up a hand to silence Jaime. "I know I have to train. That's why I'm letting you beat the shit out of me. So, do you want to toss me on the ground again or not?"

"We're done for now." Bell held out her hand for my knife. "I've been given very specific instructions to not *actually* injure you."

"Good thing a bruised ass doesn't count." I forced a grin onto my face as I handed Bell the knife, hating the weight of the weapon leaving my hand even though I knew the blade wasn't sharp.

Bell stalked away, cutting through the pairs of fighters and toward the stash of training weapons.

"She shouldn't be so hard on you." Jaime was beside me before I could think of what to do next. "You're doing really well. I didn't know you could flip someone over like that."

"It's a new trick." I ignored the pain in my back as I headed toward the far end of the cave. "The guard training program wasn't entirely useless."

"You were training to be a guard?"

It took me three steps to realize Jaime had stopped following me.

"Not by choice." I untied the string that had been holding my hair back. "The Domes Council made me join as punishment."

"Those sick fucks." Jaime spoke through clenched teeth, like he was barely holding back the urge to go pound his way into the glass to tear through the Domes Council's necks.

"It's not as bad as it sounds. I punched a guard, and they made me join the guard training program so I could learn respect and discipline. Honestly, my punishment could have been a lot worse."

"Worse than making you train to kill people?"

"I was never—" I dug my fingers into my sweaty hair and started walking again. "Just trust me. Having to run laps in the halls and learning to shoot kep guns is far from the worst thing the kep have made people do."

He didn't say anything for a moment. I wouldn't let myself glance back to see if he was still following me.

"You could tell me about it, you know." There was no anger left in his voice as he stepped up to walk beside me. "If you want to talk about anything that happened—"

"There's not really anything to talk about." I cut to the left of the entrance to the lower cavern, careful not to go where Jaime couldn't follow.

"Demetrius brought me to his tent once. He had me watch a video they'd stolen from the kep. I saw the speech you gave about Project Progeny." Jaime sank down to sit beside the wall.

"Which one." I sat next to him, leaving just enough space between us that our arms didn't touch. "There were speeches and photoshoots. All kinds of fucked up shit."

"The one with the kep holding your hand."

"Gideon." I pressed my palms to the stone beneath me,

needing to prove to myself that I really had escaped the domes. "He didn't want to do the speeches or pictures any more than I did. The Incorporation was keeping him locked in a room in the medical corridor. They probably still are."

"I'm sorry I couldn't get you out before Project Progeny ever started."

"Gideon's dad is the captain of the Outer Guard and the kep still locked him up. They'll assign him a new partner for Project Progeny. They'll force him into that sterile white room." I took Jaime's hand without even looking at him, like our palms were magnets, meant to be drawn together. "I escaped the Incorporation and Project Progeny, but Gideon's still trapped."

"You're free. That's all that matters." Jaime knelt in front of me, tipping my chin up to make me meet his gaze.

"Freedom is great. It's just..." I tried to swallow the grief that pressed against my throat, but it only made the knot worse.

"You can tell me anything, Lanni."

"Me, and Mari, and Harper, and Walsh—we got out." My breath shook in my chest. "But that isn't going to stop Project Progeny from happening."

"Does it matter? What the kep do to other kep isn't our problem. They want to breed kep babies, let them."

"They don't want to." I held Jaime's gaze, needing him to understand. "That's the thing. The students in my class hated Project Progeny. One of the boys took a dart to the neck trying to keep his girlfriend from being dragged away. She didn't want to go, but he couldn't stop them from taking her."

"I would have fought with everything I have to protect you." He trailed his fingers across my cheek. "I always will."

He leaned in, kissing me like he could somehow kill the grief that made me want to scream.

For a moment, he was right.

The ache of my guilt dulled as heat rose to my cheeks,

promising me that losing myself in Jaime's arms would make every pain and worry fade away.

I dipped my chin, easing away from our kiss.

"What's wrong?" Jaime furrowed his brow, staring at me like he thought I might be sick.

"I can't do this. I can't kiss you."

He sat back on his heels.

I missed having him closer.

"You're Jaime. You're my best friend who crossed half a continent to get to me."

"But you'd rather be kissing someone else." The line of his jaw hardened.

"No. I just—I thought I'd lost you forever."

He held his hand out to me. "I'm right here."

"And I don't want to lose you again. That means I have to do this right." I laid my hand in his. "I need time to deal with everything that happened in the Arc Domes. I can't just drag you into your tent and rip off your clothes because I want a chance to forget how fucked up the world is."

"I mean, that doesn't sound so bad." His face relaxed into a crooked smile.

"But you deserve better." I laced my fingers through his. "And I need to get my shit together."

He kissed the back of my hand. "We're going to be okay."

I let myself smile for him.

"Lanni."

I looked up to find the doctor standing over us.

"Is Mari okay?" I leapt to my feet. "Did she get an infection?"

"She's awake." For the first time, the doctor actually looked happy. "She's agitated and uncomfortable, but Mari is awake."

"Thank you!" I threw my arms around the werewolf's neck without even considering the consequences of hugging someone with the instincts of a predator.

A little growl rumbled in the doctor's throat.

"Sorry." I let go of her and ran for the tunnel.

"Lanni," Jaime called.

I skidded to a stop.

"Are you going to tell Mari I'm here?" Jaime said.

"Of course." A true smile filled my face. "She's awake."

"Go." Jaime shooed me down the tunnel. "Give her a hug from me."

"No hugging." The doctor rounded on Jaime.

A laugh of joy bubbled in my throat.

Mari alive. Jaime alive.

I sprinted all the way to the infirmary, not stopping until one of the guards stepped sideways to block the door.

"The doctor came to find me," I said. "My sister is awake."

"No one enters the infirmary without the doctor's supervision," the guard said.

I looked back at the tunnel.

The doctor walked toward me, not bothering to use any of her unnatural speed to reach the infirmary.

"Come on." I bounced from foot to foot, like Mari did when she was excited. I laughed again.

"You're going to have to stay calm while you visit my patient," the doctor said. "You may touch her hand, but no hugging. No touching her torso at all. Do you understand?"

"Yes, ma'am." I dug my nails into my palms and planted my feet on the ground. "Whatever you say, as long as I can see her."

"Briefly. You may see her, briefly."

"Yes, ma'am." My heart rocketed around in my chest as I followed the doctor into the infirmary.

Mari had been propped up in bed. Her skin was pale, and there was still a tube attached to her arm, but her eyes were open.

"Mari." All the air rushed out of my body as I said her name.

"Lanni." Mari reached for me.

"Do not lean away from those pillows, young lady," the doctor said.

"Lanni." Mari didn't stop reaching for me. Tears streamed down her cheeks. "I woke up, and you weren't here. And I don't know where I am."

"Mari, if you start sobbing, I'll have to sedate you," the doctor said. "You are still healing."

"You're okay, Mar." Tears sprang to my eyes as I took my sister's hand. "We're with Walsh's people. We made it."

"We're okay?" Mari said.

"Yeah." I squeezed her hand. "You got shot, Mar. The doctor had to keep you asleep for a little while so you could heal."

"Is that why I hurt?" Mari looked at her stomach. "It feels really bad."

"Is there anything you can give her?" I glanced to the doctor.

"Everything I have would knock her out," the doctor said. "And I don't want to keep her sedated any longer."

"I need you to be brave, Mar." I pushed Mari's hair away from her face, daring the doctor to yell at me. "The pain will go away, but it's going to hurt for a little bit while you heal. I'm so sorry, Mar. I'm sorry I can't fix it."

"It's okay." Mari coughed through her tears.

"Calm breaths," the doctor said.

"I can be brave as long as you're safe," Mari said.

"We're both safe," I said. "Harper and Walsh are safe, too. And guess who else is here?"

"Did Alec come find us?" Mari looked toward the door.

"Jaime did." I leaned sideways, looking right into her eyes. "He escaped the city back home and traveled all the way here just to find us."

"Jaime's here? Did he bring Mom?"

CHAPTER TWENTY

"I need you to try and think, Mari." Demetrius sat beside her. "Think as hard as you can for me."

If he hadn't been speaking in such a kind tone, I might have told him to back the hell off.

"Just let me be quiet for a minute." Mari furrowed her brow.

It felt like half the camp had been called into Demetrius's tent for Mari's turn at being questioned.

The doctor had carried Mari up to the main cavern herself and had stayed in the tent, glaring at Demetrius as though wanting to be sure he knew she'd snatch her patient away if he pushed Mari too hard. The doctor had started growing on me.

Harper stood with me, right behind Mari like we were her guards.

Walsh lurked in the corner, staying as far away from me as the space would allow.

Is he trying to keep his scent off me, or is he angry that I smell too much like Jaime?

The thought was both disgusting and sad.

Walsh was my friend, my partner in defying the Incorporation. He should be standing beside me, not hiding in the shadows.

But the Lycan had twisted Walsh's mind and convinced him he'd fallen in love with me.

But if he loved you before you left the Arc Domes—

"Okay." Mari glanced up at me before looking to Demetrius. "So, in the dome with all the farm-type animals, there's the part with the stalls and the part with the feed and the part where some of the animals can live all together, which is the best bit.

"When I was scared they were going to find out Lanni and I weren't kep, I figured out that I could hide behind the stalls in the place where the glass meets the walls. It would be tight for Lanni, but we could milk the goats at night and have that for food so we'd be able to survive for a little while."

"Do you remember anything about the guards," Demetrius asked. "Anything they did that seemed strange?"

"When they locked us in the bunkers when the siren went off, they always locked two guards in with us," Mari said. "If the kep are so sure their bunkers are safe, it seems like a waste of two guards to me."

"Do you have any information that doesn't involve hiding?" Bell asked.

"I'm seven," Mari said. "Hiding is my only defense."

"Great." Bell stood from her seat at the round table and went to join Walsh in the corner.

"Sorry I don't know more." Mari reached back to take my hand.

"Don't lean," the doctor said. "You'll tear your stitches."

"You're not going to get better information than we have right now." Walsh stepped closer to the table. "Between the data from the Incorporation's computers and what the four of us have given you, we need to make our move."

"It's not up to you to decide how this camp proceeds," Demetrius said.

"No, it's not." Walsh bowed. "The choices are yours to make,

Alpha. But if we start laying out what the next step is, we can ask Mari more specific questions."

"Yeah," Mari said. "'Cause if you wanted to hide in the tall grass in the Marsh Dome, then I know which way you should swim to get to the biggest island patch, but that doesn't seem like it matters since I don't know why you're asking me questions."

"Shh." I squeezed Mari's hand.

"Nobody tells me anything," Mari said. "I don't even know why Walsh's eyes aren't red like the rest of the werewolves."

"Mar," I warned.

"They tattooed my eyes before my mission in the Arc Domes began," Walsh said. "They were red when I first became a wolf, but I had to blend in with the rest of the people inside the domes."

"Tattoos on your eyeballs?" Mari wrinkled her nose. "That sounds awful."

"It was," Walsh said. "But I believed in the importance of my mission, so it was worth the pain."

"Is your mission why Demetrius wants to know more about the Arc Domes?" Mari looked at Demetrius, putting on a confused pout anyone who knew her could have seen right through.

Demetrius stood, staring at Walsh for a moment before heading to the computers on the far side of the tent.

"Once we tell the pack, they won't want to wait," Demetrius said.

"Is it that bad?" Walsh asked.

I studied Walsh, wishing I could peek into his mind to find out what information he was still missing.

"You may be my beta, but that doesn't separate you from the rest of the pack," Demetrius said. "Werewolves are not known for their patience. You'll all want blood."

"And we'll get it," Bell said.

"Show them the map." Demetrius looked to the woman sitting at the computer.

"Yes, Demetrius."

It only took a moment for the woman to pull up the image.

Reds, oranges, blues, and purples covered the map. Small spots of green broke through the other colors, seeming out of place among the more violent hues.

"What does it mean?" Mari whispered.

"It means the Incorporation is capable of far greater evil than even I imagined," Demetrius said. "It means the success of Project Afterworld was more than a myth."

"Those sick fucking bastards." Walsh strode all the way up to the screen. "Murder—no genocide—that's what they fucking did."

"You're right," Demetrius said.

"What's Project Afterworld?" I peeled my hand away from Mari's to move closer to the screen.

"They should burn," Walsh said. "They should suffer every pain they've forced us to bear."

"The demons call *us* monsters," Bell said. "How many people died because of their greed?"

"What is Project Afterworld?" I shouted.

"Holbeck needs to pay!" Walsh rounded on Demetrius.

"Quiet." Even though Demetrius barely whispered the word, Walsh and Bell both fell silent.

"The world didn't crumble with one quick blow. The people who were watching saw the end coming far before acid rain began burning through crops." Demetrius kept his gaze fixed on the screen. "As the seasons started shifting and deserts ate fertile land, a team of scientists began mapping the destruction, searching for patterns in the decay and places where the least damage had occurred. Those scientists created Project Afterworld.

"The project didn't begin with the Incorporation. The Afterworld team had nothing to do with the domes. But eventually, the

Incorporation stepped in to finance the project, and all of a sudden, talk of Project Afterworld disappeared."

"Why?" I reached out, touching the point on the map where the Plains Domes were surrounded by a sea of lethal red.

"Most people assumed the project had failed," Demetrius said. "The world had never seen weather patterns, or fires, or migrations, or species extinctions like the ones that devastated our global society. Predicting patterns amidst unprecedented chaos seemed impossible. But there were rumors that Project Afterworld had succeeded, giving the Incorporation a glimpse into the future."

"Is that how the Incorporation decided where to build all the domes?" Mari tried to stand up.

The doctor lifted her, carrying her closer to the screens.

"That was a theory," Demetrius said. "The Incorporation chose the ideal places for their future citizens to emerge into a cleansed world, generations after the rest of us had died, giving the environment time to heal."

"Live in safety and watch the rest of us die off," I said. "Enjoying the apocalypse from the comfort of the domes."

"It's worse than that," Walsh said.

"How?" I asked.

"There were some of us who believed the Incorporation had maps that charted our world now, pinpointing places where humans could survive without needing glass to protect them." Demetrius tapped a green spot on the map. "The Afterworld team found havens that might allow human survival, and the Incorporation hid them."

"Places to live outside without fires burning?" The screens blurred as the ground swayed. "Without soot killing our lungs? Places with clean water?"

A hand gripped my arm, steadying me.

"They watched us die," Bell said. "They herded us toward the places they needed workers to build their domes and hid the havens where settlements could have actually survived."

"Those sick fucks." An arm wrapped around my waist as I stepped closer to the screen.

"This is the information you got for us, Lanni." Walsh held me tighter. "We have this map because of the chip you planted."

"The Incorporation keeps saying their people will be the only ones to survive," I said. "But they made sure of it. The Incorporation wiped out humanity."

"No," Demetrius said. "They tried to wipe out humanity by hiding the findings of Project Afterworld. But now the Alliance has the map. We know where humans can thrive in the open."

"You changed the fate of the world when you planted that chip, Lanni." Walsh turned me to face him. "The demons aren't going to get to watch us die."

"Does that mean we get to go to one of the safe places?" Mari asked. "Will there be trees and places to grow food?"

I twisted away from Walsh to take Mari's hand.

"The Alliance's dream has always been to build a future free from the evil of the Incorporation." Demetrius smiled. "Now, the future we fight for will be one of plenty, not bare survival."

Tears welled in my eyes as Mari beamed.

"When can we go?" she asked.

"Not until we make sure the Incorporation can't hurt anyone ever again," Demetrius said. "Take Mari back to the infirmary to rest."

"Yes, Demetrius." The doctor gave him a little bow.

I kissed Mari's forehead. I wanted to make Demetrius let her stay, but something in his smile sent shadows of fear brushing against my skin. "I'll visit you soon. Get some sleep, Mari."

"Save the world, Lanni."

No one spoke until the doctor had carried Mari away.

"I didn't know." Harper stood at the back of the group, like she was terrified of the maps coming to life to devour her. "Every class I ever took, every lecture they ever gave us, they told us surviving on the outside was impossible. Living outside the glass was a death sentence."

"Because they made it that way," Walsh said. "The Incorporation wanted us dead. They herded us into hells we couldn't survive."

"I'm sorry," Harper said. "I did…I didn't know."

"You just lived in the paradise the Incorporation murdered hundreds of thousands of people to create," Bell said.

"The kep don't know that," I said. "The Incorporation is better at lying to their own people than you could possibly understand."

"Bodies in the streets don't lie," Bell said.

"Normal kep don't wander around outside. They don't understand the kind of suffering we've seen." I cut through the group to stand beside Harper. "When can I take my sister to one of the Afterworlds?"

"Our work here is far from over," Demetrius said.

"Then let's get it done." I took Harper's hand. "You just showed my sister a map with little green spots of paradise on it. What do I have to do to get her there?"

"We have to make sure the demons of the Incorporation can never hurt anyone again," Demetrius said. "Then we'll salvage the supplies we can and build our new home."

CHAPTER TWENTY-ONE

Harper and I spent two days trying to plot out paths through the Arc Domes, sitting at the table in Demetrius's tent, poring over the maps again and again.

Walsh paced along the back wall, stalking through the shadows like a predator waiting to slaughter its prey.

I stared at the web of corridors, looking for a way down to weapons storage for the hundredth time. "I don't think it can be done."

I closed my eyes and tipped my head back.

"I don't think there's a way to get the equipment out of the vehicle repair shop, either." Harper leaned against the table, staring at the rectangle that represented the vehicle bay. "The tunnel through the mountain is collapsed. Unless the Incorporation magically cleared and repaired the tunnel, there's no way to get a truck out of the Arc Domes."

"We don't want a truck," Walsh said.

"No, you want us to break in and steal supplies from mechanical," Harper said. "If you want to snatch enough to make it worth fighting your way down to the vehicle bay, you either need to steal a truckload's worth of supplies or have trained mechanics hand-pick what would be most useful."

"It's going to be werewolves going down there," Walsh said. "They can carry more than normal humans."

"Not really." I dug my knuckles into my eyes. "Not when the guards try to stop them and they need their hands to fight."

"We'll make it work," Walsh said.

I opened my eyes and looked toward the tent flap. Jaime hadn't been invited to any of the planning meetings for breaking into the domes. Demetrius had kept the group to Walsh, Harper, and me. Just the three of us in Demetrius's tent while I tried not to notice Walsh keeping as much distance between him and me as possible.

"I think it's time to stop trying to come up with ways to get into weapons storage and the warehouse below the Arc Domes." I laid my hands flat on the table. "None of us have been to the warehouse, and I've never seen past the cage in weapons storage. And even trying to get to the easy stock of guns would be a stupid plan. As soon as the guards figure out the domes have been breached, they'll set off the siren, which will mean people running right past weapons storage and into the bunker by seed storage. There will be too many people around.

"And even if we managed to get into the cage to steal weapons, which I don't think we could, I'm pretty sure getting to whatever destructive shit the kep have through the door in weapons storage that requires a palm print to unlock would be fucking impossible."

"It's not worth the risk either," Harper said.

"Neither of you is qualified to decide what risks the pack should take," Walsh said. "We're talking about gaining the necessary supplies to set up an Afterworld settlement. This is our one shot to get the things we need."

"You don't need kep guns," I said.

Walsh glared at me.

"I'm sorry, but you don't. The kep use tranq guns, which I'm pretty fucking sure means they can't be used for hunting. Which means you'd want the guns for shooting people. You're were-wolves and vampires, you can defend yourselves without guns."

"And what about you?" Walsh stepped closer to the table. "What about Mari and Harper? Can you defend yourselves without guns?"

"Who are we supposed to be defending ourselves against?" I stood.

"You're going to be living surrounded by vampires," Walsh said.

"Can you two please not do this right now?" Harper said.

"I'm used to vampires," I said.

"I want to protect—"

"Just stop." I banged my fist on the table. Walsh didn't flinch. "If you want to lurk in the corner so you don't have to smell me, fine. You want to avoid me, fine. But don't let the wolf in your head convince you I'm some helpless creature. I survived changed humans in the city. I can do it in the Afterworld, too."

"If we're done with that awkward moment, the vehicle bay and weapons storage are out," Harper said. "Seed storage is out. The warehouse below the domes is out. We're not going to be able to convince Demetrius to wait much longer. We have to give him a plan today. We need to stick to the levels that actually have glass we can breach from the outside. So what on those levels is the most useful?"

"We're going to the vehicle bay and weapons storage." Walsh backed away as he growled the words, like he needed to put distance between himself and Harper.

"It's not—" Harper stood.

"We can't afford to let the demons keep the arsenal they have stored," Walsh said. "Your people have been hoarding weapons that can burn cities and melt forests. If we let them keep those weapons, no Afterworld settlement will ever be safe. If we let them keep their trucks and helicopters, no Afterworld settlement will ever be safe. It doesn't matter how many people die, we've got to get it done."

"And if no one makes it out of the Arc Domes alive?" I asked.

"The Alliance will carry on without us." Walsh didn't look at me. "Now get back to work."

"I need a minute." Harper cut around the table toward the tent flap.

"We don't have time to waste," Walsh said.

"I'm not really okay with plotting how people are going to die. Give me a fucking minute to breathe." Harper stormed out of the tent.

"Harper." I started to chase after her.

"It's for the good of the Alliance," Walsh said. "We have to attack."

I didn't turn back.

None of the guards even flinched when I burst out of the tent chasing after Harper.

But why should they be startled? They were all werewolves, trusted members of Demetrius's pack who were more than capable of hearing everything said inside the tent.

I caught sight of Harper as she stormed toward the tunnel that led to the lower cavern. Refusing to let my panic show, I slowed my pace as I followed her. I cut through the tents along Demetrius's side of the cavern, staying well away from the sparring space.

"Lanni."

I glanced toward the sound of Jaime's voice. He was running fast enough I didn't have to stop for him to be beside me in a breath.

"They finally let you out?" Jaime smiled, but it wasn't a crooked smile. It was symmetrical and forced.

"Nope. I'm just going to check on Mari." The lie stung my

tongue. "I've got to run down there and get straight back to the big tent."

"It'll get better soon." Jaime caught my hand. "I know you jumped out of a kep-filled Hell and into a cave of monsters—"

"You're not a monster."

"Now you're helping Demetrius, and I know that can't be easy for you." Jaime pulled me toward him, stopping me before I reached the wolves guarding the tunnel. "But it is going to get better. We'll get out of here, and it won't all be one fight after another."

"Life has always been one fight after another. Even when we were kids."

"I know." Jaime let go of my hand and held his arms out to me, inviting me to take comfort in the person who'd gotten me through all the chaos back home.

I leaned against him, letting him hold me for just one moment, just long enough to remind myself that, even with the world burning around us, Jaime and I had had lives worth living.

"I've got to go to Mari." I eased away from my comfort. "I'll find you if I'm ever done with Demetrius."

"Right." He gave me another symmetrical smile. "You know where to find me."

I headed toward the tunnel, not letting myself look back to see how quickly Jaime's false smile faded.

The guards didn't stop me from entering the tunnel.

I gave them both a nod as I passed. A kep nod. I hated the gesture for feeling so easy and normal.

I tried not to think as I walked down the tunnel.

Water had always been the thing I worried about most in the city. Water and food, really.

Our apartment had been granted to us by the Plains Domes so we would have a place to live while we worked ourselves to death in their fucking factories.

But there wouldn't be apartments in the Afterworld settlements. There wouldn't be electricity. Not even the shitty kind that shuts off with no warning. There wouldn't be women in alleys selling shoes for Mari, or trade halls where Jaime could barter whatever he'd managed to get his hands on.

There would be no tablets for lessons. No solar panels for growing plants.

No kep to kill us when they decide we aren't useful anymore.

What would happen when everyone's shoes fell apart? Or their clothes. How would we cook? Had Demetrius even thought through how much unchanged humans needed to eat? How many unchanged humans would the Alliance send to the Afterworld settlements?

The questions kept banging through my head.

If I could get into my old room in Bloom Dome, I could steal some extra clothes, but they wouldn't last forever. I could take the pot we'd used to cook, too. Then I could boil drinking water. We'd need blankets in case our Afterworld haven got cold.

By the time I reached the tent I'd been sharing with Harper, I knew damn well the list I'd made in my mind would be too much for me to carry a long distance, even if I didn't have to worry about keeping Mari safe and helping her through whatever terrain stood between us and the new home the Alliance wanted to build for their people.

I stopped just outside my tent and really looked at the cavern.

The camp had an infirmary. They had weapons stored in one of the shacks and supplies in another. Almost everyone in the main cavern had a tent to call their own, even though vampires and werewolves didn't sleep very often. Demetrius had been keeping his camp fed and healthy for months as they hid in the mountains the Incorporation called home.

"What the hell else do they really need?" I whispered.

I couldn't come up with an answer worth dying for.

"Harper." I knelt to unzip the tent. "You in here?"

"Where the fuck else would I be? It's a cave," Harper said.

"Just think of it as a dome made of rock. That should make it feel more homey." I crawled into my tent and zipped it closed behind me.

"I'm not looking for *homey*." Harper sat on her sleeping bag, staring down at her hands. "I never want to feel like I'm in the domes again."

"Well, you're in luck." I sat on my own sleeping bag. "Wherever we end up, I'm sure it will be nothing like the domes."

"What if it is?" Harper crawled over to sit beside me. She leaned close to my ear as she whispered, "What if Demetrius is exactly like the Incorporation?"

"Harper—"

"They're talking about invading the Arc Domes." She kept whispering. "They're going to break through the glass, and they don't care how many people die. To get down to the lower levels, they'll have to slice through dozens of guards."

A shadow of fear twisted around my heart.

"And if they meet students on their way to the vehicle bay, what do you think Demetrius is going to order the pack to do? Is he going to let the kids get to the bunkers? And the seed storage bunker is near weapons storage. If they want to get rid of the weapons, the easiest solution would be to blow them up. What would that do to the people hiding in the bunker?"

"The bunkers are safe." I took Harper's hand. "The Incorporation built the seed storage bunker and the atrium bunker to protect the kep. The kids will be all right."

"Walsh said it was worth sacrificing everyone to destroy the Incorporation. Do you really think *everyone* doesn't include every single person living in the Arc Domes?" Harper's hand trembled in mine. "They're going to kill everyone, Lanni. And they want us to help them do it."

CHAPTER TWENTY-TWO

There is a hatred in my mind I don't want to see. But the darkness lures me further into her trance than I knew I could fall.

If I let myself tumble into that sweet embrace, I know I can never be redeemed. The wolf inside me screams that the darkness is my sanctuary. There is no other cure that can soothe the scars on my soul.

But a faint voice calls from far away, promising there is light floating just out of sight.

I recognize the voice. It doesn't speak of comfort or peace, but there is beauty in her words. She offers me the promise of a life worth fighting for.

In the quiet moments, I know I would give anything to follow that faint voice. Those moments are far too brief.

The hatred returns, and the voice is nothing but a whisper I am too weak to understand.

I will try to keep writing to you, to prove to myself that some part of my mind still belongs to the person I was.

If I turn into the monster the darkness asks me to become, I won't write you again.

I'll have lost the last part of me that was the boy you loved.

Forgive me for the things I must do. If the universe has any mercy, I

*will become the innocent you knew in the moment before I die. Then I will
be burned as the one you loved, and your ashes will greet mine.*

*I hope whatever comes after I am gone will be worth the sacrifices I've
offered to our cause.*

See you in the embers,

~C

CHAPTER TWENTY-THREE

I knew something was wrong when the pounding carried down from the upper cavern.

I scrambled out of my tent and ran for the infirmary, needing to be with Mari even though there was shit I could do to save her if the Incorporation had found base camp.

"Lanni. Harper."

I tripped over my own feet at the sound of Walsh's voice.

He stood just inside the tunnel, his hands behind his back, looking more like a soldier than I'd ever seen him. "Demetrius wants you there for the announcement."

Everything in my chest went numb. I knew I should be overwhelmed by relief that the kep hadn't come to kill us, but all I could feel was cold.

"Harper." I looked toward our tent.

She stood beside the ratty material. She had her hands tucked behind her back, too, but she'd locked her gaze above Walsh's head like she couldn't stand the sight of him.

"What about Mari?" I didn't move.

"Demetrius didn't say to bring her," Walsh said. "Let her stay in the infirmary. She's a child, not a member of the pack."

"I'm not a member of the pack, either." I walked slowly toward him, like there was a sea of fragile ice between us instead of a floor of solid stone. "I'm your friend. You trusted me to help you plant the chip. I trusted you to help Mari and me escape."

The sound of the pounding in the upper cavern got louder.

"You're right," Walsh said. "Demetrius hasn't just called the pack together. He's called the camp. We are a cell of the Alliance. Werewolves, vampires, even plain humans. We fight together against the Incorporation."

"Why does Demetrius want us to come to the upper cavern now?" I reached for Walsh.

"He got tired of waiting." Walsh turned and strode up the tunnel before my fingers could even graze his arm.

"Lanni." Harper took my wrist. "What if I'm right?"

"Don't react." I slipped out of Harper's grip and took her hand, keeping her by my side as we walked up the tunnel just like I would have if Mari had been made to face the rumble above us. "Don't tip your hand in public. Don't show fear. Don't show anger."

"Just smile and nod as Demetrius decides murder is the best idea?"

"Get a group of normal humans riled up, and it's close to impossible to change their minds. It's worse with vampires, and I doubt we'd have a fuck of a chance with werewolves. So listen, stay silent, and wait until things have calmed down to try and speak."

"Are you sure?" Harper squeezed my hand.

"I used to sell stolen syringes to a vampire." A weird little smile curved my lips like it was a happy memory. "I went into the dark corridor most nights to sell him what I'd snagged or visit Jaime at the trade hall. I dealt with vampires all the time."

"But never with werewolves."

The thumping from above became clearer, solidifying into a steady rhythm.

"Werewolves are new territory for me," I said.

The thumping started to shake my lungs before we even stepped out into the upper cavern.

The entire camp had gathered around one of the niches in the cavern wall. Everyone was stomping their feet, creating the pounding that seemed like it might bring the stone ceiling down on our heads at any moment.

Walsh cut around the outskirts of the group, leading us right up to the rock wall.

The few people in our path stepped out of his way with a deference that drove a nauseating knot into my stomach.

We stopped just below the niche, like Walsh wanted us to have front row seats for whatever the camp had gathered to see.

The rhythm of the stomping quickened as the horde parted, creating a path to the niche.

Demetrius strode through his people with a placid look on his face, like he was a benevolent ruler instead of a warlord ready let a river of blood flow through the mountains.

The stomping stopped as Demetrius jumped up into the niche. The cavern stayed silent as he took a breath before turning to face the mob.

"Brothers of my pack"—his voice rang through the space—"vampire allies, today I must give you news that is both wonderful and heinous. To the horror of the Alliance and all living souls with decency in their hearts, we have discovered the Incorporation has long known of safe havens where humans could successfully survive. The Incorporation knew, and they hid the information. The demons let our families suffer and die so they could have workers to build their glass palaces."

A palpable wave of rage swept through the crowd.

"The children we have lost," Demetrius pressed on, "the family, the friends, the lovers, every person we have mourned should have had a chance to live. The Incorporation stole that chance. The Alliance has deemed this act genocide."

"Kill them!" The shout came from the back of the crowd.

I tried to find who'd spoken but couldn't see over the horde.

"They all deserve to die," a second voice shouted.

"Drain them dry."

"We'll rip out their guts."

"They have to be punished."

The calls for vengeance jumbled together into one massive roar.

Then a howl cut through the chaos.

Another added on.

Another. And another.

Walsh threw his head back, howling with the rest of the pack.

I clung to Harper's hand as the sound threatened to toss me into a spiral of panic.

Demetrius raised his hand. The howling still rang in my ears even as the cavern fell silent.

"The monsters living high up on the mountain murdered the people we loved and robbed us of our humanity," Demetrius said. "We are werewolves and vampires because of the evil of the Incorporation."

Another round of howling rang through the cavern.

My heartbeat quickened as instinct screamed I should run.

Demetrius raised his hand again. "It is time for us to take the world back. We will not suffer under the sword of the Incorporation. We will build a new world. We will remake society in the Alliance's image."

Harper gripped my arm as a new chorus of howling threatened to choke the air out of my lungs.

"Our world will begin with the Incorporation's end," Demetrius said. "The time has come to attack!"

Demetrius punched his fist into the air, and it was like all the fear and grief and anger everyone in the camp had ever suffered transformed into one massive shout. For more than a minute, he stayed in the niche, basking in the bloodlust of his people.

Even when Demetrius jumped back to the ground, the cheer roared on and on.

Demetrius stopped in front of me. He looked at Harper and me clinging to each other like two babes lost in the woods.

He took my hand, kissing it before I could think to pull away.

Then he turned to Walsh, saying something I couldn't hear before walking through the crowd and disappearing behind his mass of soldiers.

Walsh jumped up into the niche. "Vampires will be leaving tonight and burrowing until we attack. Report to your unit commander immediately for preparation. Pack brothers, we win or we die. Prepare your weapons."

He threw his head back and howled.

I shut my eyes, trying to convince myself I hadn't fallen into a nightmare.

This is how we face the end of the world.

"Go!" Walsh shouted. "Prepare!"

I opened my eyes as he landed in front of us.

"What are we supposed to do?" I stepped into Walsh's path before he could disappear into the horde. "We're not wolves. We're not vampires."

"Come with me." He stepped around me, leading us toward his tent.

I kept hold of Harper's hand as we followed him.

"What plan of attack did Demetrius choose?" Harper said.

"You'll be given your orders by your unit commander." Walsh led us into the tent where we had spent so many hours working on maps.

"But what's the big picture?" Harper said. "Shouldn't we know what to expect?"

"Your unit commander will give you the information you need." Walsh pulled a metal case out from under his cot.

"Is everyone only getting to know their unit's assignment?" I asked. "Do you know the whole plan?"

"I have to. I'm Demetrius's beta." Walsh opened the case.

Two lines of vials lay nestled in blue padding. Half the vials held milky white liquid, the other half golden.

"Vamp." I reached for the white vials. "Is that Vamp?"

"I wondered if you'd recognize it." Walsh trailed his fingers along the row of gold-filled vials. "I didn't understand what Lycan would truly do to me before I joined the pack."

"Would you still have done it?" I asked. "If you'd known what being a werewolf would really mean?"

"We found the Afterworld map." He held my gaze. "That's worth any sacrifice."

I nodded, too afraid my soul might snap if I tried to speak.

"Demetrius wants both of you with us at the domes," Walsh said. "You're members of this camp. You'll fight with the rest of us."

"I'm not a fighter," Harper said.

"But you can guide a unit to the vehicle bay," Walsh said. "That's invaluable."

"And if I refuse?" Harper stepped away from me.

"Then you stay in the lower cavern under guard until we're done with the Incorporation," Walsh said. "At that time, you'll be free to leave the protection of the pack and make your own way in the world."

"See how fast I can starve or get eaten by a wild animal?" Harper tipped her head back, staring at the top of the tent.

"Wolves don't fear other predators," Walsh said.

"Is that what Demetrius wants us to be?" I touched the golden vials. My heart raced. "He wants us to inject Lycan and become werewolves to fight the Incorporation?"

"We have Vamp, too," Walsh said.

"Would we even be fit to fight so soon after dosing?" Every nerve in my body screamed for me to run.

"You'd be stronger than you are now," Walsh said. "You wouldn't be as capable as vampires and wolves who have grown accustomed to the changes, but you wouldn't die from getting stabbed in the gut."

Mari. You can get through anything for Mari.

"You'll still be needed in the battle, whether you change or not," Walsh said. "What I'm offering is a choice."

An alpha giving orders inside my head. Commands I wouldn't be able to disobey. Demetrius could order me to fight and kill.

He could make me leave Mari.

I looked to the white vials.

Vamp would mean never feeling the sunlight against my skin again. It would mean living off blood. Having to stay away from Mari when she was hurt in case the scent of her blood overpowered my reason and made me see my little sister as food.

Bile rose in my throat.

Any kep could become my food. A meal for the ravenous beast the Vamp would make me.

"The vampires are leaving tonight and burrowing during the day." I pushed the words past the sick in my throat. "Are they going to have time to hunt before the attack?"

"Their feeding habits aren't my concern," Walsh said.

I backed toward the tent's opening. "You're sending hungry vampires into the domes?"

"Demetrius—"

"There are kids in the domes," I said. "Even in Incorporation Headquarters, there are kids."

"Incorporation spawn." Walsh stepped closer to me, still holding the fucking box out in front of him. "The Incorporation has slaughtered entire cities. We're making sure they can't hurt anyone ever again."

"The kids—"

"Our fight will ensure the safety of the Afterworld settlements," Walsh said. "Isn't that what you want for Mari?"

"Of course it is!" My whole body trembled as I forced my lungs to drag in air. "But there's a difference between fighting against the Incorporation and sending hungry vampires into a place filled with children."

"No, there isn't."

I stared into Walsh's eyes, searching for any hint of the ally who'd helped me escape the Arc Domes. The friend who had protected Mari and me even when it went against his orders.

That friend was gone.

"I'm not taking Vamp or Lycan." I bit the inside of my cheek, trying to banish the heat pooling in my eyes. "I don't want Demetrius in my head, and I'm not going to let myself rip out a kid's throat because they smell like a snack."

"You're leaving yourself vulnerable." Anger hovered beneath the surface of Walsh's words. "I'm trying to keep you alive."

"I'm staying human," I said.

"Me too," Harper said. "If I die, I die. The domes tried to brainwash me into believing their bullshit. I'm not letting an alpha control what goes on in my head."

"The alpha's orders are for the good of the pack." Walsh's words grated in his throat like a growl.

"The scary thing is, you might actually believe that," Harper said.

"You are here at his—"

"Don't." I stepped between Walsh and Harper. "We're going to be fighting as humans, which means we need to pack some things before we're ready to leave. All of us could be dead before this is over. It would be a waste of time for you to murder Harper and me in your tent."

Walsh snapped the box shut and backed away from me.

For a split second, I thought I saw the boy I'd known in the Arc Domes flicker through his eyes.

"You'll be given vests for your protection," Walsh said. "Be ready to travel with the pack."

"Yes, sir." I took Harper's hand and yanked her out of the tent.

CHAPTER TWENTY-FOUR

"Fuck," Harper said as I dragged her toward the back of the cavern. "Fucking fucks."

"Yep." I jumped back, barely avoiding being run over by a vampire carrying a crate an unchanged human wouldn't have been able to manage.

"How soon are the vampires leaving?" I called after him.

"Less than an hour," he called back.

"Shit." I let go of Harper's hand and pushed her toward the tunnel to the lower cavern. "You go find food. Water bottles, too. Nothing too big. I don't think we'll be able to carry much."

"Why aren't you coming with me?" Harper grabbed my arm. There was fear in her eyes. Genuine, Mari-like fear.

"I have to find Jaime. I'll be down soon." I gave Harper a quick hug and bolted toward Jaime's tent.

It seemed like everyone in base camp was getting ready for the fight, and no one had gone back into their fabric homes. I'd never seen everyone moving around the cavern all at once. The reality of how many fighters Demetrius had in his camp crashed into my chest.

Between the Dome Guard, Outer Guard, and Incorporation

Guard, the Alliance fighters would be outnumbered. But how many guards really equaled one hungry vampire?

I sprinted the rest of the way to Jaime's tent.

"Jaime." I smacked my palm against the faded orange fabric. "Jaime."

He didn't answer.

I closed my eyes and dug my fingers into my hair.

Weapons. He was leaving soon. He would need to collect his weapons.

I ran toward the front of the cavern, weaving between tents, trying not to get in the way of anyone preparing for battle.

I started at the back of the line of people waiting for weapons, trying to find Jaime, but he wasn't there.

"Shit." I headed for the short tunnel that led to the open air where a few vampires had already gathered. He wasn't with them either. "It's a fucking cave. Where the hell else is there to go?"

"Lanni!"

A glimmer of relief burst through the panic pounding in my chest as I heard Jaime shout my name.

He ran toward me, coming from the far side of the cavern.

I opened my arms, launching myself at him as soon as he reached me.

"I tried to find you." Jaime held me tight. "I was ready to fight my way into the lower cavern, but Harper said you were looking for me."

"I needed to see you before you left."

"Everything is going to be okay. I burrowed during the daylight the whole way here. I'm a good fighter, and I've got Vamp on my side. I'll be back before you know it."

"I'm not waiting here. I'm coming to the Arc Domes."

"You can't heal like the rest of us." Jaime kept one arm around my waist as he pulled me away from the other vampires. "I know you're capable, Lanni. I know you've trained to fight, but it's just too dangerous."

"It doesn't matter. Demetrius wants me to go to the Arc Domes. I have to go."

"That filthy fucking wolf." Jaime looked toward Demetrius's tent like he wanted to rip the alpha's throat out with his teeth. "Find a way to stay at the back. Hide until the fighting's over. Where is he sending you? Who's leading your unit?"

"I don't know." I took Jaime's face in my hands and made him look at me. "I promise I'll be careful. But I need you to do something for me."

"We can take Mari and run," Jaime said.

"I need you to hunt on your way to the Arc Domes. You have to eat before daylight. You have to get all the vampires to eat."

"Vampires don't need to feed every night. I'll be fine."

"Not once the fighting starts. What's going to happen when people start to bleed?"

"When the kep bleed?"

"Yes. If you go in there hungry, are you going to be able to resist feeding?"

"I would never feed on you. And I know Harper's scent now, I can keep myself away from her."

"I'm not talking about me and Harper, I'm talking about the kep."

"What?"

I tightened my grip on his face as he furrowed his brow. "It's not just guards and monsters living inside the glass. There are kids, too. There are people who have never held a weapon in their lives."

"Because they're too privileged to need to."

"Their privilege isn't their fault. They were born inside the glass. They don't know what it's like on the outside. They don't know anything about Project Afterworld."

"Ignorance doesn't make them innocent."

"But it's not a good enough reason to kill them."

Jaime pulled away from me.

"The other students in my class, they hate the Incorporation. When the orders for Project Progeny came down, they wanted to fight back. They wanted to protect each other. They're decent people. They just—"

"How can you say that?" Jaime stared at me. I wished I could read his black eyes. "How can you say that anyone inside the glass deserves mercy? After what they did to us? After they slaughtered all those people in our city?"

"Guards did that." I reached for him. "Guards working on Incorporation orders. The kids had nothing to do with it."

"The guards didn't spare the city scum kids when they culled the population. They shot them. They let them die of dehydration. Lanni, your mom is gone. You'll never see her again because of what those butchers did to our city."

The air whooshed out of my lungs, like it was making room for the flood of grief that didn't come. "I'll never know what happened to my mom. I'll never have a decent answer when Mari asks where Mom is. The kep who destroyed our city deserve to burn. I would gladly kill every kep guard from the Plains Domes with my bare hands. I would cry tears of joy while their blood seeped into my shoes.

"Those guards are evil. They have to be stopped, but that doesn't mean everyone inside the glass is a monster. There are good people in the Arc Domes. People who don't deserve to have their throats ripped out by hungry vampires."

"Ha." Jaime looked up at the stone ceiling. "You genuinely believe that, don't you?"

"Yes." I took his hand. He didn't move. "Let the kids get to the bunkers. Fight the guards. Make a meal of Director Holbeck."

"I spent so long being terrified I'd lost you forever. I gave up sunlight and walked halfway across a continent to get to you."

"I know." I took his other hand. "And you found me. I'm right here."

"You're not my Lanni." He finally looked at me. "My Lanni

would never defend the glass butchers. They slaughtered us. There is not a single kep that can be called innocent."

"Jaime—"

"We'll figure it out." He tucked my hair behind my ears and kissed my forehead. "I'll find a way to fix the lies the kep shoved into your head, just as soon as every last one of them is dead."

CHAPTER TWENTY-FIVE

I have faded into the darkness before. It was a comfort then.

The wolf I became wasn't the same boy who had loved you. He hadn't held you in his arms as the life faded from your eyes. His heart hadn't shattered as he faced a world without you in it.

The wolf freed me from my pain.

The beast is once again devouring my mind. He craves blood and vengeance. He follows orders without thought. He won't let me protect her.

Now I hate the wolf inside my head.

I love her. I fought it for so long, but I love her.

The wolf does not. The wolf covets her. Longs to claim her.

But he will sacrifice her for the good of the pack, and my heart will shatter again.

I am not strong enough to fight the wolf or the orders that echo through my mind.

I am weak. She is in danger.

And I cannot stop loving her.

I will love her even as the wolf tears her apart.

I am beyond redemption.

-C

CHAPTER TWENTY-SIX

I watched Jaime join the rest of the vampires. I just stood there, desperately trying to come up with something to say to convince him I hadn't been brainwashed by the kep.

I couldn't think of anything, not a single way to argue that the kep kids deserved to live. At least not in a way Jaime could understand.

Vampire Jaime. The Vamp changed him. Made him hungry for blood and death.

I couldn't convince myself of that either. He was still my Jaime, and I'd seen the horrors that had taught him to hate the kep. I couldn't blame him for his anger.

I'm not sure how long it took me to make myself move.

I ran toward the far end of the cave, heading straight for the infirmary, bolting down the tunnel like it was my throat Jaime wanted to tear out.

The normal guards weren't at their posts. I didn't let myself wonder if it was because the vampires were leaving.

Taking a breath, I knocked on the infirmary door. "I'd like to see Mari," I called through the crack.

I glanced back to my tent as I waited.

Harper knelt outside the open flap, rolling something into a ball.

The doctor finally opened the door. She glared at me before speaking. "Isn't there something you're supposed to be getting ready for?"

"Yes, but I needed to talk to you." I stepped back, bowing the doctor out of her own infirmary.

"Lanni!" Mari shouted from inside. "Come here. I want to show you something."

"Just a minute, Mar," I said. "I need to talk to the doctor."

"But you'll be proud of me. I've been practicing giving stitches, and I'm getting really good."

"You've been practicing what?"

The doctor shut the infirmary door, blocking my path to Mari. "Why did you need to speak to me?"

"What kind of stitches has Mari been practicing?"

"I had to keep her busy, and she has an interest in medicine." The doctor held out her arm. A line of neat stitches ran along a non-existent wound on her forearm.

"She's been practicing stitches on you?" I shouted.

"Would you like to volunteer?"

"No, but she's just—" I pressed the heels of my hands to my eyes. "Demetrius wants me to go to the Arc Domes. I'm going to fight the Incorporation. Harper and Jaime and Walsh are all going, too." I made myself look into the doctor's red eyes. "I need to know there will be someone to take care of Mari."

"Mari is my patient. She is under my care," the doctor said. "I'm staying in base camp, and she'll be staying with me."

"Good." I blinked away the stinging in my eyes. "I'm glad you'll be with her. But I...if I don't come back, if Harper and Jaime and Walsh don't make it back, can you still take care of Mari? Even when she isn't your patient anymore?"

The doctor looked back at the infirmary door.

"Please," I whispered. "I have to go to the Arc Domes.

Demetrius isn't going to let me stay behind, not if I want to get Mari to one of the Afterworld settlements. But she's so little, she can't make it all the way there on her own. Please."

"I've been meaning to find an apprentice. Even away from the Incorporation, there will be people who need medical care. If the worst happens, she'll stay with me."

"Thank you." The words cracked in my throat.

"Just make sure the worst doesn't happen. I don't want to tell that girl her sister isn't coming back." The doctor opened the infirmary door and stepped out of my way.

I wiped the tears from my eyes before going in to see Mari.

"Lanni, did she show you my stitches?" Mari sat up in bed, mismatched pillows piled behind her.

"She did." My voice stayed steady as I took Mari's hand. "They look great, but I'm not sure how I feel about you stitching up somebody who isn't hurt."

"She was hurt. She made a cut on her arm so I could practice getting the skin to pull together the right way. The cut healed before I finished, but she still said I did a good job."

"I'm really proud of you, Mar." I wanted to sit beside her, or hug her, but I knew it wouldn't be allowed. "You're going to be able to help a lot of people."

"But that's not why you're here." Mari furrowed her brow.

"There's one more thing Demetrius needs to do before we can leave here and go to our new home." I hated the smile I forced onto my face. "He wants me to go with him so I can help."

"What does he want you to do?" Mari squeezed my hand with both of hers.

"We're going to get supplies for our new settlement. And I know about the Arc Domes."

"I know about the Arc Domes, too." Mari leaned away from her pillows. "I can help."

"Sit still, young lady." The doctor spoke from the corner.

"Let me go with you." Mari gripped my hand even harder as

she settled back onto her pillows. "I can help, and then we can leave sooner."

"You're still healing, Mar. You've got to stay here with the doctor. She promised she'd take good care of you while I'm gone, and I'll come back as soon as I can."

"You're not going to be safe are you?" Mari glanced toward the doctor, then pulled me closer to whisper, "Going to the Arc Domes is dangerous. Tell them you have to stay with me."

"I wish I could." I kissed her forehead. "But I have to go with Demetrius, so I've got to go get ready."

"We're supposed to stay together." Tears glistened in Mari's eyes. "You promised."

"I'll be back soon, okay?" I kissed both her hands. "I love you, Mar."

"I love you too, Lanni." She threw her arms around me.

"You're still healing," the doctor shouted.

I held onto Mari for a moment, trying to make sure that, if this was the last time she ever got to hug someone from her family, she would remember how much I loved her and that I would do anything to protect her.

"I'll be right back." I pried her arms from around my neck and settled her back onto her pillows. "You'd better rest. You need to be ready to go to our new home."

I kissed her on the head one more time and stepped away, making my feet keep moving as I headed toward the door.

"Let me check your stitches," the doctor said. "You probably ripped something moving around like that."

I glanced back before I stepped out of the infirmary.

I couldn't see Mari. The doctor blocked her from view.

Shutting that door was one of the hardest things I'd ever done. A sob hitched in my throat.

I headed toward my tent, forcing air in and out of my lungs like that could somehow stop the overwhelming panic from swallowing me whole.

Harper knelt beside our tent, two filled backpacks in front of her.

"I think I got everything we need. Food, water, an extra layer so we don't freeze before we even get to the Arc Domes." She looked up at me. "What's wrong?"

"I—" I coughed on my tears.

"It's okay. You're okay." Harper stood and gripped my arms.

"After everything we've been through, I'm leaving Mari with a werewolf I don't even know."

"Think of it as hiring a babysitter." Harper wiped my tears away with her sleeve. "We're going to go, fuck up the Incorporation, and come right home. No big deal."

"We're going into the Arc Domes with a pack of altered humans who want to kill everyone inside the glass."

"I was hoping you'd forget about that for a minute." Harper wrinkled her nose. "You and Mari have both been through hell and you're still alive. You two can make it through this. Just keep your head down and focus on getting back to Mari in one piece. You've got this."

"Thank you." I hugged Harper. "But we can't let them—"

"I know." She pulled away from me and tossed me a pack. "Let's just get to the Arc Domes. We won't even make it that far if Demetrius decides he wants to keep us away from the fight. Step one: get to the glass. We can worry about how fucked up everything else is later."

I shrugged my backpack on. "Get to the glass."

We walked side by side toward the tunnel.

"You know I'd never want to go back to living in the domes," Harper said. "But I really do miss my brewing supplies right now. A couple glasses of my fine wine would make this shit a hell of a lot easier."

"Once we get to our Afterworld settlement, maybe you can become the official brewmaster."

"Can werewolves drink alcohol?"

"No idea."

We kept the easy chatter going as we made our way up the tunnel and into the upper cavern. Even as we weaved through the werewolves preparing for battle, we talked about what fruits she'd want for brewing and what sort of space she'd need to let the wine age.

"What do you want to do in the Afterworld?" Harper kept her voice cheerful as we joined the group of werewolves waiting for weapons.

"I don't know," I said. "I've been thinking about it, but I don't really have any skills that will be useful for the rustic life."

"That's not true." Harper nudged me with her elbow.

"I'm a thief who can punch people. I don't think those are useful skills for building a settlement."

"You also know how to grow plants. And...do many other things that will also be useful."

"Thanks. I feel so much better now." A wave of dread rolled through my gut as we reached the front of the pack.

The weapons woman glared at us.

"What the hell am I supposed to do with you?" She looked from me to Harper and back again like she was hoping we'd giggle, tell her we were joking, and run away.

"No fucking clue," Harper said.

"Give Lanni a guard's gun." Walsh appeared from the pack like the wolves had parted to grant him access to the weapons.

"Yes, Walsh." The weapons woman didn't look happy, but she opened the black case behind her and pulled out a guard's gun for me without arguing.

"They'll each need a vest as well."

"Yes, Walsh." She passed him the gun.

He took a moment, examining it before handing it to me.

"Thanks." Part of me hated how familiar the weapon felt in my hand, but the weight of it was too comforting for me to resent being given a kep gun.

"What do I get?" Harper said.

"A guard's gun," Walsh said.

"We have normal guns, Walsh," the weapons woman said. "If you'd prefer for her—"

"My preference is for my orders to be followed." Walsh pulled a belt with a holster from the stack and handed it to me. "Harper will be given a guard's gun."

"Yes, Walsh." The woman opened the case again. Her jaw tensed as she pulled out a gun for Harper. "If you could bring me any weapons you claim, I would be glad to rebuild our stock."

"For the good of the pack." Walsh gave the woman a nod and stepped over to the stock of knives.

I fastened the belt around my waist. It was dome-issued, I recognized the make from the Outer Guard, but this belt had been worn. The material on the holster had cracked, and a slit on one side had been stitched up, like the belt had been damaged in a fight and the pack member who'd pulled it off a kep corpse had tried to fix it.

I tucked my gun into the holster.

"Harper, can you use a knife?" Walsh passed two blades to me. Both had sheaths. Both were sturdy and well-balanced.

He wants me to survive.

I tucked one knife into the ankle of my boot and hooked the other onto my belt.

"Drivers in the domes get basic hand-to-hand and crowd control techniques." Harper fastened on her own gun belt. "I'm better with a club than a knife."

"So the glass demons can beat us to death with their fancy sticks." The weapons woman bared her teeth as she growled.

"Don't insult allies." Walsh opened a box that had been tucked behind the weapons, almost like its contents had been deemed worthless.

"Yes, Walsh." The woman looked to the next people in line.

I took Harper's arm, pulling her around the weapons stash to stand by Walsh.

"We still don't know what we're supposed to be doing," I said.

Walsh handed me five clips of darts.

"Are these tranqs or lethal?" I tucked the clips into my pockets.

"Does it matter?" Walsh pulled out a club and gave it to Harper.

"Yeah," I said. "I don't know who I'm supposed to be aiming for or what my weapon will do to them, and none of that is fucking okay."

He rounded on me, his eyes seeming to glint like red was trying to break through their golden brown. "You will fight for the good of the pack."

"I'm not a member of the pack, Walsh." I kept my hands in front of me, palms up like I was trying to convince a kep guard I wasn't going to attack. "I understand I have to go with the pack if I want to get Mari to an Afterworld settlement. But I need to know what you want me to do once we get to the Arc Domes. You know me, Walsh. You know I can get myself out of a tight spot, but I need to know what kind of hell you're throwing me into."

Walsh blinked and shook his head. "You'll be with me."

"While we do what?" I asked.

"Harper, you're going with Bell," Walsh said. "You'll be going to the vehicle bay."

"Great," Harper said. "Just the place I wanted to revisit."

"Stay in the upper cavern until the pack is called outside. Find a place near the entrance and get whatever sleep you can. We leave the moment our alpha gives the order." Walsh tucked two extra knives into his belt and strode through the thinning horde into the tunnel that led to the open air.

"Why won't he tell you what you're going to do?" Harper tucked her club into her backpack.

"Because he knows I'll try to stop it."

CHAPTER TWENTY-SEVEN

I tried to sleep in the upper cavern, but the energy of the pack filled the air and made resting impossible.

My chances of sleeping didn't get any better when Demetrius gave the order for everyone to go outside. The sun had already risen, but the chill of the morning burrowed through my sweater.

I finally started slipping in and out of sleep when the afternoon sun crept into the sky. Even with the puffs of cloud hovering on the horizon, it seemed like the evening had vowed to be beautiful and clear.

I sat leaning against the trunk of a tree, keeping to the shade as the werewolves split off into small groups of five to ten fighters. Each group would go to where Demetrius held court by the river, like they were receiving his blessing before bolting off into the trees.

Bell had come to collect Harper. She gave me one more hug before joining the eight others under Bell's command. The wolves all looked confident and strong.

They'll keep her safe. Harper will be fine.

I closed my eyes and tipped my head back, letting myself take comfort in the lie as I tried to make myself drift to sleep for a few more minutes.

"You'll be able to rest once we reach our position," Walsh said.

I opened my eyes to find him standing right above me. "If I'll have time to rest, why don't we wait here and travel in the dark like the vampires?"

"Because the alpha has ordered us to travel during the day." Walsh took my hand, pulling me to my feet.

"Did the alpha tell you why we're traveling during the day?" I slipped my hand from Walsh's grip, trying not to look like I wanted to run from him.

"It's not—" Walsh shook his head. "Our attack begins just before sundown.

Walsh started toward Demetrius.

"Why didn't we get into position last night?" I darted around him to block his path. "It's a simple question, Walsh."

"Wolves can't see in the dark as well as vampires." His fists tensed. "We have to run twenty-five miles through thick woods and over steep slopes. If we want to cover that much ground quickly, the pack needs daylight."

"Twenty-five miles." I tightened the straps on my backpack. "Sounds like fun."

Walsh's shoulders loosened as he smiled. "Don't worry. I haven't forgotten you're still plain human."

"Good."

He placed his hand on my backpack, herding me toward Demetrius.

Someone had cut a fresh stump, making a little altar for the alpha to stand on as he sent his wolves off to battle.

"Walsh. Lanni." Demetrius nodded.

"We're ready, Alpha." Walsh bowed.

"Actually, I'm not." I stepped sideways, out of Walsh's reach. "I still don't know what exactly it is you want from me. I can't just run blindly into the Arc Domes and hope for the best."

"You've kept your word." Demetrius looked to Walsh.

"Yes, Demetrius." Walsh bowed again.

"What does that—"

"You're not going into the Arc Domes." Demetrius spoke over me.

I backed away a step.

Walsh was behind me in an instant. He slipped his hand between my backpack and my shirt, his palm pressing me forward, toward Demetrius.

"While I appreciate your willingness to fight, one more blade won't change the course of this battle." Demetrius acted like he hadn't noticed me trying to run away. "Your usefulness comes with your image. You are the face of Project Progeny."

"I never wanted any of that," I said. "They wouldn't let me see Mari."

"And that's exactly what you're going to tell the world." Demetrius took my hand. "The Incorporation broadcast a video of you promising all the young people of the domes that Project Progeny would bring them joy and prosperity. Today, you are going to have a chance to tell the truth. You will stand in front of the flames of our battle and tell the world why the Incorporation deserves to burn.

"Your new message will be broadcast to every set of domes in the world. The young people will learn the depths of the evil that abused their bodies and stole their choices. And none of them will mourn the end of the Incorporation."

"Why didn't you tell me sooner?" I asked.

"There was no reason for you to know." Demetrius looked to Walsh. "I'll see you inside the glass."

"Yes, Demetrius." Walsh bowed.

Demetrius beckoned the next group forward.

Walsh pressed on my back, steering me away from the stump altar.

I kept my chin raised, trying to look calm even though all I wanted to do was scream that I wasn't a member of Demetrius's damn pack.

"We should get moving." Walsh kept pushing me away from the stump.

"He could have told me," I whispered.

"You know now, let that be good enough. We have a lot of ground to cover. Are you ready to run?"

"If you want me to travel twenty-five miles, I'll have to be. Good thing you just want me to stand in front of a camera. If you actually wanted me to use the weapons you so kindly gave me, I'd be screwed. I don't think I'll be able to walk by the time we make it to the Arc Domes."

"You'll be fine." Walsh stopped, sliding his hand away from my back to check the knives he'd attached to his belt. I hated how small and alone I felt without his touch. "Give me your pack."

"Why do I have weapons if all I'm supposed to do is talk? Walsh, please." I grabbed his wrist. "I've been lied to and kidnapped and pushed around and shoved on camera so I could lie for the Incorporation. All I'm asking for is the truth."

He lifted my hand away from his wrist. "Give me your bag."

"Does Demetrius not want me to carry it?" I took off my pack and shoved it against his chest.

"I'm trying to make sure you have a comfortable trip." Walsh put my pack on and checked the knives on his belt one more time. "You won't have to worry about your legs getting tired."

My stomach jolted as he scooped me into his arms.

He started running through the trees before I could ask if he was serious.

I clung to his neck, trying not to flinch as we weaved between branches.

"Are you really going to carry me the whole way?" I squeaked as he leapt over a stream.

"Are you regretting not taking the Lycan?"

"Never."

He shifted his grip, cradling me closer to his chest.

"But I am wondering who's going to carry Harper." I closed my eyes as he sprinted up a slope of loose rocks.

"Bell. Don't worry. She'll take care of Harper."

"Just for the run, or once they get inside the Arc Domes, too?" Walsh didn't answer.

For the first few slopes, I clung to him, afraid he might corner around a boulder too quickly and lose his grip on me. But soon, I relaxed into his arms, trusting him to protect me as I watched the forest pass by.

One type of tree gave way to another as we raced through the mountains. I'd never seen such a large stretch of plants before. Everything seemed wild and old. Even the decaying trees that had fallen to the ground seemed somehow like they belonged.

The vibrant scent of the forest smelled more like the domes than the city. I caught sight of birds flying away as they heard Walsh sprinting toward them, and what looked like a rabbit diving into the brush to hide from us.

"Is this a green spot on the map?" I held my breath as Walsh leapt over a gap where part of a ridge had crumbled away.

"It's a blue spot," Walsh said. "The winters here are harsh, long, and unpredictable. It's only going to get worse over the next hundred years. So, people could survive, if they could find a way to not freeze or starve, but it's not a great place for a settlement."

"The Afterworld scientists knew so much, and those Incorporation fuckers just hid it."

"Keep your eyes open." Walsh picked up speed as he charged toward the edge of a rise.

"Why?" My question was swallowed by my scream as Walsh leapt off the cliff.

A river flowed beneath us, churning violently as the rock walls on either side narrowed its banks.

Before I'd run out of air to scream, Walsh landed on the rocks on the other side, not even breaking his stride.

"The fuck was that?" My voice trembled.

"The easiest way to cross the river. It's only a fifteen-foot gap."

"Why did you tell me to keep my eyes open?" I smacked him on the chest.

"Lycan has more to offer than just being able to heal, Lanni." He cut back into the trees, winding us down yet another slope. "I'm faster, stronger, I can jump over a river while carrying you."

"You have an alpha in your head."

"You're a decent fighter," Walsh said, like he hadn't even heard me. "With Lycan, you'd be able to protect yourself."

"Why do I need to protect myself? Why does the pack care about my safety once the video is recorded?"

"It's not about the pack."

"Everything is about the pack, remember?"

Walsh's steps slowed. "I want you safe. For me."

"Put me down."

"I can't. We're not to our position yet. We can't stop until we're there."

"Not even for a minute?"

"My orders are not to stop."

"Okay." I settled my head on his shoulder, letting myself nestle close to him like I had chosen to seek safety in his arms. "Is his voice that loud?"

Walsh's shoulders trembled.

"Then keep running. Get us into position. Don't fight him when you don't have to."

"I would never fight the commands of my alpha."

His shoulders shuddered again, like Demetrius's orders were pounding through his brain, drowning out the part of Walsh that had bent his alpha's commands to help Mari and me escape the Arc Domes.

A sharp, awful pain dug into my chest. I leaned up high enough to kiss Walsh's cheek.

"You're going to be okay," I whispered. "You didn't abandon me. I won't abandon you."

I kept my head on his shoulder as he ran, laying my hand on his chest so I could feel his heartbeat. He should have been soaked in sweat, his heart racing just from sprinting through the mountains. But, even with me in his arms, his heart stayed slow and steady, like he was strolling through the woods.

The sun had shifted to the west before he finally slowed, picking his path more carefully as he cut through the trees.

The forest around us thinned, letting more of the sky peer between the branches, and making it feel like we were being watched from every angle.

Walsh stopped, taking a deep breath to scent the air before shifting our path.

"What do you smell?" I whispered.

"On you? Vampire."

"Don't be an ass."

"Fireweed." He ducked beneath a thick cluster of branches.

"You can put me down if we're just going to walk."

"We're here."

We'd reached the edge of the trees.

Beyond the shelter of the forest, the slope curved to join with the neighboring peak. A field of flowers coated the mountainside, painting the ground with a wide purple streak.

The beautiful sea of blooms rustled in the breeze. It took me a moment to look past the flowers to what lay beyond—the Arc Domes nestled into the slope with Incorporation Headquarters rising above, reaching up toward the peak of the mountain.

Walsh had brought us level with the Incorporation's atrium. The massive dome should have been beautiful as it glimmered in the late afternoon sun.

"Now we just have to wait." Walsh set me on my feet but kept his hand on my back.

I'm not sure if he knew that the world had started to sway

around me, or if he was panicking at being so close to the Arc Domes, too.

"The domes are too big." I took Walsh's free hand, locking my fingers through his. "Whatever Demetrius is planning, there's no way it can work. The kep have better weapons. They'll pick the pack off before the wolves even get near the glass."

"No, they won't." Walsh's voice held a terrifying certainty.

"Tell me what Demetrius is planning." I turned to him.

"We're going to make a video and broadcast—"

"Why are you so sure the pack will make it into the glass?"

His shoulders shuddered. He shut his eyes, wincing like Demetrius's voice was slashing through his mind.

"Just breathe, Walsh. You can tell me. Demetrius isn't here."

"Yes, he is." Walsh opened his eyes, meeting my gaze. "He's in my mind, and I can't make it stop." He stepped away from me, doubling over as he gripped his head.

"You can't fight it like you could in the domes?"

"I just left the pack. What do you expect from me!" He lunged toward me. His hands grazed my shoulders like he was going to grab me before he pulled away. "You should eat and rest." He took off my pack, dropping it by my feet.

"You need to eat, too."

"I'll be fine." He leaned against a tree, sliding down to sit on its knobbled roots. "I'm a wolf."

CHAPTER TWENTY-EIGHT

The wind picked up as the evening sky shifted to a gentle red, bringing a chill that made me grateful for my sweater. I'd pulled the tattered material down over my hands, keeping my nails from cutting into my palms as my fists clenched tighter and tighter while the sun faded.

I watched the shadows on the slope change, searching for any hint of the other wolves hiding in the woods. I took a drink from the flask Harper had packed for me. I hoped she'd remembered to pack water for herself.

"Can I ask you something?" I looked at Walsh.

"You can ask. I probably can't answer." He kept his eyes closed as he traced his right forefinger over his left palm in a steady stream of curls.

"What are you doing?"

"Waiting."

"I mean with your hands." I crawled closer to him.

"Writing something no one is ever going to see."

"Why?"

He stopped writing and pressed his palms together, hiding the imaginary words.

"Okay then." I knelt beside him. "How is Harper going to get to the vehicle bay?"

He stayed silent.

"How will we know when it's time for us to move?" I took another drink of water, not knowing if it would be the last sip I got before the chaos began.

"You won't be able to miss it." Walsh held his hand out for the flask.

My fingers brushed against his as I passed him the water.

He twined his pinky around mine, keeping our hands locked together with the gentlest touch.

"Why did you say you were in love with me?" I whispered.

"It doesn't matter."

"Yes, it does."

"You have your vampire." He looked at me with a sadness in his eyes that hollowed out my lungs.

"I didn't ask because of Jaime." I took the flask from him, setting it down so I could properly hold his hand. "I just need to know why you said it. Were you really in love with me?"

He tipped his head back, looking up to the darkening sky. "I still am."

"Walsh—"

"It started in the atrium. You should have been terrified when I told you how much I knew about you and Mari. But you didn't run. You held your ground like you were the most powerful force in the world. Maybe you are. I poisoned a man, and you didn't run. You found out what I am, and you didn't even flinch."

"Is being too stubborn to run a reason to fall in love with someone?"

"You're brave and stubborn, and loving, and you make it feel like maybe the world is still worth fighting for." He held our hands close to his chest.

"Do you need the world to be worth fighting for if you're just following Demetrius's orders?"

"No. But it helps."

"Then there's more than just the wolf in your head. If you're in love with me, that means the Walsh from the domes is still in there."

I placed his hand on my hip, easing myself closer to him when he didn't pull away.

"I followed that Walsh out of the Arc Domes because I trusted him." I trailed my fingers along his cheek and tipped his chin up, bringing his lips closer to mine. "I need that Walsh, *my* Walsh, now. I'm not stupid. I know we're not just going in there to steal supplies and destroy the kep's weapons. Demetrius wants more than that. I need to know that whatever he's planning is worth fighting for. If you say what's going to happen here tonight is worth it, then I'll trust you."

He closed his eyes. His jaw tensed beneath my touch.

"Please be the person I can trust." I pressed my forehead to his. "I'm scared, Walsh."

I froze, ready for him to shove me away as he shifted his hand from my hip.

But he pulled me into his lap, holding me close as he whispered in my ear, "Demetrius wants everyone dead, whether or not we get any supplies."

He gasped, clinging to me as his shoulders shook.

"Breathe. Just breathe, you're okay."

"He's sending in groups. Two teams are aiming for supplies as their primary mission. Every other team has orders to pick the domes' people off and try for supplies after—" He swallowed his scream, tipping his head back, his whole face screwed up against the pain in his mind.

"Don't say anything else. Just breathe."

He gagged on the air.

"Shh." I pressed my cheek to his. "You're going to be okay. I'm right here. You're okay."

"He's going to kill them all. I'm sorry. I'm so sorry."

"Don't." I brushed his sweaty hair away from his forehead. He hadn't sweat at all when he'd carried me through the mountains.

"I wanted to get you away from the Incorporation. I wanted you to be safe. I'm sorry." Tears filled the corners of his eyes. "I couldn't leave you behind."

He shut his eyes again, panting from the pain.

And I kissed him. Just brushed my lips against his, needing to kiss him one more time. In case resisting Demetrius's orders destroyed his mind. Or killed him. Or stole that last bit of the Walsh who loved me.

Or in case we both died in the hell we were about to face.

Or maybe those are just lies I tried to make myself believe. Maybe I kissed him because I needed one more thing worth fighting for.

He kissed me back, so carefully, like he knew how close everything was to shattering.

"I love you, Lanni." His lips brushed against mine as he whispered, "Even when the wolf swallows my mind, I love you."

"Then fight to stay with me." I kissed him again, twining my fingers through his hair, hoping that somehow loving me would be enough to change everything.

I forgot how to breathe as he kissed me. Not for the cameras or as any part of a lie. Just Connor Walsh kissing Lanni Sampson.

A blissful hum filled my body as he lifted me, still kissing me as he set me down so we were both kneeling. I ran my hand up his back, my fingers tingling as they traced the ridges of his muscles.

He tipped his chin down, stealing his lips from mine. "If things go badly, I want you to run. I won't be able to—"

Boom.

Walsh leapt to his feet, lifting me with him, twisting to shelter me behind him.

Boom, boom, boom, boom.

"What's happening?" I stepped sideways, looking toward the sounds.

Boom, boom.

Crack.

The ground tipped. But it wasn't the ground beneath my feet. It was the peak of the mountain above Incorporation Headquarters.

At first, it looked like the massive stone of the mountain's summit would fall all in one piece, but the peak shattered as it tilted, breaking into boulders the size of houses as it slid toward the glass domes nestled into the mountain's slope.

"No!" I lunged forward, like I could somehow stop the horror.

Walsh caught me around the middle, keeping me in the shelter of the trees as the first rock crashed into Incorporation Headquarters. The stone smashed through the glass, caving in the Incorporation's precious atrium.

"Stop!" The scream ripped from my throat.

The boulders kept sliding down, slamming into the Arc Domes' atrium, shattering the housing domes where families would already be in their homes for the night. Tearing into the growing domes, destroying the safety that had allowed the kep to grow food.

A flood of water rushed from the Salt Dome, washing down the slope as the glass gave way, letting the kep's little ocean loose.

The damage didn't stop once the shattered summit had fallen. An avalanche of stone and dirt cascaded down the slope.

In my head, I could hear the Arc Domes' siren blaring. I wasn't sure if I was imagining the sound. With so much destruction, I didn't know if the siren would still work.

Tears burned down my cheeks as I fought against Walsh's grip.

Little dots moved on the sides of the slope. Members of the pack shifting into position, getting ready to attack.

"Stop them." I kicked back, catching Walsh in the knee. He didn't let go of me. "There are kids in there. We have to get the kids out."

"Our orders are to make the video." Walsh shifted his grip on me, holding me more like he was trying to keep the girl he loved from shattering and less like I was a rabid animal he was trying to control.

"Fuck the video." My sobs shook my words as another wave of rock and earth swept down the mountain and the pack members crept closer to the chaos. "Mari's classmates are in there. Our classmates are in there."

"The damage is done."

"They have to get to the bunkers." I twisted in Walsh's arms, needing to see his face. "The kep never showed any mercy to the people in my city, but we don't have to be like them. I don't want to be like the Incorporation's butchers. How can I face Mari if I have to tell her I did nothing while her friends died?"

"We have to make the video."

"Walsh—"

He kissed me, like he knew there was no coming back from the choices we faced. The blood that lay in front of us would change everything, even the things we'd never wanted to risk.

"My orders are to make the video, get into the domes to upload and send the file, then join the fight." He loosened his hold on me. "I have to start with the video. I can't go into the domes until it's done."

"Okay." I don't know how I stayed on my feet when Walsh let go of me.

He pulled a little camera from his pocket, smaller than anything the Incorporation had ever used to film me.

I looked back toward the domes. "What am I supposed to say?"

"Tell the world the Incorporation has fallen. Tell them why it had to be done." Walsh pressed a button. A red light on the front of the camera blinked to life.

"The Incorporation has fallen." I stepped aside, giving the camera a view of the ruined domes in the last of the evening light. "After all the horrible things the Incorporation has done to the people outside the glass, after the Incorporation chose to torment their own people with Project Progeny, their paradise has come crashing down." A desperate laugh bubbled in my throat. "Their precious home was ruined by the Alliance—a group of people so desperate to stop the Incorporation, their violence has proven they are barely better than the monsters they set out to destroy.

"The human race is dying off. There are so few of us left alive. And this—" I looked back to the domes. A huge swath of flames burst to life on the slope, swallowing the Incorporation's atrium. "This is what we do to each other. The Incorporation murdered outsiders. They abused their own people in vile ways. The fate of humanity must not be left for them to decide.

"But whatever new leader manages to claw their way to the top of this shit show needs to be better than the demons who came before them. We're out of chances. We're out of time. If the human race can't get its shit together and stop murdering each other, then maybe the world is better off without us."

I swiped the tears from my cheeks. "Turn the camera off. I'm done trying to convince people any of us are worth saving."

Walsh pressed a button and the red light on the front of the camera disappeared. "I need to connect to an Arc Domes' computer to upload the video."

"Will the computers even be working after the mountain fell on them?" I wiped my tears one more time before grabbing my bag.

"There are backups for the backups inside the domes. The computers in the tunnels will be working."

"Then we can get down into the corridors together." I checked the clip of darts in my gun, trying to pretend it didn't matter if they were tranqs or poison. "I'll try and keep the paths to the bunkers clear for the kids to evacuate, you upload Demetrius's precious video."

"If you want anyone to survive, you have to get them to the

bunker below the atrium." Walsh tucked the camera into his pocket. "The bunker below seed storage won't be safe."

"We've got to get to the stairs. Force everyone toward the atrium."

"We're already too late." Walsh grabbed my arm, swinging me around onto his back. "The battle's begun."

I clung to him as he sprinted toward the domes, watching the pack charge through the mangled glass to begin their attack on the kep.

CHAPTER TWENTY-NINE

I had witnessed chaos and violence before, but never anything like the scene that waited inside the domes. The world should not survive with such monsters in it.

See you in the embers,

~C

CHAPTER THIRTY

The pop of kep guns carried from inside the Arc Domes, but no one fired on us as we neared the shattered glass.

Walsh kept me on his back as we approached the concrete base that supported one of the domes. The boulders that had crashed through that dome hadn't crumbled the whole structure. The edges of the glass still stood.

He jumped up onto the base and sidestepped away from the slope, aiming us toward a spot where the remaining glass was only seven or eight feet high.

He took a breath before jumping up and grabbing the edge of the shattered dome.

"Careful." I watched blood drip from his hands as he pulled us up and over the glass.

"I'll heal." Walsh ducked low as he darted toward the nearest shelter—a stand of tall grass that seemed out of place with the pops and screams that carried through the darkening night. By the time he put me down, his hands had already healed. He knelt beside the water to wash the blood off his palms.

I peered through the grass where Walsh had hidden us, trying to figure out where we were.

A massive boulder had smashed through the nearest house. A woman knelt beside the building, screaming for help even though two others were already digging through the wreckage.

The siren hadn't started blaring. The lack of its overwhelming sound somehow made everything seem worse. More desolate and desperate.

"I need to get to a computer station." Walsh pulled his knives out of his belt.

I looked beyond the damage, trying to make my brain process where we actually were.

Channels of water cut between grass islands. He'd brought us into the Marsh Dome.

"We aren't too far from the stairs people will be trying to take to reach the bunker by seed storage." I crawled toward the edge of our patch of land. "Can you come with me? You're just as likely to find a computer if we stay together."

Walsh gripped my wrist. "If we're staying together, then I'm going in front."

"I have a vest on." I still let him slide in front of me as we crept toward the nearest bridge.

Pop. Pop. Pop, pop, pop.

The sound seemed to be coming from near the stairs leading down into the concrete corridors that connected the domes.

"Help! We need help!" The woman beside the crushed home was still screaming, not even trying to dig through the rubble to reach whoever had been trapped inside. Blood and dirt covered her face. The people helping her were coated in filth, too, like they'd been caught in the storm of dirt that had cascaded down the mountain.

"Stop." I dragged my hands through the dirt that covered the bridge, coating my palms. I rubbed the dirt over my face, then grabbed a handful and mashed it into my hair. "Want to donate some blood, or should I just cut my head?"

"I don't want you smelling like human blood." Walsh sliced his palm back open. The feel of him smearing his blood onto my temple sent sour surging into my throat.

"Now let's go." Walsh grabbed two handfuls of dirt, coating himself as we ran across the bridge.

"I need a doctor," a man called from the next island.

I wanted to change our path, but Walsh kept running toward the voice.

"Someone call a doctor!" The man lay on the walkway, like he had been taking an evening stroll when the world had gone to hell. Blood oozed from the wounds on his back where glass had rained down on him, and his leg was broken, twisting at an angle that made fleeing impossible. "Get a doctor, please." He reached for us as we ran past.

I tucked my chin, picturing the people back home I'd watched beg the kep for help as they died. The kep had never tried to save any of the city scum.

"Down to the bunker!" The shout came from near the steps. "Anyone who can move, get down to the bunker."

"She can't walk!" The shout came from our left.

Pop. Pop.

The next bridge we came to had been smashed by debris.

Walsh scooped me into his arms, jumping over the canal and landing on the far side before I could warn him to act like a plain human. He set me back on my feet and we kept running.

"You! Help me!" A woman had a man on a bedsheet. She was trying to drag him to the next bridge. She should have left him behind. From the blood surrounding the glass that had ripped through his stomach, there was no way the man would survive, even with fancy kep medicine. "I said help me." The woman looked me square in the face. "It's you. You ran away. Guards! Gua—"

I shot the woman in the chest with one of my darts.

You had to. She was screaming. You can't afford to be caught. Not now.

"The hall is clear!" The shout came from the stairs. "Everyone out, now. Move. Move!"

"Act hurt." Walsh scooped me into his arms again.

I clutched my gun to my stomach, hunching around it as though I was protecting a wound.

"I'll get you to a doctor." Walsh looked down at me, keeping his face away from the guards.

I curled my head toward his shoulder. "It hurts. They have to make it stop hurting."

"You'll be okay." Walsh carried me down the stairs at a human pace, keeping clustered with the others who had made it that far.

"Medical will be waiting in the bunker," the guard said. "Go straight to the bunker."

Pop. Pop. Pop.

The sound came from the left, toward the other housing domes.

"Who the hell are these people?" A man shoved his way to the front of our fleeing group.

"Keep moving. Get down the stairs. Don't stop until you reach the bunker."

"They're herding everyone toward the seed storage bunker," I whispered just loudly enough for Walsh to hear. "We have to make them go the other way."

His shoulders shook. He held me tighter. "I have to upload the video."

A terrible shriek came from behind us.

Bang. Bang.

The kep screamed, panicking at the sound of the old-fashioned gun.

Walsh cut through the fleeing kep as we reached the stairs. He kept me in his arms as he ran down the steps to the level with the vehicle bay and medical corridor.

"Go back," he shouted up the stairs. "Get to the atrium bunker! It's not safe this way. Go back!"

He didn't stop to see if his shouting had worked. He darted through an open door and into a room, setting me on my feet before lunging toward the computer screen in the wall.

"Guard the door." He started tapping on the computer.

I saw the screen blink to life before I looked to where a door should have been. Singe marks surrounded the doorframe, like someone had blasted their way into the room.

A stream of people ran by. I hoped they were heading toward the medical corridor and not trying to find a safe path to the bunker by seed storage. I wanted to shout for them to go back, but I couldn't make myself do it, not while Walsh and I were cornered.

"Tell me you're almost done." I glanced back at Walsh. My gaze caught on the desk.

Captain Tate's desk. A smear of blood led from her desk to the blown-apart door.

"Why Captain Tate?" I backed toward Walsh, keeping the gun in my hand by my side, like that would somehow make me look like less of a threat.

"You said there was a hand scanner to get through the door in weapons storage," Walsh said. "Orders are to take both Tate and Pace to weapons storage. A team was assigned to find each of them, but every wolf who came into the domes knows they need to be brought to weapons storage. It's top priority for all of us. We just need one of the captains to open the door."

"So you can blow the weapons to hell and kill everyone in the seed storage bunker right above the blast."

"The weapons have to be destroyed. No one will ever be safe from the Incorporation while they have the ability to dissolve forests. You can't build a home for Mari while the demons have the power to melt her to less than ash."

"Fuck." I tightened my grip on my gun. "Fuck."

"I'm almost done."

"Then where do we go?"

He didn't answer.

"I'm not a fighter, Walsh. Where do we go?"

I glanced toward him again.

He'd screwed up his face against the pain.

"Breathe, Walsh. You're not disobeying your alpha. You're supposed to join the fight. We just need to make the fight funnel the kep toward the atrium bunker."

"We go up. Back to the housing level. We're not going to be able to convince anyone to leave the bunker by seed storage—their fate is their fate—but we can stop the flow of people going there. Bring the fight to the staircase that leads this way, and people will have to head toward the atrium."

"Sounds great."

"Then let's go." Walsh stepped around me, tucking the camera into his pocket and pulling his knives from his belt.

The screen he'd been using had gone blank. If everything had worked, a video of me standing in front of the ruins of Incorporation Headquarters was being sent to domes all over the world.

The kep would panic. Try to figure out what had happened to Incorporation Headquarters. They wouldn't be celebrating that the Incorporation had been destroyed.

The kep would mourn first. If not for the kep who had died, then at least for the feeling of being protected by something beyond their domes. They'd hate me.

Kep all over the world would hate me. Some might never realize the world was better off without the Incorporation, and they would spend their entire lives hating me. They would never know it was Demetrius who'd brought down the top of the mountain to smash through the safety the Incorporation had spilled so much blood to build.

They would all blame me.

"Lanni." Walsh stood in the doorway, a knife in each hand. "Are you okay?"

"Yeah."

He flashed me a smile and headed into the corridor. "Keep up."

I stayed right on his heels as we started down the hall.

The flood of people fleeing the housing domes had slowed.

"Go back!" I shouted to the four kids coming down the stairs. "Tell everyone to go to the atrium bunker. Run!"

"We can't," a little girl sobbed.

"Go!" Walsh shouted at her. "Now."

All four kids bolted back up the stairs.

We followed behind them.

"Why aren't there more people?" I asked. "Are they already heading toward the other bunker? Is there no one—"

Shouted orders came from the medical corridor.

"Gideon." My feet froze. "Is he still locked in the medical corridor?"

"If he's locked in, he's safe." Walsh kept climbing the stairs.

"They'll evacuate him. He'll end up in the seed storage bunker."

Pop. Pop.

The sound came from the hall leading to the vehicle bay.

"I'm sorry." I turned and ran back down the stairs.

"Don't!" Walsh shouted.

I kept running.

The fourth door on the left. That was where they'd made me take pictures. But I didn't know if that same room was Gideon's prison.

I slipped, falling backward onto my pack. My flask banged into my spine, but the thickness of my pack saved my head from cracking against the floor.

I rolled sideways onto my knees.

Blood. I'd slipped in a pool of blood. Was kneeling in a pool of blood.

"All of it. Get everything into the bag." The orders came from a room in front of me. "Where's the rest? Where is it!"

I got to my feet, stepping around the blood, trying to avoid the red footprints others had left behind.

The door to the room that held the voices hung off its hinges, like it'd been kicked in.

Two doctors frantically grabbed things from the cupboards of medical supplies, stuffing them into the bags two werewolves held.

A third wolf stood behind them, tossing his knife from hand to hand.

The body of a guard lay on the ground. He was wearing a normal uniform, without any of the riot gear that might have helped him survive a fight with a werewolf.

I walked past the door, heading farther down the hall.

Most of the doors didn't have any hint of a lock on them.

Bang. Pop. Pop.

The sounds came from the vehicle bay corridor.

A man screamed.

"Shit." I shut my eyes, trying to think of a better plan. "Gideon! Gideon!"

"Who the fuck is out there?" The wolf with the knife stepped out into the hall.

"Shh." I pressed my finger to my lips. "Demetrius gave me orders."

The wolf grinned.

"Gideon!" I shouted again.

"In here." Banging came from a door to my left. "I'm in here."

I ran to the door and tried to shove it open. It wouldn't budge. Gideon had been left locked in. Abandoned and trapped in the chaos.

"Break the door down." I looked to the wolf. "Demetrius wants this one alive for questioning."

"Funny thing to send a weakling to do." The wolf narrowed his eyes at me.

"The boy inside knows me." I tried to picture Gideon as

someone as disgusting and violent as his brothers, letting my hatred for them ooze into my voice. "He'll follow me out of here. His father is the captain of the Outer Guard. He'll have information that can help the Alliance."

Boom!

The floor shook. The lights in the corridor flickered.

I couldn't tell where the explosion had come from.

How many people just died?

"Open the fucking door!" I shouted at the wolf.

I leapt out of the way as he charged toward me, ramming his shoulder into the door at full speed. The door cracked. The wolf pushed his shoulder back into its socket and kicked the crack.

Pop, pop.

The wolf kicked the crack again, and the door gave way, swinging open into Gideon's prison.

Gideon stood inside the sterile room, backed against a bed with a white fitted sheet.

Panic gripped my throat.

"Have fun." The wolf winked at me and ran back to steal more medicine from the doctors.

"Lanni?" Gideon shook his head, blinking at me like he thought he was imagining me. "You can't be here. You ran away."

"I came back." I reached for Gideon. "I need you to come with me."

"But there's something bad going on. The ground shook. I heard screaming, and I think something exploded."

"Bad things *are* happening, and it's going to get worse." I kept reaching for him. I couldn't make myself step into that room. "Please, Gideon. I'm trying to help you. I need you to trust me. You have to come with me, now."

Bang, bang, bang.

"Where did you go when you ran away?" He stepped toward me.

"It doesn't matter."

"Why did you come back?"

"I'm trying to save your life! You have to come with me, right now, or you're going to die."

"I want to leave the domes." He took another step toward me. "Wherever you escaped to, take me there."

"We have to—"

"If you won't help me escape, then leave me to die."

Boom.

The floor shook again. Not as much as the first time. Not enough to be weapons storage.

"Fuck." I looked down the hall, past the blood smeared on the floor. "Fine, just keep up."

CHAPTER THIRTY-ONE

Two guards lay dead on the ground. Both had been stabbed, their bloody corpses tossed aside in the corridor that led to the vehicle bay.

"No, no, no." Gideon ran toward the bodies.

The way the guards had been slashed, it could have been Walsh who'd killed them.

"Warren." Gideon knelt beside Guard Warren. She'd been stabbed in the throat.

"We have to go." I grabbed Gideon's arm, making myself look at the faces of the dead guards.

They were enemies who would have killed city scum without hesitation. Who had dragged their own people into sterile rooms to be abused in the worst ways.

Their deaths made the world a better, safer place.

I still couldn't feel grateful they were gone.

"We need to find a doctor." Gideon let me haul him to his feet.

"It's too late for them."

An earsplitting scream came from the stairwell.

"What the hell is going on?" Gideon backed down the hall.

"We have to keep moving." I tried to drag him toward the stairs.

"Why are we being attacked?" He yanked his arm away from me. "Are you here to kill people?"

"I am trying to help you."

"Lanni—"

"We're running out of time!" someone shouted from near the vehicle bay.

"A lot of people are going to die today." I backed toward the stairs. "I am trying to keep as many kids alive as I can. Do you want to come with me, or do you want to stay here?"

"We need help!" The scream came from the staircase.

"Time's up. Good luck, Gideon." I ran toward the stairs, focusing on the weight of the gun in my grip to keep my hands from shaking.

Pop, pop, pop, pop.

"Filthy fucking demon!" a man shouted.

Then a woman screamed.

I reached the top of the steps and bolted into the corridor.

Bang.

The gunshot echoed through the hall, pounding into my ears and muting the sound of the woman's screams as she fell with a fresh bullet hole in her shoulder.

For a second, I wanted to help the woman, but Walsh and four of Demetrius's people blocked my path to her.

"We need more guards!" The shout carried over the woman's screaming.

"That's enough," Walsh said. "Grab them all."

He held his ground, keeping his gun aimed down the arc of the corridor as the rest of Demetrius's people darted past him toward the seven kep that lay on the floor.

I couldn't tell if most of them were alive or dead.

A vampire reached the screaming woman first. He grabbed her

leg, dragging her closer to the stairs. He chucked her against the wall.

"What are you—"

Before I could finish shouting at him, the vampire had sunk his teeth into the woman's neck.

She scratched at his face as her blood dripped from his chin.

"Toss them down the stairs," Walsh ordered.

Pop, pop.

Walsh grabbed me, pinning me behind him as a dart pinged off the cement wall beside us. I didn't even know he'd seen me.

He fired his gun at the guards as they pulled back along the arced hall. The bullets sprayed fragments of concrete from the kep's perfect walls.

A guard leaned back into sight to fire at us.

Pop. Pop.

I ducked behind Walsh as he shot back.

"Leave him." Walsh grabbed me, flinging me toward the stairs.

I caught a glimpse of the corridor as I stumbled around the corner.

The kep bodies weren't in the hall anymore. But the vampire lay on top of the woman he'd been draining. A silver dart stuck out of his shoulder.

"It's a shitty barricade." One of the wolves threw a kep corpse onto the stairs leading toward the medical corridor and the bunker below seed storage, scattering it with the other bodies they'd tossed onto the steps, creating a grisly warning that only death would greet the kep who fled that way.

"It's a deterrent, and it's the best we can do." Walsh dragged me the opposite direction, to the steps that led up to the atrium.

"Thank you." I got my feet under me, finally managing to make my legs move. I ran up the steps beside Walsh, focusing on the sounds coming from above us rather than the growing screams from below.

"How much time do we have left?" one of the wolves asked.

Pop, pop, pop, pop, pop.

The pops from below were faster and louder than a normal kep gun.

"No fucking clue." Walsh scooped me into his arms, cradling me close as he sprinted up the steps at a speed I wouldn't have been able to match.

"If they can't go down to the seed bunker, they'll be okay?" I spoke into the crook of his neck.

"Only if they find a place to hide."

Boom.

The stairs shook.

"Was that it?" one of the wolves asked.

"I don't think so," Walsh said. "With what the Incorporation has stored in this mountain, the explosion in weapons storage should be enough to knock us off our feet."

Two levels up to the Council chamber, through the corridors, and down a different set of steps to reach the bunker below the atrium.

Too far. Too many halls. The wounded kep won't be able to make it.

There's nothing more you can do.

A howling rang through the air.

I gritted my teeth, swallowing my need to scream as Walsh and the wolves behind him joined the cry.

He carried me past the Council chamber level. I twisted, trying to see if there were any wolves blocking the path to the atrium bunker. Part of the ceiling had crumbled, but there was no blood on the floor.

Someone on the stairs below us screamed. It sounded like a kid.

The howling from above started again.

"What the hell is that?" I shrank into Walsh's arms.

"The battle's moved to the atrium. Our alpha wants us there." Walsh stepped up into the atrium and set me down behind him. "Stay in the shadows. You don't belong in this fight."

"Neither do you." I touched his arm.

He didn't try to stop me as I followed him toward the center of the atrium.

The damage to the Marsh Dome was nothing compared to the destruction of the atrium. Nearly all the glass had shattered when giant boulders slammed down on the dome, crashing through the trees that had once made the place so maddeningly peaceful.

The other wolves flanked Walsh as he headed down the path. Moonlight glinted off the glass that crunched beneath my feet as I followed them. I kept behind the wolves, knowing they would be better off without me blocking their path to the fight, even as I tried to think of a way to make the whole thing stop.

A boy lay beside the path. A massive chunk of glass stuck out of his back. I recognized the boy from my class. He'd sat in front of me. He'd died with his eyes open.

A chorus of pops and the clang of metal crashing against metal grew louder as we reached the center of the atrium.

"Back them up!"

"Demetrius." Walsh cut around the crack in the ground that had been the pond, sprinting through the trees toward the entrance to Incorporation Headquarters.

Pop, pop.

A shard of bark flew off the tree beside me.

Pop.

One of the wolves fell to the ground.

The wolf beside them charged silently toward the shooter, knife raised.

Walsh didn't slow down.

"Hold the line. Hold the fucking line!" a woman shouted.

We reached the edge of the trees and the little clearing that surrounded the entrance to Incorporation Headquarters.

Kep had barricaded themselves in the corner where Gideon and I had announced Project Progeny. They'd dragged over smashed-up trees, shoving the wood between the four massive hunks of rock that had fallen from the ceiling, building themselves a shitty shelter.

A rhythmic crashing came from behind the barricade.

"Wear them down." Demetrius stood behind a tree, arms crossed, blood from an already healed wound smeared across his cheek. "Fire again."

A round of bangs and pops shot out of the trees as the pack fired on the kep.

Someone behind the barricade screamed, but the rhythmic crashing didn't stop.

Walsh grabbed my wrist, tucking me behind his back as he bowed to his alpha. "Demetrius, the video has been sent."

"Good." Demetrius frowned as the guards behind the barricade fired back. "They're trying to break through the door to Incorporation Headquarters."

"It won't do them any good," I said. "There's an elevator through the door that won't work without the right palm print and chip band. Same as the door. If they can't open one lock, they can't open the other."

"You're still alive," Demetrius said. "I'm impressed."

I flinched as another round of darts shot out from behind the barricade.

"They probably don't know they can't get up the elevator," I said. "Tell them. Maybe they'll surrender and we can—"

"I don't take prisoners, and I don't allow survivors," Demetrius said. "We are removing a cancer from the world. Leave any trace behind, and it will come back to kill us."

"Without weapons? Without trucks or helicopters?" I tried to step around Walsh. He let go of my wrist and looped his arm around me, keeping me pinned to his back. "The Incorporation will never be able to rebuild what you've managed to destroy today. Take the pack and get out of here before weapons storage blows."

"We won't know if we've successfully demolished their

weapons until the whole mountain shakes." Demetrius pulled a knife from his belt, aiming the point at Walsh's heart. "We will not leave until our work is done."

Walsh kept his gun aimed at the barricade even though his other arm was behind his back holding me in place. His chest was exposed to the alpha's weapon, leaving Demetrius a clear path to stab him in the heart—a wound not even a werewolf could survive.

"I appreciate your contributions to our mission, Lanni, but do not stand against me." Demetrius touched the tip of his blade to Walsh's chest. "I don't want to give the order for Walsh to kill you, but I will."

Pop, pop, pop.

Demetrius pulled his hand away as the barricaded kep shot at us again.

"We should burn them out," Walsh said. "Catch the trees in front of them on fire, and they'll have to come out."

"Is it just guards back there?" I pushed against Walsh's arm, but he didn't loosen his hold on me.

"It's better than wasting time and ammunition picking them off," Walsh said.

"There's no chance of getting through that door?" Demetrius asked.

"Didn't you already mas—"

A wave of shouts came from behind us.

Walsh let go of me as he turned toward the sound.

Pop, pop, pop, pop, pop.

Darts flew from the barricade.

I leapt sideways behind the shelter of a tree, raising my gun toward the shouts that were still racing closer.

Kep guards charged through the trees, pinning us at the edge of the clearing.

"Shit." I sprinted sideways, racing toward the edge of the attack.

Pops and bangs and screams filled the air.

"Lanni!"

I heard someone shout my name. I glanced behind, slowing my pace just a little, just enough to watch Walsh slice through a guard's throat.

A spray of bark shot off the tree in front of me.

I knew I needed to dodge for cover but didn't know which way to go.

A dart grazed the front of my vest.

"No! Not her!"

I looked toward the shout.

Paul Pace had his gun aimed at my neck. I watched him pull the trigger as something crashed into me, knocking me to the ground.

I kept my grip on my gun as I rolled away from the impact, keeping my sights on Paul.

"No!" Fear filled Paul's face. He aimed at me again.

I shot first, sinking a dart into Paul's stomach. I scrambled to my feet as he fell to the ground. I stepped on something soft and looked down.

Gideon.

He lay sprawled on the ground beside me, a silver dart sticking out of his side. I'd stepped on his hand. His arms were reaching out in front of him. He'd pushed me out of the way.

Gideon Pace had saved me again.

"Gideon, no." I fell to my knees and yanked the dart from his side. "Gideon, wake up. You have to wake up."

I looked at the dart in my hand. I couldn't tell if it was poison or tranq.

"Paul, what did you—" I looked to Paul, but he was sprawled on the ground where I'd shot him.

A dart struck the tree beside me.

"Fuck. Fuck. Gideon." I shook his shoulders. "Gideon, we have to go. Please, Gideon."

A blur of silver streaked past my face as a knife flipped end over end, flying toward some enemy I couldn't make myself care about.

"Gideon, don't do this. Just wake up."

An arm wrapped around my waist, lifting me away from Gideon.

"No. No!" I tried to grab the front of his shirt. "Let go of me!" I kicked, catching my captor in the knee. Their grip didn't falter as they carried me toward the rock wall on the side of the dome.

"You can't help him." Walsh's voice was low and calm as he spoke in my ear, but there was something about it that made me believe him when he said, "I'm sorry."

"He might be tranqued." I tried to break free from Walsh's grip. "I can't leave him. He saved me."

Walsh shoved his way through a thick cluster of trees that hid a row of small vents carved into the rock wall.

"If Gideon's tranqued, he's better off if we're not near him." Walsh kept his hold on me. "If he's dead, there's nothing we can do for him."

"It shouldn't be like this. Destroy the weapons, destroy the vehicles, get out. Gid"—his name caught in my throat—"Gideon shouldn't have been shot by his own fucking brother."

I sagged against Walsh, clinging to him as fear and loathing wrung tears from my eyes. "We shouldn't have tried to herd people toward the atrium bunker. Demetrius is going to kill them all anyway."

Walsh wrapped his arms around me, holding me close like people weren't killing each other a hundred feet away.

"All the kids. All our classmates." I gave in to Walsh's strength, letting him hold me up, unable to carry the burden of death on my own. "Demetrius is a monster. I helped a monster break into the domes so he could slaughter children."

Walsh gasped as his shoulders shook.

"I don't blame you." I took Walsh's face in my hands. I didn't know when I had lost my gun. "Just promise if I don't make it out, you won't let Mari become a monster like him."

"I ca—" Walsh choked on the words, his face screwing up in pain.

"I know you can't make him stop." I smoothed out the lines beside his eyes. "That only makes me hate him more."

"I love you, Lanni." Walsh's face relaxed. He opened his eyes, a faint smile lifting his lips as he looked at me. "I thought I was too broken to care about anyone ever again, but I fell in love with you."

He tipped my chin up and kissed me. I'd never been kissed like that. So gentle in his longing that I knew I was precious and craved all at the same time. He pulled me closer, like he wanted to memorize the way our bodies locked together.

I leaned into his longing, completely sure he would never let me fall. My breath caught in my chest as wanting flared from my gut to my fingertips. I laced my fingers through his hair, viciously unaware that a battle still raged just beyond our tree-made sanctuary.

Walsh. The whole world was Walsh. Needing him. Wanting him. Safe and strong with him beside me.

He stole his lips from mine. "Promise you'll remember the me you knew inside the Arc Domes?"

"What?"

He lifted my hands away from him. "Whatever happens, know that the Walsh who kissed you in the domes loved you with everything he was."

"What are you talking about?"

"Stay in the trees." He handed me his guard's gun. "When it's over, get the hell out of here. Mari needs you."

"Walsh."

"I love you." He kissed my hand and bolted through the trees, running back into the battle.

CHAPTER THIRTY-TWO

I stared at the leaves rustling behind him, trying to make my mind accept his words.

Stay in the trees. Stay hidden. Let the boy who loves me run into danger to do I didn't fucking know what.

I needed Jaime. Needed to talk to Jaime and tell him that Gideon had gotten shot to protect me and Walsh really did love me and people were dying and I couldn't convince myself that every drop of blood spilled wasn't my fault.

I had joined a monster to battle against demons.

Pop, pop, pop, pop, pop, pop, pop, pop.

I scrunched my eyes shut.

Screams of terror came from the back corner of the dome.

"Fire! Help. Someone help me!" a man shouted.

The sounds of the battle shifted, heading toward the barricaded kep.

Walsh wanted me to stay hidden. But he knew I could fight. He'd given me a weapon.

Crack!

A sound like a tree being split in two came from where the fighting had been.

Shouts moved toward the sound as another crack cut through the pops and screams of pain.

"Fuck." I opened my eyes.

A howl echoed over the chaos.

"Fucking Walsh." I checked the gun Walsh had given me and patted my pockets to make sure the spare clips were still there. "Shit."

I dove into the tree branches, forcing my way through the same path Walsh had followed.

A haze of smoke rolled over the bodies on the ground. I didn't let myself look at Gideon as I stole Paul's gun, tucking it into my holster in case I fucked up and lost my weapon again.

"Keep them pinned!" The shout came from the eastern side of the dome.

A line of Demetrius's people ran toward me.

I stared them down, making sure they could all see my face so none of them would mistake me for a kep.

"Walsh's human is still alive." A wolf winked at me as she ran past.

"Where is he?" I called after her.

Another howl came from right in front of me.

Bang, bang, bang, bang.

Pop, pop, pop.

The rounds of gunfire didn't slow as I ran toward the howling.

Crack!

The tree in front of me shook as a body struck the trunk with enough force to splinter the wood. But the person who'd been thrown didn't crumple to the ground like they should have. He landed on his feet.

I didn't recognize Demetrius until he pulled his shoulders back to stand upright.

"You're a fool." He tipped his head from side to side like he was checking to make sure his neck hadn't broken. "I am on the brink of the most glorious victory the Alliance has ever achieved, and you choose this moment to challenge me?"

"You haven't given me a choice." Walsh stepped into view. Blood stained his chest around a long slash through his shirt. "I would have followed you until the earth finally ended, Demetrius. But I can't let you make our pack into nothing better than blood-soaked monsters. We are not the Incorporation. Our pack shouldn't be butchering children."

Demetrius charged Walsh, aiming his blade for Walsh's heart.

A scream rose to my throat, but I couldn't make any sound. I raised my gun, aiming for Demetrius's back, but Walsh leapt up, grabbing a tree branch and pulling himself above Demetrius's blade.

Walsh swung forward off the branch, landing behind his alpha.

"Tell them to call off the attack." Walsh pulled a knife from the ankle of his boot as Demetrius turned to face him.

"Keep them pinned!" Demetrius shouted to the wolves still fighting the kep.

"You can end this before anyone else dies."

"You have betrayed me, Walsh. I will never suffer a traitor to live within my pack." Demetrius leapt toward Walsh, his head brushing the tree branches as he raised his knife.

Walsh lunged sideways, sweeping his blade behind him to slice Demetrius's hip.

Demetrius staggered forward.

Walsh turned toward him.

I waited for Walsh to plunge his knife into Demetrius's back, but he didn't move as the alpha rounded on him.

"Demetrius, don't make us the monsters," Walsh said. "I've seen too many dead children in my life. I don't want to see any more."

Demetrius threw his knife, the blade spinning end over end toward Walsh's stomach.

Walsh dodged out of the way. The blade sank into the trunk of a tree.

"Out! Everybody run!" a woman screamed.

The sounds of the fighting shifted closer to us.

"Bring me my knife." Demetrius held out his hand.

"Let the children flee," Walsh said.

"As your alpha, I command you to bring me my knife." Demetrius smiled.

Walsh gasped, his shoulders rounding forward as he staggered like he'd been punched in the throat.

"Do not try to fight my commands, Walsh." Demetrius stepped toward him, his hand still outstretched. "This is the way we werewolves work. My orders are absolute. I am your alpha, and I am ordering you to hand me my knife."

"No." Walsh pressed his knuckles to his temples, like squeezing his own brains out would be less painful than resisting his alpha. "Just let the kids go."

"Give me my knife, Connor Walsh." Demetrius stopped two feet in front of him. "And then go and kill as many of the domes children as you can."

Walsh's knees buckled. His knife slipped from his hand as he hit the ground.

"Walsh!"

Demetrius turned his glare toward me. Danger and loathing glinted in his red eyes.

I aimed my gun at his chest.

"Don't test me, Lanni," Demetrius said. "Or Project Progeny will seem like heaven."

"She is protected." Walsh threw himself forward, catching Demetrius around the knees and knocking him to the ground.

Demetrius kicked up, tossing Walsh into the air.

Walsh crashed back to the ground with enough force to break bones.

I aimed for Demetrius, ready to shoot, but they were moving too fast.

Demetrius dove for Walsh before Walsh even made it to his feet.

Walsh swung his fist, catching Demetrius in the cheek, sending him stumbling sideways, then kicked Demetrius in the ribs, knocking him into a tree.

The tree shuddered, but Demetrius didn't seem to feel any pain as he pushed off of the trunk and brought his elbow down on Walsh's shoulder.

Walsh's arm sagged in its socket.

Demetrius kicked behind Walsh's legs, knocking him to the ground.

Walsh rolled away and leapt back to his feet, using his good arm to land a punch in Demetrius's chest.

Boom!

The sound swallowed the screams of the battle.

I toppled over as the atrium shook like the whole mountain was going to crumble.

The tree beside me crashed to the ground as the last of the glass in the dome rained down on the battle in the atrium.

When the rumble of the boom stopped, the screaming got worse. They were a different sort of screams, too. Less anger and pain, more pure terror.

But the fight in front of me hadn't paused.

Glass sliced into my palms as I pushed myself to my knees.

Demetrius had Walsh pinned to the ground, punching him in the face over and over.

"Walsh!" I tried to aim my gun, but my hands were too slippery with my own blood.

Walsh dug his heels into the ground and flung himself sideways, knocking Demetrius off him.

And then it happened. The fate of hundreds of lives decided in one quick moment.

A sharp twist, then a snap.

Walsh let go of Demetrius's head, and the alpha fell to the ground, limp and lifeless.

Walsh coughed out a sob.

My whole body shook as I forced myself to my feet. "Walsh, are—"

"I need a knife." He staggered like an awful weight had crashed into his head. "He can heal from a broken neck."

I picked up Walsh's knife, coating the hilt with my blood as I passed it to him.

Tears coursed down Walsh's cheeks as he drove the blade into his alpha's heart.

Walsh fell sideways, screaming in pain like he'd plunged the knife into his own chest.

"What can I do?" I knelt beside him, lifting his head into my lap.

Sweat beaded on his forehead.

"Walsh, you have to tell me how to help you." I took his hand, ignoring the blood that coated both our palms. "Please tell me how to help you."

A horrible howling filled the ruined atrium.

Walsh screamed again, curling in on himself like pain had carved out his gut.

"You have to be okay." I clung to him as the howling came closer. "I won't lose you. I can't. Please."

He gasped, his chest arching toward the moonlit sky before he sagged and went still.

The howling stopped.

"Don't you fucking dare." I pressed my fingers to his neck, but they were shaking too badly for me to find a pulse. "You don't get to tell me you love me and then get yourself killed." I leaned over, trying to feel his breath against my cheek. "I've lost too much. Don't make me grieve for you."

His lips brushed against my cheek. "I'll do my best."

"Walsh." My tears fell onto his face as I sat up enough to look into his eyes. "Tell me you're okay and mean it."

He gripped my hand. "We have to go. The pack is still fighting under Demetrius's orders."

"How do we stop them?" I stood, ignoring the pain in my sliced hands as I hauled Walsh to his feet.

He let go of me, gripped his elbow, and shoved his shoulder back into place. He grimaced against the pain. "We give them an order from their new alpha."

"What?"

"I killed Demetrius. The pack is mine now." He yanked Demetrius's knife out of the tree. "My pack doesn't kill children."

He threw his head back and howled. A chorus of howls answered his as he strode through the trees.

I wiped my palms on my pants, making sure I could grip my gun before following him.

"Let the children retreat," Walsh shouted. His words seemed heavier than normal, like the weight of being the alpha had somehow changed his voice.

Pop, pop, pop.

A silver dart sank into my vest.

I ripped it out and ducked behind a tree. I held my breath, waiting to see if the dart had nicked me and searching for whoever had shot me.

Walsh threw one of his knives up through the leaves of a tree. A guard fell from the branches, the knife sticking out of his eye.

"Let the children and civilians retreat," Walsh shouted again as he ripped his knife from the guard's face. "We fight guards and those who attack us. We do not murder children."

"Alpha." A wolf ran toward Walsh.

I stepped out to stand beside him, raising my weapon to aim for the wolf.

She ignored me as she bowed to Walsh. "What's the cutoff age for children?"

"Anyone who could be considered a child," Walsh said. "And any non-combatant, let them retreat. We've already accomplished the mission the Alliance gave us. Everything else is vengeance."

She winced, like she wanted to scream that vengeance was what she craved.

"Spread the word," Walsh said. "Now."

The wolf bowed again and ran back toward the fighting. "Allow the children to retreat! Kill anyone holding a weapon."

A wave of heavy fatigue washed over me, threatening to knock me off my feet.

Two girls not much older than Mari ran past us. They clung to each other, both of them sobbing as they fled the battle that had spilled so much kep blood.

"Where are they going?" I watched the girls disappear. "They don't have anywhere to run to."

"The explosion in weapons storage shouldn't have hurt the atrium bunker," Walsh said.

"Demetrius gave the order to kill everyone in the atrium bunker. They're running toward a bloodbath." I sprinted away through the bloodstained trees, not waiting to be told the kep weren't mine to save.

CHAPTER THIRTY-THREE

The stairs had been cracked by the blast from below. Whole chunks of the steps had crumbled in a way I didn't think the kep would ever be able to repair.

Drops of red spattered the ground, and smears of blood stained the walls, marking the path of the people who had fled from the atrium.

Most of the lights in the corridor leading toward the atrium bunker had gone out, and the few that remained flickered like they were fighting desperately to stay lit.

I leapt over a body that lay in the center of the hall, careful not to slip in the pool of blood that surrounded the kep corpse.

Footsteps pounded up behind me.

I spun toward the sound, ready to sink a dart into whoever was chasing me.

Walsh didn't slow his pace as he reached me. "They might have closed the bunker before our people got there. The door could still be sealed."

"Then whoever fled the atrium and ran to the bunker for safety will be trapped outside." I sprinted behind Walsh. "They'll be slaughtered."

"Better the few people outside than everyone inside the bunker."

"Shit." I should've turned and run the other way, snuck out through the glass and waited for it to be over. But I heard screaming carrying up the steps that led down to the bunker, and I couldn't make myself stop running toward the bloodshed.

Three guards' corpses lay at the bottom of the steps, flopped on top of each other like someone had wanted to display their kills.

Violent chaos filled the hall that led to the still-standing bunker door.

The two girls we'd followed were crouched against the wall, screaming as a guard tried to defend them from a wolf.

"Fall back," Walsh shouted. "Our work here is done. Fall back."

The wolf kicked up, knocking the guard's club from their hand before running toward the stairs.

Three more wolves followed, each of them abandoning the guards they'd been fighting.

With them gone, the carnage in the hall was easier to see.

Bodies littered the floor. Children, guards, civilians. All of them dead.

Blood everywhere. On the walls, the floor, staining the necks of the corpses.

But the bloodshed in the hall hadn't stopped when the wolves followed their alpha's orders.

At the end of the corridor, a mass of people still fought.

Guards held the line in front of the bunker door, defending the kep who cowered behind them.

"Fall back," Walsh shouted again.

None of the fighters at the end of the hall moved.

Walsh shoved me against the wall as a chunk of concrete flew toward us.

"As your alpha, I am ordering you to leave." He kept me

pinned against the wall, planting himself between me and the fight.

Bile shot into my throat as a man gave a gurgling scream.

"Fuck." Walsh glanced toward the stairs. "Lanni, go to the atrium. Find a way out of the glass and to the pack."

"I'm not leaving you."

A guard hit the floor. Blood poured from a wound on his wrist. The one who'd tossed him to the ground looked our way. Red stained her mouth.

"Shit." I wiped the fresh blood from my palms onto my pants.

"The battle is over." Walsh walked toward her, holding his knives to his sides. "It's time to go."

She turned away from him, diving back into the fight to find her next snack.

None of the kep fired on her, like somehow in the chaos of the attack, they'd run out of darts or lost their guns. Or maybe they hadn't had time to reach proper weapons after the mountain's peak had crashed into their home. The why didn't matter. The guards had nothing left that could actually protect them from the blood-crazed vampires.

"Stop!" I shot the vampire in the back, hitting her right between her shoulder blades.

She stumbled forward and fell.

The vampire beside her glanced away from the guard he'd been fighting, looking straight at me. He stabbed back, catching the kep in the arm. Blood stained his teeth as he grinned. "Bitch."

He charged toward me.

Walsh bolted in front of me, grabbing the vampire by the neck and slamming him into the wall.

I ran past them, toward the rest of the fight, trying not to see the corpses I leapt over as people who hadn't needed to die.

I stopped at the edge of the fight. I didn't know who I should be aiming my weapon at.

"The battle is over!" I echoed Walsh's words. "It's time to go!"

More of the vampires looked my way.

"We've gotten what we came for," I shouted. "Your commander has ordered you to leave."

A flicker of movement caught my eye as one of the vampires dropped the girl he'd been feeding on.

Dark hair. Red smeared across his lips. He'd already taken two steps toward me before my mind could accept that it was Jaime.

Jaime had been drinking from that girl. She was younger than me. She'd worn her hair in two braids.

Jaime took a deep breath, and a smile lifted one corner of his mouth, like whatever he had scented brought him joy.

"Jaime, we have to go." I reached for his hand. "It's time to leave."

He lunged toward me, grabbing my throat.

My gun slipped from my grip as he lifted me off the ground.

"Lanni!"

A club crashed into Jaime's head.

He let go of my neck, and I fell to the ground, landing in a pool of someone else's blood.

The guard who'd hit Jaime swung again, catching him in the back of the neck.

"Lanni, run," the guard shouted. His bright blond hair was matted with blood.

Jaime grabbed the guard's arm, tossing him across the hall and slamming him against the wall.

"Go, Lanni." The guard met my gaze. His swollen face had been covered in bruises and blood, but I recognized Alec's emerald green eyes. He raised his club as Jaime ran forward with his knife.

"Jaime, no!" I screamed.

He hesitated for split second.

"Not him. Jaime, please." I fumbled with my belt, trying to grab the gun I'd stolen from Paul. "Let's just go."

Jaime turned toward me.

"Alec is my friend." My legs shook as I got to my feet. "Just like you're my friend. You have to come with me, okay?"

He stepped toward me, and for one stupid second, I thought everything was going to be okay. But he grabbed my arm, yanking my wrist up to his mouth.

"Jaime!" I punched him in the neck, but it didn't stop his teeth from digging into my skin.

Pop.

His bite faltered. He swayed and fell to the ground.

Alec knelt behind him, holding my gun. He turned toward the fight, taking down three vampires with three shots.

Two more vampires still fought at the end of the hall.

"Give me a clean shot!" Alec shouted.

The guards at the end of the corridor ducked, leaving the vampires standing alone. Both vampires were slicked in blood from their mouths to their knives. They charged toward Alec.

Pop, pop, pop, pop.

Both of them fell.

"We have to go." Walsh grabbed me around the waist, pulling me away.

"No. Jaime. I can't leave Jaime!" I fought against his grip, even though I knew I couldn't win.

Alec turned to me, aiming my gun at me.

"Jaime, wake up!" I screamed, hoping that something in his vampire blood would let him hear me shouting for him.

"Just run." Walsh shoved me toward the stairs.

He grabbed Jaime, tossing him over his shoulder before I could find my footing.

"Lanni." Alec staggered as he struggled to his feet, still aiming my gun at my neck. "She's alive. He hid her in the bunker in the plains with Jac. She's safe."

"My mom?" I stepped toward Alec. "How did—"

"We have to go!" Walsh spun me toward the stairs with his free hand as the other kep guards charged toward us.

I bolted for the steps, ready for a dart to sink into my back with every heartbeat. But the dart didn't come, and Walsh's footsteps stayed steady behind me.

CHAPTER THIRTY-FOUR

The wolf pack waited just beyond the domes, all of them ready to defend their new alpha.

My legs shook as I climbed over the shattered glass and onto the concrete base that supported the place that had been the kep's perfect atrium.

Walsh jumped down onto the slope and passed Jaime to another wolf. "Get him to camp before sunrise."

"Yes, Alpha." The wolf disappeared into the darkness.

Walsh reached up for me, taking my waist and lifting me down.

My legs shook when he let go of me.

Walsh looked to one of the female wolves. "Bandage her wrist and keep her safe."

"Yes, Alpha." She pulled a med kit out of her bag. Bundles of bandages had been packed in around extra syringes of Lycan.

"We need to get back to base camp and prepare to leave." Walsh addressed his pack. Less than half of the people who'd left the caverns that morning stood with him on the slope.

Pain shot up my arm as the woman wound a bandage around my wrist.

"The sooner we get out of these mountains, the better," Walsh said. "Take the safe ways back. Don't make it any easier for them to find the camp."

The wolves ran into the darkness.

The woman stuffed the med kit back into her bag.

My stomach rolled as she scooped me into her arms.

Walsh held up a hand, stopping the woman before she could bolt down the mountain. "You run with me."

"Yes, Alpha."

He glanced back at the atrium, then sprinted down the slope.

"What about the other vampires?" I looked up toward the shattered domes as the wolf followed Walsh.

In the moonlight, the broken glass seemed like teeth surrounding ravenous voids in the mountainside.

"I can't risk my pack hunting down vampires who chose feeding over orders." A dull pain crept into Walsh's voice.

I wanted to take his hand and tell him I didn't blame him, but I couldn't, not while trapped in the woman's arms.

"Harper." My heart banged into my throat. "Did Harper make it out?"

"Angry ginger human?" the woman who carried me asked. "Burned the shit out of her arm but was alive enough to swear about it when Bell hauled her out. They ran her straight back to the doctor."

"Good." I let myself sag into the woman's arms.

"I'm Liz, by the way." The woman jumped over a downed tree without breaking her stride. "You're welcome for the ride, and yes I expect you to wash your blood out of my clothes."

Liz kept me safely tucked in her arms as she ran behind Walsh, protecting my head from the branches that appeared out of the darkness so quickly, I wouldn't have known to flinch if she hadn't twisted her shoulders, letting the trees scrape her instead of me.

I tried to keep my gaze fixed on Walsh, focusing on catching glimpses of him in the shadows, rather than let my mind wander to the horrors we'd just left behind.

The vampires we'd abandoned were doomed, but I didn't know how the kep would kill them. If they were smart, they'd question them first, find out where our camp was hidden.

The kep would have bodies to burn. How many dead would Alec have to carry? Would Gideon be burned, or had his brother only tranqued him?

"She's shaking, Walsh," Liz said.

"I'm fine." I dug my nails into my sliced-up palms, trying to ignore the pain in my wrist where Jaime had bitten me.

Jaime with blood on his face. My blood in his mouth.

The shaking got worse.

Walsh. Watch Walsh.

The moonlight glinted off the glass stuck in his hair. He weaved between the trees, leading us back to Mari.

She'd see me covered in blood, and—

"Walsh, your human's broken," Liz said. "You've got to calm down, Lanni."

I tried to take a deep breath, but it caught in my throat, threatening to suffocate me.

"Walsh." Liz stopped. She held me in front of her, offering me to her alpha.

"I ne—need to walk." I rolled sideways, tipping myself out of her arms.

Walsh caught me before I hit the ground.

"I don't need to be carried." I couldn't make myself fight against him as he wrapped his arm around my waist, helping me to my feet.

"You're exhausted." He kept to a slow human pace as we walked through the woods. "You haven't slept, you've lost blood. You need to be carried so you can close your eyes and rest."

"I don't want to close my eyes. I don't need rest." A weight pressed down on my chest.

"We need to move faster than you can run," Walsh said. "I'm sorry, but you have to be carried."

"Fine. Give me back to Liz. I won't ask the alpha to carry me."

"It's better for her to carry you." Walsh tightened his hold on me.

I tried to push away from him, but he kept me locked beside him.

"Not for my sake, for yours," Walsh said.

"But I'd rather be with you."

His jaw tightened, not like there were orders stabbing through his head. More like there was some new kind of pain I couldn't recognize.

I touched his cheek. He leaned into my hand.

"I'll keep you safe." He scooped me into his arms, holding me close enough that no one would be able to tear me away. "Whatever happens to my mind, I have to keep you safe."

I wrapped my arms around his neck, nestling my head closer to his shoulder. "I believe you."

"Rest, Lanni."

I think he kissed my forehead as I fell asleep.

CHAPTER THIRTY-FIVE

The tent that protected the entrance to the cave had already been taken down by the time we reached base camp. In the early morning light, with just a wooden door to keep intruders out, the cavern seemed hopelessly vulnerable.

Four wolves flanked the door, all with blood staining their clothes and weapons in their hands. They bowed as Walsh approached.

"Are you packed?" Walsh asked.

"Yes, Alpha." A wolf opened the door. "We're ready to leave as soon as you give the order."

"Good." Walsh hesitated before stepping into the tunnel. It was only for an instant, so quick I don't think I would have noticed it if I hadn't still been in his arms. He took a deep breath and entered the camp he now commanded.

"How soon will you have them leave?" I asked.

"As soon as we can. I don't want to risk what's left of the Arc Domes' guards finding our camp and trying to hit back." Walsh twisted sideways in the narrow part of the tunnel, keeping my head away from the wall.

"I can walk," I said.

"I know."

The main cavern rumbled with werewolves hurrying to pack up the camp. Most of the tents had already been taken down. Litters had been loaded with supplies. Voices filled the space as the people who had destroyed the domes tried to make sure they'd gathered the precious few things they owned.

But even in the chaos it was easy to see how many people were missing. We'd lost so many in the fight. It didn't seem right that so many altered humans could be lost to the kep.

I looked up into Walsh's face, needing to be sure he really had survived, even though his arms were locked around me.

His face stayed stony as he walked through his pack, acknowledging them with a nod as they bowed to him.

"I can get to medical on my own," I said. "You have to make sure everyone's ready."

"I'm not letting you out of my sight until you're in the doctor's care. I can't."

"Okay." I laid my hand on his chest. An itching pain burned in my wrist.

"I could've lost you too many times today. I should've fought Demetrius before we ever went to the domes. If I'd been the alpha, you could've stayed here and—"

"Don't." I touched his cheek. "It's not worth it. We have to leave and build an Afterworld settlement, and you have to lead your pack. There's no time for wondering what could have happened."

He turned his head just enough to kiss my bloody palm. "I'll make sure your tent gets packed while the doctor takes care of you. I'll make sure she cleans your hands and..." He shut his eyes and shook his head, almost like he was trying to fling Demetrius's words from his mind. "You'll be taken care of."

He carried me into the tunnel that led down to the lower cavern.

"Walsh, what you said during the fight"—I pressed the words

past the fear pounding in my chest—"when you said that you love me, and then ran to fight Demetrius—"

"I shouldn't have given you that burden."

"Walsh—"

"Lanni!" Mari screamed as Walsh carried me into the lower cavern. "Are you hurt? Do you need stitches? Doctor Gloria is done taking care of Harper's burns, but she didn't pack up all her equipment since she didn't know if you'd need medicine. Are you going to need stitches? I can do them for you."

"I'm not sure if I need stitches, but I know I'll be fine." I squirmed, trying to climb down from Walsh's arms. I might as well have been trying to wriggle out of a stone cage.

"Everyone's packing to go to our new home." Mari stayed beside Walsh as he walked to the infirmary. "But I don't think I'll be able to run fast enough to keep up with everyone else. I had to promise not to twist or bend or jump or run or reach or bounce just so Doctor Gloria would let me walk out here to meet you. She didn't even want me to walk! I think she only agreed because I'm really good at whining."

"You'll be carried while the pack travels," Walsh said.

"Can I pick who I get to ride on?" Mari opened the infirmary door.

"We'll ask for volunteers." Walsh carried me right over to the bed where Mari had slept after being shot.

"Tell me not all this blood is hers," the doctor sighed.

"It's not," I said. "I'm not too bad off."

"Cuts on her hands and a bite on her wrist." Walsh stared down at the bed like he was trying to convince himself to let go of me. "I want the rest of her checked as well."

"Yes, Alpha," the doctor said. "She'll be safe in my care."

"I'm okay," I whispered.

He didn't move.

"Alpha, she's still bleeding," the doctor said.

Walsh set me down. "I'll send help to pack up your supplies." He strode out of the room, slamming the door behind him.

"Cranky." Mari pushed a tray of tools closer to the bed.

"He's really the alpha?" Harper groaned as she stood from her seat in the corner. Her right arm had been swallowed by bandages and a sling.

"Yes, he's the alpha," the doctor said.

I wanted to ask if she knew because she'd heard from other pack members or if she could somehow feel the change in leadership deep in her Lycan-filled brain, but when she peeled the bandage away from my wrist, too much bile shot into my mouth for me to risk speaking.

"One of ours?" The doctor took a tub of blue goo from the tray.

"Yeah." Tears burned in the corners of my eyes.

"This is why access to the lower cavern is restricted." The doctor smeared the cooling goo onto my wrist.

"Why?" Mari asked.

I lifted my arm out of her view. "Nothing, Mar." I offered her my other palm. "Do I have any glass left in here?"

"Hmm." Mari studied my hand. "Yep. But I can get it out."

"Thanks."

The doctor held my gaze, giving me a look I hoped was approval. "As long as this is the worst of it, we should have you ready to travel before the pack gets antsy."

"I don't like the idea of antsy werewolves." Harper sat on the end of the bed. "Not after seeing how they fight."

"Was it bad in the bay?" I asked.

"We got in pretty quick. But then a bunch of Outer Guard swarmed us while we were grabbing the tools Demetrius wanted us to take. The guards took down a few from our group. Bell made me leave them behind when we ran. The tools were more important than the people—Demetrius's orders. We blew up the bay with three wolves still inside." Harper brushed the tears from her cheeks. "Guess I'm lucky they weren't ordered to leave me behind."

"And the people who went down to destroy the weapons?" I asked.

"None of those pack members returned." The doctor's hands were steady, even though her voice shook. "Our pack paid a high price for the Alliance's victory."

Pain pricked my hand as Mari dug a shard of glass from my palm.

"Just keep breathing. You're doing really well," Mari said.

"Thanks, Mar." I let myself smile as I watched her furrow her brow while she dug for the next bit of glass.

"But it won't be like that anymore, right?" Mari said. "Because Walsh is the alpha and he won't order people to be left behind."

"Only time will tell what sort of alpha a wolf will become," the doctor said. "Lycan alters a person's mind and senses, drawing them to the pack. For most of us, the Lycan demands we obey our alpha. For the alpha, the Lycan shifts their entire being, turning them into a wolf that is meant to lead."

I sat quietly while they bandaged my wounds and the doctor checked the rest of me for damage. Focusing on the pain in my body helped. Every cut and bruise was another distraction to keep me from screaming *how long?*

Had the alpha in Walsh already changed him into a person I didn't know? Would it?

I needed to see him, to thank him and say I didn't even know what. Goodbye, I guess. But I wanted to say it to the Walsh I knew. How long until the ally who had saved me disappeared?

What if the wolf devoured the boy who loved me?

The pack had cleared most of the supplies from the infirmary by the time the doctor declared me fit to travel. As soon as Harper, Mari, and I were out the door, they started pulling the boards apart, ripping up the infirmary so it could be reassembled someplace else.

"Our tent's gone." Harper stopped, staring at the spot we'd briefly called home.

"It's okay." Mari took Harper's unburnt hand. "When we get to our new home, we'll find a place for the three of us to stay together. Lanni and I won't leave you."

"Thanks, Mar." Harper didn't wipe away the fresh tears on her cheeks.

The tunnel leading to the upper cavern was strangely quiet. My mind couldn't process the lack of weapons clanging and people shouting as too many wolves existed all crammed together.

We stepped out into the cavern, and everything was just...gone.

A few scraps of discarded trash littered the ground, but every tent, sleeping bag, and weapon had been cleared away.

"Maybe we'll be able to put our tent out in the open in our new home." Mari bounced from foot to foot, barely managing to not run as she led us toward the last few people lingering by the tunnel to the outside. "Or we could build a hut. Doctor Gloria said some of the pack were trained to be builders, but we'd have to see who survived the fight in the Arc Domes before we'd know what kind of infirmary she was going to get."

"Maybe I should be your babysitter from now on." Harper shot me a sideways glance. "More brewing, less death."

"Lanni." Jaime stepped out of the shadows of one of the stone niches in the cavern wall.

"Jaime!" Mari let go of Harper's hand and ran toward him.

"Mar—" She was in his arms before I could stop her.

"I'm so glad you're okay." She hugged him around the middle.

"You're still healing." I took Mari's shoulders, ready to rip her away from Jaime. "You have to be careful. Remember what the doctor said."

Jaime looked at me. He'd washed the blood off his face, even changed into clean clothes.

I glanced down at the dried blood that still covered me.

"You should head outside." Jaime ruffled Mari's hair. "Everyone's getting ready to go."

"Come on." Mari took Jaime and me by the hands, pulling us toward the tunnel to the outside world.

"I'll catch up to you," Jaime said. "Do you mind if I talk to Lanni for a minute?"

"Okay." Mari let go of us and took Harper's hand instead. "I'll find someone good to carry Lanni."

"Thanks, Mar." I watched her and Harper leave the cavern.

Only Bell and three other wolves were left lingering by the tunnel. Each of them had a guard's gun in their hand.

"Lanni, I'm sorry." Jaime reached for me.

I flinched. It was a tiny movement, but Bell aimed her gun at Jaime.

"I'm sorry." He stepped away, tucking his hands behind his back, like that might somehow make me forget the feel of his teeth tearing through my skin. "Did the doctor...How badly did I hurt you?"

"I'll heal." I held up my bandaged wrist. "Just have to keep it clean."

"I really thought I could never hurt you." Pain lowered Jaime's voice. "But everything just became this blur of hunger and blood, and I knew it was you and I couldn't make myself stop. I could've killed you. I'm so, so sorry, Lanni. I will never forgive myself for hurting you."

I held my wrist close to my chest as the weight of having to carry a scar from Jaime for the rest of my life crashed down on me. "If you'd fed before you went into the domes, would it have been different?"

"I don't know." Tears glistened in Jaime's eyes. "They were right to keep me away from Mari while she was hurt. You're right to be scared of me. I need to stay away from both of you."

I stepped closer to Jaime, testing my daring as much as trying to comfort him. "I'm not afraid of you."

"You flinched." Jaime backed away from me.

"Well, you just bit me last night. My wrist still hurts."

His shoulders rounded like I'd torn out part of his chest.

"I just need time." I held his gaze, trying to make myself want to hold him and comfort him. "Let's get to the settlement, and we'll figure everything out."

"There's nothing to figure out. I thought we had a chance together, but I ruined it."

"Jaime, just—"

"I'll always be afraid of hurting you, and you'll always be afraid of me hurting Mari. We were supposed to take care of her together, and I blew it."

Pain pinched the front of my throat.

"I'll never forgive myself for ruining what we could have been," Jaime whispered.

"That's it?" Tears ran down my cheeks. "You're just giving up?"

"I will always love you, Lanni Sampson. But I know you better than anyone. There's no coming back from what I did. Asking for that kind of forgiveness would only make things worse for you." He looked toward the tunnel and the wolves that still waited for me. "You should go. The pack will be ready to move by now."

"Okay." I swiped my tears away and started toward the tunnel. It took me a few steps to realize Jaime wasn't following me.

When I turned around, he was still standing by the niche, tears sliding down his cheeks.

"I know you're fast, but you don't want the pack to leave without you," I said.

"It's daylight." Jaime tried to give me a crooked smile. "I'm stuck in here."

"Well then they have to wait." I walked back to him. "The pack has to stay here until you can travel, too."

"The pack needs to move. Walsh can't risk the kep finding the cavern."

"He's just going to leave you behind?" I looked to Bell. She stared back, her gun calmly leveled at Jaime. "I'll talk to him. We'll find a way to keep you with the group."

"I'm not sure I should be with the group." Jaime tucked his hands into his pockets. "It might be best for everyone if I find my own path from here."

"What do you mean?" I stepped right up to Jaime, stopping a foot in front of him.

He looked up at the ceiling.

"No, I'm serious, Jaime. What the fuck is that supposed to mean?"

"I can find somewhere else to be." He kept his gaze above my head. "I can go back to our city, see if there are any people left I might be able to help. Or I could go to a different city. Find another branch of the Alliance."

"Is that what you want?" The words cracked in my throat. "You traveled so far to find me, and now that *you've* decided you don't think we should try to be together anymore, you're just going to leave?"

"I want you to be safe and happy, and that will be easier without me."

"You're family." I shoved him in the chest, ignoring the pull of my tearing stitches. "You're my best friend. Yes, you fucked up, and yes, things aren't going to be the same, but you don't get to disappear. You're not a coward, Jaime. You don't get to run away because you're scared.

"You are coming with us to the Afterworld settlement. If you're not happy there, then you can go *after* you've explained to Mari that you're leaving. But you do not get to take the shitty way out and tell me to just walk out of this cave and never see you again."

"You're impossible." He swiped the tears from his cheeks with his knuckles, still keeping his gaze over my head.

"Yeah, I am. I'll go tell Walsh we have to figure out how you can travel with the group."

"I can catch up after dark. I'll be able to follow the scent of the pack. And I'll be able to run faster on my own than the wolves can carrying all the camp's supplies."

"Are you sure?" I looked to Bell again.

"We have a ton of shit." She nodded.

"What about the kep?" I asked. "If they find the cavern, you'll be trapped."

"I'll be fine." Jaime gave me something closer to a real smile. "If you want me to go to the settlement with the pack, I promise I'll be there."

"Okay. Then I'll see you soon." I turned and strode toward the tunnel.

"Please be careful, Lanni," Jaime called after me. "If anything happens to you—"

"No more speeches." I waved over my shoulder. "See you soon." I managed to get the words out before tears tightened my throat.

CHAPTER THIRTY-SIX

I'd managed to fall asleep, curled up on the litter that held a bunch of the camp's bedding.

Harper, Mari, and I were assigned litters to ride on as the pack ran. The wolves had said it was better than someone carrying each of the unchanged humans in their arms. They didn't mind our weight, and it kept more hands free for fighting if the kep managed to find us.

By the time I woke up, darkness had swallowed the sky. The terrain around us had changed, shifting from mountains to rolling hills. There were no shouts of attack. Just the steady, thundering thump of the pack running to freedom.

I lay on the litter, listening for the pop of guards' guns as the Incorporation raced to kill us. But the kep hadn't found us.

A sad sort of fear seized my chest.

Jaime is a vampire. He can track the pack in ways the kep can't.

I studied the stars, trying to make out their patterns while the bouncing of the runners shook the litter.

A new place none of us had ever been. A fresh landscape with no factory sludge, or acid rain, or kep to fight. No apartment buildings or factories to work in, either.

I tried to picture what our home would look like, but I couldn't think of anything other than green. I'd seen the inside of the Arc Domes, been up to Incorporation Headquarters, but all I could imagine for our Afterworld paradise was a sea of green.

The pace of the runners slowed.

I sat up, searching for figures surging out of the darkness.

The wolves carrying my litter stopped.

"Half rest, half guard," Walsh called to the pack. "Everyone needs to eat and drink. We have days left to run."

"I get front on the next stretch." The wolf carrying the back of my litter said as they lowered me to the ground.

"If there's anything I can do to help." I rolled off the blankets and onto the dirt.

The soil I landed on smelled of soot.

The stink won't be able to reach your new home.

"Unless you want a dose of Lycan, then riding quietly is the best you can do." The wolf carrying the front of my litter handed me a flask of water and a hunk of dried meat.

"I'll stick with quiet." I took the meal and stepped away from the wolves, needing just a moment to breathe without feeling like someone was watching me.

I leaned against a tree. The bark smelled of soot, too, and creaked under my weight, like the tree had thought it was done being bothered by people and resented my presence.

"The trees in our new home will be like the ones in the domes, but with no kep," I whispered, trying to convince myself it was possible.

"There should be a lot of maples and birches where we're going." Walsh stepped out of the darkness.

"A forest of birch trees. That would be beautiful." I took a sip of my silty water.

"It *will* be beautiful." Walsh shifted in the shadows, staying just far enough away he could pretend he hadn't come to check on me. "How are your hands?"

"Sore."

"Do you feel safe riding on the litter?"

"How do you mean?" I sniffed the meat.

"Are they protecting you?" He leaned against the tree opposite me.

"They haven't tipped me over the side." I stepped closer to him, holding out my dried meat. "What is this?"

"Rabbit." He didn't even have to look at it to know. "Do you need more to eat? Would you rather someone else carry you? We could take a longer stop so you could sleep without moving."

"Did you really find me to make sure I was comfortable? I'm alive, and we're getting away from the Incorporation for good. Being bumped around doesn't bother me."

"They're bumping you around?" Walsh straightened up, looking toward the wolves who'd been carrying me.

"They're lugging my useless ass to the Afterworld." I took Walsh's chin, tipping his face toward mine. "I promise you, I'm fine."

"I know, it's just"—he shut his eyes tight—"the wolf in my head wants you safe and happy and needs to tear apart everything that might hurt you. And I know you're strong and a survivor, but I can't make the wolf stop." He backed away from me. "I'm sorry I bothered you."

"Don't go." I tucked my flask of water and half-eaten rabbit meat into the pockets of my bloodstained pants.

"I'm the alpha of my pack now."

"I know."

"I don't know what that will do to my mind. I want you. I'm in love with you, and I want you to be happy. But the wolf in my brain wants you to be my mate, and what if being the alpha makes it worse?" He clenched his fists, like he could feel the power of the alpha burning through his limbs. "There is no voice in my head giving me orders, but I feel a need to command my pack, and to protect you, and I don't know what all of that is going to turn me into. I don't know who I'm going to be when we get to our Afterworld settlement, but I know that I love you, and I want you to be happy."

"I don't know who I'm going to be when we get to the settlement, either. I've been a factory rat and a thief and a fake kep and none of that will help me where we're going."

"That's not what I mean. It's in my head, Lanni. I'm the alpha until I die."

"I know." I held my bandaged hand out to him. "You have to take care of your pack. I have to take care of Mari. I have to figure out how to be useful. We have to build a settlement and learn how to survive, and I don't know how any of that's supposed to work."

"Everything will be okay." He reached out, his fingers barely grazing mine. "The pack will make sure—"

"You don't know that. Neither of us knows how this is going to end up." I twined my fingers through his.

He sighed, his shoulders relaxing like a relentless pain had just been whisked away from his mind.

"But I know that I trust you." I moved closer to him. "I know that I care about you and the world is a better place with you in charge of this pack. And maybe that's what matters right now."

He put his hand on my waist, his fingers settling onto my hip like they'd been made to fit there.

"I don't know who we're going to be, but I know I want you around while we figure it out." I laid my head on his shoulder, and my fear and pain crumpled, shrinking to a size I was strong enough to carry.

"There's a lake where we're going." He rested his cheek on top of my head. "And a river that runs down from the mountains. We'll have water and a place to grow crops. I keep trying to picture what it will be like, but I can't."

"Me neither. But we'll be free, and that's a good place to start."

We stood together, hiding in the shadows until it was time for the pack to move on, taking the next leg of the journey to reach our new home.

"Mom, it's me, Lanni." I closed my eyes, shutting out the rustling of the tall grass around me, trying to picture myself sitting in our apartment in the city. I tightened my grip on the handheld radio. "I needed to tell you that Mari and I are alive, and we're doing really well."

He laid his hand on my shoulder. I took comfort in the familiar warmth.

"We've made a new home away from the Incorporation and the hell they turned this world into. Mari's training to be a doctor, and me"—I let out a long breath, trying to keep my tears out of my voice—"I teach and help plan our crops, and I'm happy. Actually, really happy.

"A friend told me you were alive and hiding from the kep. I hope you're still there. I hope you're healthy. But I can't come and find you. Not yet. I can't leave Mar for that long. But I needed you to know that we're alive and that..."

He sat beside me, wrapping his arm around my waist.

"I needed to tell you that I'm choosing to believe you didn't know what you were condemning Mari and me to when you sent us away. I have to believe that. Because if you knew what the kep would try to do to us or how evil the Incorporation was, I wouldn't want to come find you. I need to believe you'll be happy that we're free. I can't deal with the pain of you thinking the kep were better for Mar and me than freedom.

"Because it's all worked out okay, Mom. Mari and I are happy, and Jaime found us and he's doing really well, and our new home is beautiful, and my life is more than I ever thought it could be."

He kissed the side of my head.

"So I need you to stay safe, Mom, because someday soon, I'm going to come get you. I'll bring you to our home, and you'll get to see the life your daughters have built." My tears blocked my throat. I looked up to the sky, letting the colors of the sunset soothe me. "This message is for Lyssa Sampson. If anyone knows where she is, please pass it on. Her daughters want her to know they love her."

I let go of the button on the radio and lay back.

The tall grass blocked out the world, making every problem seem small enough to be conquered. I wiped my tears from my cheeks and took a deep breath. The scent of healthy, fertile earth filled my lungs.

"Are you okay?" He lay next to me, leaving his arm to his side so I could nestle my head into my place on his shoulder.

"Better than I ever should have been." I kissed his cheek and curled up beside him.

Our world is not a perfect one. My story does not end with splendor and bliss, but I am happy. And that's more than a girl surviving the end of the world should ever hope to be.

CHAPTER ONE

Nola dug her fingers into the warm dirt. Around her, the greenhouse smelled of damp earth, mist, and fresh, clean air.

Carefully, she took the tiny seed and placed it at the bottom of the hole her finger had made.

Thump.

Soon the seed would take root. A sprout would break through to the surface.

Thump, bang.

Then the green stem would grow until bean pods sprouted.

Bang, thump!

The food would be harvested and brought to their tables. All of the families would be fed.

"Ahhhhh!" the voice came from the other side of the glass. Nola knew she shouldn't look, but she couldn't ignore the sounds any longer.

It was a woman this time, her skin gray with angry, red patches dotting her face. She slammed her fists into the glass, leaving smears of red behind. The woman didn't seem to care as she banged her bloody hands into the glass over and over.

"Magnolia."

Nola jumped as Mrs. Pearson placed a hand on her shoulder.

"Don't pay her any mind," Mrs. Pearson said. "She can't get through the glass."

"But she's bleeding." Nola pushed the words past the knot in her throat.

The woman bashed her head against the glass.

"She needs help," Nola said. The woman stared right at her.

Mrs. Pearson took Nola's shoulders and turned her back to her plant tray. "That woman is beyond your help, Magnolia. Paying her any attention will only make it worse. There is nothing you can do."

Nola felt eyes staring at her. Not just the woman on the other side of the glass. The rest of the class was staring at her now, too.

Bang. Thump.

Families. The food she planted would feed the families.

Bang.

Pop.

Nola spun back to the glass. Two guards were outside now. One held his gun high. A thin spike protruded from the woman's neck. Her eyelids fluttered for a moment before she slid down the glass, leaving a streak of blood behind her.

"See," Mrs. Pearson said, smoothing Nola's hair, "they'll take her where she can't hurt herself or any of us ever again."

Nola nodded, turning back to the tray of dirt. Make a hole, plant the seed, grow the food. But the streaks of blood were burned into her mind.

The setting sun gave the greenhouse an orange-red gleam when the chime finally sounded.

"Students," Mrs. Pearson called over the sounds of her class packing up for the evening, "remember, tomorrow is Charity Day. Please dress and prepare accordingly. Anyone who doesn't come ready to leave the domes will be sent home, and their grades will be docked."

"Thank you, Mrs. Pearson," the students chorused as they drifted down into the hall.

"Magnolia."

Nola pretended she hadn't heard Mrs. Pearson call her name as she slipped in front of the group leaving the greenhouse. She didn't want to be asked if she was all right or told the sick woman would be cared for. And she didn't want to see if the glass had already been wiped clean.

Lights flickered on, sensing the group heading down the steps. Hooks lined the hallway, awaiting the gardening uniforms. Nola pulled off her rubber boots and unzipped her brown and green jumpsuit, straightening her sweater before shrugging out of the dirt-covered uniform. The rest of the class chatted as they changed—plans for the evening, talk of tomorrow's trip into the city. Nola beat the rest of them to the sink to scrub her hands. The harsh smell of the soap stung her nose, and the steaming water turned her hands red. But in a minute, the only sign of her time in the greenhouses that remained was a bit of dirt on the long brown braid that hung over her shoulder.

"Nola." Jeremy Ridgeway took his place next to Nola at the sinks, shaking the dirt from his light brown hair like a dog. It would have been funny if Nola had been in the mood to laugh. "Are you ready for tomorrow?"

"Sure. It's our duty to help the less fortunate." She sounded like a parrot, repeating what their teachers said every time Charity Day came around. Nola turned to walk away.

Jeremy stopped her, taking her hand.

"Are you okay?" Wrinkles formed on his forehead, and concern filled his deep brown eyes.

"Of course." Nola forced herself to smile.

"Do you want to come over tonight?" Jeremy asked, still holding her hand. "I mean"—his cheeks flushed—"my sister and my dad are off-duty tonight, and she hasn't seen you in a while."

"I've got to get home. My mom leaves tomorrow. But tell your dad and Gentry I said hi." Nola pulled her hand away and half-ran down the hall. More lights flickered on as she sped down the corridor. She made herself breathe, fighting her guilt at running away from Jeremy. She liked being in the greenhouses better than the tunnels that dug down into the earth. There might only be a few feet of dirt on top of her, but knowing it was there pressed an impossible weight on her lungs.

The hum of the air-filtration system calmly buzzed overhead. The solar panels aboveground generated power so she could breathe down here. She pictured the schematics in her head. Lots of vents. Great big vents. The air would be filtered, cleaned and purified, and the big vents would bring oxygen down to her.

Blue paint on the wall read *Bright Dome* above an arrow pointing to a corridor on the left. Nola ran faster, knowing soon she would be aboveground. In a minute she was sprinting up the steps. She took a deep, gulping breath. The air in the tunnels might be the same as the air in the domes, but it felt so different.

The sun had set, leaving only the bright lights of the city across the river and the faint twinkle of the other domes to peer through the glass. Nola squinted at the far side of Bright Dome. The other homestead domes glowed gently, but if she tried, she could almost make out a few stars. At least that's what she told herself. It might only have been wishful thinking.

Tall trees reached almost to the roof of Bright Dome. Grass and wildflowers coated the ground around the stone footpaths that led from house to house. Nola followed the path through the buildings to the far side of the dome. Twelve families shared Bright Dome, each of them lucky enough to have been granted independent housing units.

The trees in the dome hung heavy with crisp, green leaves. The flowers had begun to close their petals for the night. A squirrel darted past Nola's feet.

"A little late getting home, buddy." Nola's pulse slowed with each step closer to home.

The birds were all flying back to their nests. Bright Dome had been assigned robins and blue jays this cycle. The birds and the squirrels shared their home to be kept safe from contamination. The domes provided them all protection from the toxic air and tainted water.

The lights were on in Nola's house as she swung open the door.

"Hey, Mom," Nola called.

"Mmmhmm." The sound came from her mother's office in the back of the kitchen.

"How was your day?" Nola pulled the pot of steaming vegetables from the stove, knowing they would be overdone without having to lift the lid.

"Fine," her mother said, running her fingers through her shoulder-length, chestnut hair, which had been graying quickly of late. "We've been running samples in the lab all day."

"You'll figure it out." Nola didn't ask what the problem in the lab was. Her mother, Lenora Kent, was one of the heads of the botanical preservation group. It was their job to decide what plants from the outside needed to be preserved and how to take care of those plants once they were safely inside the domes. Whatever her mother was working on was for the good of them all. Beyond that it was all vague answers about classified projects.

Nola pulled bowls down from the cabinet, dishing out steamed beans and broccoli, adding spices to make the food taste like something real.

Nola pushed the bowl in front of her mother. Only when she put the spoon in Lenora's hand did her mother seem to notice Nola was still in the room.

"How was your day, sweetie?" Lenora looked up at her daughter.

Nola's mind flashed to the woman. Pounding on the glass, shattering the serenity of the greenhouse.

"It was fine." Nola smiled. "Don't forget to pack for the conference. It'll be colder at Green Leaf, so pack your sweaters."

"Of course." Lenora nodded, but she was already looking back at the charts on her computer screen.

Nola carried her dinner up the narrow stairs to the second floor. She crept into her mother's room and found the duffel bag under her bed. Nola pulled clothes out of the tiny closet. They were lucky. The residents of the domes hadn't been forced into uniforms outside of work and school. Yet. That would come when there was no one left on the outside to work in manufacturing.

When she had counted out enough blouses and slacks for her mother's week-long trip, Nola moved the suitcase to the head of the bed, where her mother would have to see it if she went to sleep that night. A picture in a carved wood frame sat on the nightstand. Six faces beamed out of the photo. A ten-year-old version of herself sat in a tree above her mother and father. Kieran sat on the branch next to her, and below him were his parents.

Nola touched her father's face, wishing the photo was larger so she could properly see his bright blue eyes that had matched her own. But her father was dead, killed in the same riot as Kieran's mother. And now Kieran and his father had been banished from the domes. The photo blurred as tears pooled in Nola's eyes.

She slid the picture into the top of her mother's bag. Lenora would need a bit of home during the Green Leaf Conference—even if their family had broken.

Nola snuck across the tiny landing at the top of the stairs and into her room. She climbed straight into bed, leaving her dinner forgotten on her desk. She pushed her face into her pillow, hoping sleep would come before the face of the woman desperate to get through the glass.

Order Girl of Glass *to continue the story.*

THE WORLD WANTS A HERO. THE CURSE NEEDS A THIEF.

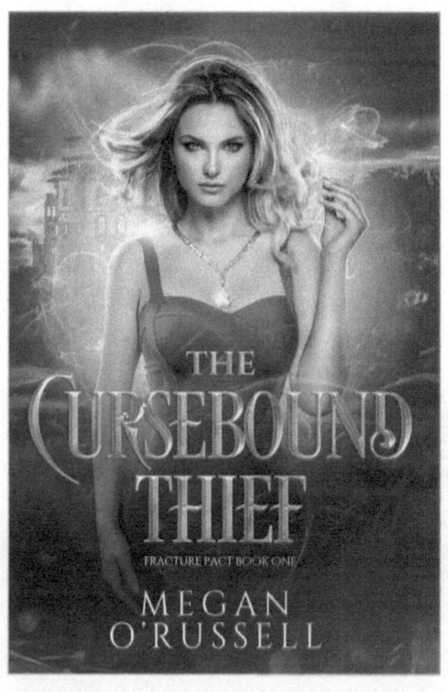

Six of Crows meets Heist Society in this New Paranormal Fantasy.

Read on for a sneak peek of *The Cursebound Thief.*

BEFORE

Ari,

    *You are hereby invited to a heist of the highest order. Danger, decep-
tion, and the salvation of the feu are promised to those who commit to
attendance.*

    Please R.S.V.P. at your earliest convenience,
    Jerek

Jerek,

    *Sounds thrilling. Who could say no to a party that delivers salvation?
Are you sending a car?*
    Ari

Ari,

    *I'm coming to you. Need your help collecting a partygoer before you fly
east.*

    In the meantime, bring our boy home.
    Jerek

JEREK

Jerek squeezed the bridge of his nose between his knuckles, closing his eyes as he waited for his computer to ding with Ari's response.

The first rumble of a spring storm shook the windowpanes. He didn't spare the glass a glance. The house would hold against any storm. The roof would stay sturdy even as everything else crumbled.

Minutes ticked past. An ache crept up the back of Jerek's neck. He stared at the red-stoned ring on his left hand, trying to distract himself from the gnawing pain in his head. His bag was packed, the plane tickets bought—the time for turning back had long since passed.

A faint mew carried up from the floor as a furry head pounded against his ankle.

"You can't come, Cas," Jerek said. "Cats and burglary don't go well together. You'll have to stay behind."

Casanova dug his claws into Jerek's calf.

"I promise I'm sending you someplace nice." Jerek shut his eyes and kneaded his temples. "The height of cat luxury. You'll never even think of missing your life here."

Jerek opened his eyes to find the white cat sprawled across his keyboard.

Purring rumbled in Casanova's chest.

"I understand." Jerek scratched between the cat's ears. "But we both know there's no other choice."

The computer dinged.

Jerek,

He's on his way. To your house by morning. The Maree aren't happy. Don't think they're just going to send him to you and forget about it. There will be hell to pay for this.

Ari

"Hear that, Cas?" Jerek lifted the cat off the keyboard. "Our brave knight Lincoln is finally coming home."

Jerek kissed the cat on the top of the head before setting him down on the armchair beside the library's fireplace.

No fire crackled in the grate.

He pushed aside the imagined chill that lapped at his neck and allowed himself one long moment to look around the room.

The shelves were packed with texts that held information many would kill to possess. The records and files that didn't need to be hidden had been sorted into an order that would be easy for others to interpret. The pictures of his family had been dusted and perfectly aligned on the mantle.

"Don't mind the sound, Cas. It'll be over soon."

Taking the box of matches from the mantle, Jerek walked through the front door and out into the rain. He didn't need to bother with placing any charges—he'd already run the fuse right up to the stone steps of the entryway.

He touched a match to the fuse and went back inside, not bothering to stay and watch the black car explode. There was too much to be done. Windows to destroy. Glass to scatter.

This was only the beginning of the necessary chaos. Saving

everything he loved would require much greater sacrifices than wreaking havoc on his own home.

Jerek Holden didn't even flinch as the boom of the explosion shook the floor beneath his feet.

Preorder The Cursebound Thief *today*.

ABOUT THE AUTHOR

Megan O'Russell is the author of several Young Adult series that invite readers to escape into worlds of adventure. From *Girl of Glass*, which blends dystopian darkness with the heart-pounding danger of vampires, to *Ena of Ilbrea*, which draws readers into an epic world of magic and assassins.

With the *Girl of Glass* series, *The Tethering* series, *The Chronicles of Maggie Trent*, *The Tale of Bryant Adams,* the *Ena of Ilbrea* series, and several more projects planned, there are always exciting new books on the horizon. To be the first to hear about new releases, free short stories, and giveaways, sign up for Megan's newsletter by visiting the following:

https://www.meganorussell.com/book-signup

Originally from Upstate New York, Megan is a professional musical theatre performer whose work has taken her across North America. Her chronic wanderlust has led her from Alaska to Thailand and many places in between. Wanting to travel has fostered Megan's love of books that allow her to visit countless new worlds from her favorite reading nook. Megan is also a lyricist and playwright. Information on her theatrical works can be found at RussellCompositions.com.

She would be thrilled to chat with you on Facebook or Twitter

@MeganORussell, elated if you'd visit her website MeganORussell.com, and over the moon if you'd like the pictures of her adventures on Instagram @ORussellMegan.

ALSO BY MEGAN O'RUSSELL

The Girl of Glass Series

Girl of Glass

Boy of Blood

Night of Never

Son of Sun

The Tale of Bryant Adams

How I Magically Messed Up My Life in Four Freakin' Days

Seven Things Not to Do When Everyone's Trying to Kill You

Three Simple Steps to Wizarding Domination

Five Spellbinding Laws of International Larceny

The Tethering Series

The Tethering

The Siren's Realm

The Dragon Unbound

The Blood Heir

The Chronicles of Maggie Trent

The Girl Without Magic

The Girl Locked With Gold

The Girl Cloaked in Shadow

Ena of Ilbrea

Wrath and Wing

Ember and Stone

Mountain and Ash

Ice and Sky

Feather and Flame

Guilds of Ilbrea

Inker and Crown

Myth and Storm

Viper and Steel

The Heart of Smoke Series

Heart of Smoke

Soul of Glass

Eye of Stone

Ash of Ages

Fracture Pact

The Cursebound Thief

Sorcerers of Ilbrea

Spell and Secret

www.ingramcontent.com/pod-product-compliance
Lightning Source LLC
Chambersburg PA
CBHW050836190726
48286CB00007B/2113